NATIONAL DARKROAST DAY

NATIONAL DARKROAST DAY

A Novel

AUGUST ADAMS

iUniverse, Inc.

New York Lincoln Shanghai

NATIONAL DARKROAST DAY

iUniverse books may be ordered through booksellers or by contacting:

iUniverse
2021 Pine Lake Road, Suite 100
Lincoln, NE 68512
www.iuniverse.com
1-800-Authors (1-800-288-4677)

This is a work of fiction. All of the characters, names, incidents, organizations, and dialogue in this novel are either the products of the author's imagination or are used fictitiously.

Cover illustrations and Darkroast logo illustration
by Shane L. Johnson

ISBN-13: 978-0-595-43465-7 (pbk)
ISBN-13: 978-0-595-87792-8 (ebk)
ISBN-10: 0-595-43465-7 (pbk)
ISBN-10: 0-595-87792-3 (ebk)

Printed in the United States of America

August Adams graduated from Emory University and earned his MA in writing and publishing from Emerson College in Boston. He lives in Washington DC.

NATIONAL DARKROAST DAY

Dedicated to all Americans who enjoy a dark roast.

Prologue

A t the turn of the 21st century, the largest and most popular corporation in America was Darkroast Coffee. Darkroast was popular because it made coffee for the American public, and made it better than anyone else.

Everyone in America knew that there was no better coffee than Darkroast coffee. They had countless different flavors, including everything from your basic cappuccino and espresso to Chocolate Bliss Mocha, Bumbleberry Crème, and Relaxo Caramelo Blast. There were so many different kinds, with such unique tastes and trendy names, it was impossible to go in a Darkroast shop and not find the perfect coffee. Their motto was "Take one sip. We'll command you forever!"

Darkroast was so popular that there were stores in every city, on practically every corner. The Darkroast coffee stores were beautifully designed with coffee-themed wallpaper, stylish lighting, cozy seating, and a central coffee counter staffed by smiling black-aproned baristas. Sometimes customers would say entering a Darkroast store was, "like entering a dream. Only better, because they served coffee. The *best* coffee." Sometimes the stores even had sampling stations inside them, so people could drink coffee while they were waiting in line to buy coffee. People couldn't get enough.

The coffee was just that good.

• • •

People loved everything about Darkroast Coffee. The stores. The coffee. Even the logo.

Some people actually wore T-shirts or ties around town that had the logo printed on them. The logo was a big black shield with a coffee bean and two machine guns. It looked sort of like a militaristic badge, which some people said was cute. The Darkroast logo was proudly displayed in Darkroast coffee stores on every corner in America, so people would always see it nationwide.

This is exactly what the logo looked like:

Supposedly, the logo was designed by Darkroast's founder and CEO: Victor Black. Victor Black founded Darkroast nearly ten years ago on what he claimed was the American Dream. As Victor liked to tell the story, he was walking along the street one day, and while passing a small coffee bean store he'd gotten a brilliant idea. Stopping and looking at all the coffee in the store window, he'd said, "What if there was a store like this on every corner in America? And what if instead of just beans, they made coffee to drink and sold it by the cup!"

Months later, Darkroast was born. Its headquarters was established in Boston, giving new meaning to the nickname "Beantown." Within no time at all, almost as if it was a miracle sent straight from above, almost as if it was all planned out with the precision of a machine, the company exploded into a nationwide money-making empire, and the rest was history.

• • •

If you had to speak generally, you could say that the entire country had Darkroast addiction. There was no such thing as too much

Darkroast, and with all this support, Darkroast's company size and number of stores grew monstrously large. There was no stopping it. There were over one million stores nationwide. Its fortune was in the untold billions. And then came the upcoming national holiday called National Darkroast Day.

Ever since Darkroast had announced its upcoming national holiday, the people were going wild. For months talk had been circulating through every office and every street in every city. "It's going to be huge," people said to one another. "A huge national party!"

The plan was this: Darkroast, the corporation that had a store on every corner in nearly every neighborhood in America, was going to host a national celebration with music, dancing, and free cups of coffee for everyone. It would be the largest, most elaborate national celebration in American history. They built a huge Darkroast Day Blimp and built a massive Darkroast Day Amphitheater in Boston and in every major American city so that people could gather and celebrate. Across the country, even in those places where there was no Darkroast amphitheater, Darkroast was sending out an army of special baristas. They'd serve free coffee all day to ensure that on National Darkroast Day, everyone in America was able to share the American dream with at least one free cup of coffee.

To make things even more special, that free coffee they'd be serving was a brand new brew called *Mind Melt*. No one had ever tried *Mind Melt* and people couldn't wait.

But Darkroast always made it a point to remind people that *Mind Melt* wasn't even the best part of National Darkroast Day.

"All across the country, at exactly 9 p.m. Eastern time," they had been saying for months and months. "There will be a show of unprecedented size and stature! And it's coming to a Moon near you!"

What they meant was that Darkroast—the richest, most successful, and certainly the most popular corporation in America—had planned a show on the Moon.

A Moon Laser Show, to be exact.

• • •

People all over loved this idea of a Moon Laser Show, and as far as Darkroast was concerned this was a very good thing. There was nothing they ever wanted more than to make sure that on National Darkroast Day, by exactly 9 p.m. Eastern time, every man, woman and child in America had downed a cup of *Mind Melt*, and was staring up at the Moon waiting for the most spectacular show in history.

It is in regards to this landmark event that our story begins. It is in Boston, a.k.a. "Beantown," a.k.a. Darkroast's hometown, that our story takes place. It concerns itself with several people of particular importance:

Victor Black, founder and CEO of Darkroast Coffee corporation.

Ted Baxter, who was Victor's Darkroast partner.

Miriam Baxter, who was Ted Baxter's wife and head of Darkroast Public Relations.

Billy London, a reporter for one of Boston's largest newspapers.

Wally and Nate, who were two baristas at a Darkroast coffee store in Boston.

Guerrero Montana, a coffee farmer and leader of a revolutionary group from Mexico.

And the Source, a person of pivotal importance who we cannot yet reveal.

Our story holds these people in particular regard because during the arrival of National Darkroast Day in Boston, during the biggest celebration in America's history, the fate of America—the survival of an *entire* nation of 300 million people—would eventually rest on the shoulders of these eight people.

And the odds were *definitely* not stacked in America's favor.

Beantown

Chapter 1

There was action happening in a downtown warehouse. Definite action. Not sure why anyone was there at this time of night. It wasn't the best neighborhood. A creepy old back alley. Lots of shadows for bad guys to hide in. And it was late, after midnight. No one should have been there. But people *were* here and something *really bad* was about to happen.

Most of the action going on had to do with the group nearest to the warehouse. A bunch of men in black camouflage suits were gathered round a truck. The truck's back door was wide open, and nothing was inside.

The other bit of action was happening at the end of the alley. There was a single man, a red-freckled private investigator named Bernard, who was crouched behind a dumpster. He had been sent here by an anonymous source, and told there would be something worth photographing. Something related to National Darkroast Day.

The Source was right. There *was* something worth photographing. The P.I. thought he was seeing it moments before when one particular truck, a much bigger truck than this one here now, had pulled up and parked in front of the warehouse. A team of these camouflaged men had gotten out of the truck and began loading wooden box after wooden box into the warehouse. Countless wooden boxes.

After the men had finished unloading, the original truck had zipped off into the night. But the men remained behind, and then this other truck arrived, the one that was here now. It hadn't been more than a minute between the two. Perfectly coordinated.

And clearly the men had been expecting the second truck.

• • •

The men now shoveled box after box out of the warehouse and back into this new truck. They hardly made a sound, and moved with rapid speed. The boxes were large—of bone-crushing size—but the men lifted them as if they weighed nothing.

Using his telephoto camera lens, the P.I. was able to see that each box had the same message inscribed on it. The message was in the top right corner, and was very small but clear. It said: *Mind Melt*.

The P.I. began snapping away.

Photo after photo recorded the event. The truck. The boxes. The *Mind Melt* label. The faces of the men in camouflage, which weren't particularly striking in any way, except that they all looked extremely young. Early twenties.

Then the P.I. saw that there was one face he did recognize. A *very* familiar male face. It was someone older—late thirties, maybe. Someone waiting in the shadows of the warehouse, smoking a cigarette.

"This is the last shipment," the man said. "It'll be in Philadelphia by morning."

He took a long drag on his cigarette.

• • •

The P.I. knew he needed to get closer. He needed some better shots of this familiar man with the boxes. He buried his camera against his chest, and like a cat, he crept to another closer dumpster. From here he had a better angle, and he started snapping away.

Holy shit … this is good, he thought. And it was. It was perfect. He never could have expected this. The scoop of a lifetime, and he was photographing it right now without them even knowing at all.

But then suddenly, he reached the end of his film. The camera, on automatic rewind, started spinning away its gears.

Everyone turned and looked. It especially made one of the young men jerk around, almost as if he had heard the noise and responded so quickly that it made him uncharacteristically clumsy. It caused him to bump into one of his nearby companions, and suddenly, one of the boxes came crashing to the ground. The wood shattered against the alley's asphalt, and the box's hidden contents spilled everywhere.

What spilled out was this: pound after pound of glowing green coffee beans.

They looked radioactive, almost illuminating the entire alley in a strange green glow. The P.I. dropped his jaw. He saw it. This was *Mind Melt*, and it was never what he'd have expected. It barely looked like coffee. He should have run straight away, but his instinct was to photograph. If he could only get one shot of this then people would pay millions.

He grabbed his other camera, and started snapping away. It was a foolish move, and he knew it. He saw the familiar man drop his cigarette, stamp it out, and look straight at him.

"Get him," the man said.

One of the camouflaged young men turned, and then ran straight for him.

The P.I. turned and ran. Down the dark alley, away from the warehouse, he sprinted, and within moments, he knew he was running for his life. This young man ran fast. Relentlessly fast. Inhumanly fast. The P.I. cleared the other end of the alley, and bolted straight across the street. Zigzagging between several parked cars, he looked for cover. He saw another alley nearby, and headed for it.

Down this alley he kept running. Harder. Harder. He ducked past a rusty fire escape. He weaved past a dumpster and some piles of trash. No stopping, until he was at the end. Nearing the alley's end, he was about to continue …

But then he turned back. He looked over his shoulder to check his pursuer …

The young man was gone.

The P.I. stopped. Nothing. No one. The alley was dark and empty.

The P.I. thought to himself: *I'm free.*

He breathed a heavy sigh, then smiled at his narrow escape. He laughed, patted his camera like he could smell that million dollars already, and then he turned … straight into the face of the young man.

The P.I. had been cut off. It was a fatal mistake. The young man grabbed his neck and the P.I. struggled to breathe. He tore at the hand to let go, tearing back the skin, ripping it off. There was no blood, and underneath, the hand was solid metal. The young man gripped his neck with the force of a machine.

The P.I. knew he was a dead man and he didn't last long. The young man lifted him into the air like he was a struggling child, and then a surge of green electricity encapsulated the P.I. It came from the metal hand. Moments later, his body hung limp, and the young man threw the dead body into a nearby dumpster. The body landed face down, unmoving. Smoke rose from his head like cooked melon, but in his lifeless fingers, he still held the flap of skin from the young man's hand.

• • •

Less than a minute later, the young man was back at the warehouse. The other men had cleaned up the shattered box and its contents, and he stepped past them to the familiar man.

"Did you dispose of the body," the familiar man asked.

"Yes," the young man answered.

"Did you get the film," the familiar man asked.

"Of course," the young man answered, handing the P.I.'s cameras to him.

The familiar man looked at the cameras, nodded with approval, then observed the young man's hand.

"Your hand is damaged," he said.

"I know," said the young man, showing no pain, nor emotion.

"Fix it," said the familiar man. "And get back to work."

So the young man turned, slid on a black glove, and returned to loading boxes.

Chapter 2

It was two days later. Late morning in the city of Boston.

• • •

Boston was a fair-sized city. Nothing like New York, or Los Angeles. Nothing like one of those cities that endlessly sprawled as far as the eye could see. Forty-eight square miles. Six hundred thousand people. Humble, yet sizeable. Boston was beautiful enough when you looked at it during the day. Some called it a city of contrasts, where ancient red-brick sidewalks wrapped around soaring steel and glass towers and row after row of bustling city shops. Now and again you would find wonderfully historic churches and old world apartments nestled in-between all this, and there were lots of parks and trees scattered around in just the right places.

One of the most beautiful and most popular places was the Boston Commons, a central park downtown that in many ways had always been the heart of the city. It was a wonderful spot of urban nature, complete with duck ponds, willow trees, flower gardens, and wide-open stretches of grassy knolls. Standing in the middle of it, looking out at the surrounding city on a perfect blue-skied day, the view had the power to change and inspire you. And now, there was practically nothing left of it.

"I hate National Darkroast Day," mumbled Billy London, sitting in his boss's office, staring out the window at all the damage being done.

"For the love of Christ," shouted London's boss. "Don't say that! And pay attention!"

London tried to look at his boss, but it was no good. He returned to looking out the window. The whole problem was the National Darkroast Day Amphitheater. Darkroast had built the largest outdoor amphitheater in existence (should have been called an amphi-city cause you could see it from space), and it was where the first National Darkroast Day celebration in Boston was going to be held. The

Darkroast Day amphitheater was an architectural masterpiece. Over sixty acres wide and eighteen stories high—constructed like a giant colosseum with a breathtaking half-shell dome—it dominated the city's central park and rivaled the surrounding buildings. Along the top, seventy-thousand giant black sails—each sail emblazoned with the image of the Darkroast shield—could be seen for miles around. Inside the amphitheater, there were huge lawns, a mega-sized central music stage with sixteen adjoining stages, multi-tiered stadium seating, and giant digital screens. A Darkroast Day Blimp hovered above it all.

Nearly every tree had been cut down in the park, and now there was hardly an ounce of natural green space left except around the edges. Only if you went up to the tallest window in any of the surrounding buildings could you see anything that resembled the old view. And even then, there was no way not to look at that giant, freakish monstrosity that'd been built directly over the *entire* park. They had obliterated where the willow trees, flower gardens, and duck ponds used to be (some ducks were still wandering the area wondering where their homes had gone), exchanging them instead for paved roads and sidewalks everywhere. The blue sky was a mess of banners and promotional artwork and the skyscraper-sized half-shell dome rivaled the local buildings. As if this wasn't enough, grassy knolls once perfect for picnics and city-watching had been covered with tons of coffee booths. Countless coffee booths. Altogether, the park had become like some monstrous, cluttered temple built for nothing but worshipping Darkroast. A monument to Darkroast, built right on top of the park.

Even as construction crews finished the last details onsite right now, and put up the final advertising posters beyond the park on the surrounding office buildings, the whole thing's potency seemed to grow bigger and bigger. It might have consumed the entire world. All so that Victor Black and the people could have their Darkroast Day.

"It's horrible," said London. "They've ruined the park."

"FOR THE LOVE OF GOD," shouted London's boss. "PAY ATTENTION OR I SWEAR I'LL …"

London turned around and his boss went quiet. His face was bright red, on the verge of exploding.

London thought about turning back to look out the window, but it was no use. Some man on a scaffolding ladder had just come down and slapped up the bottom half of a giant Darkroast Day poster over the window. London saw the big black Darkroast logo. The one with that dark militaristic shield. The one that always made London wonder, why use *such* a militaristic logo, and why the hell does everyone love it so much?

"Now …," said London's boss, calming down, but not really. His face was still red. "About Darkroast Day …"

London's boss's name was Lewis Burns. London called him Lewie for short. Lewie ran one of the biggest newspapers in town, known as the Boston City Spotlight, and like all Boston newspapers, it made a habit of covering Victor Black and Darkroast. Almost one-half of coverage was always given to Darkroast, because that's what people wanted to read. Even if it was something totally insignificant—an article on a new door chime one of the coffee stores had installed—people wanted to know. Everyone could never get enough of Darkroast, including Lewie himself.

London knew what Lewie was going to say. He had been harping on London about it for the past three weeks. He wouldn't say anything else to him, and though Lewie could be a nice guy, it was really starting to creep up his ass, with permanent chaffing already setting in.

What's your story on Darkroast Day, was the question. *What's your angle?*

"How about," said London, doing his best to pretend he had a good idea. "Darkroast Day: What's that again?"

London watched Lewie's temples bulge. His skin tone was reddening again. If London didn't say something else quick, Lewie was gonna pop.

"Okay, okay," said London. "How about ... Darkroast Day: Should anyone care?"

Lewie nearly had an aneurism.

"Come on, London," he shouted, pounding his desk. "What's the holdup? You've had three weeks. The freakin' holiday is tomorrow, we're running a cover to cover on the event. Everyone's gonna read it, and you're the only one of my reporters who hasn't turned in his article. Every paper in Boston's got a cover to cover going on, and every staff writer's chipping in. How am I gonna look when I can't rally my team for the cause?"

"I've tried. But I can't do it," said London. "Look what they've done to the park."

"Screw the park," said Lewie. "The park doesn't pay your salary!"

"It's not my style," said London.

London had two basic beliefs: that there was such a thing in the world called *morals*, and that if people stuck to them, the world would be better off. He probably cared for humanity more than anyone else ever had cared for anything, and he wanted to see it turn out in good shape. This was London's style. This was who he was and how he wrote his articles. He wrote from the heart, and he wrote the truth. Always had, and always would.

After all, that's why he got into newspapers: because he wanted to save the world.

Unfortunately, he came along at a time when the entire country devoted half its news coverage to Darkroast and it was nothing but fluff, PR coverage. It was like ice cream and kisses—honestly, no one could get enough.

As far as London was concerned, Lewie and the rest of America saw things backwards, namely in that they had lost touch with everything that was important. There were problems in the world … *real* problems like starvation, homelessness, pollution, disease, economic inequality, and park obliteration … and here everyone, the entire city, the entire country, seemed utterly obsessed with Darkroast. Non-stop Darkroast.

And then Darkroast Day came along, and it simply made things a hundred times worse. No one would stop obsessing over the fact that their favorite corporation was going to have a holiday with a big national party, where they'd give away tons of free coffee (they were giving out a brand new brew called *Mind Melt* … a ludicrous name), and were hosting a Moon laser show, clearly just a blatant PR stunt that was going to waste tons of money that could have been put to good use.

London wished they'd all just get over it already.

As far as he was concerned, any group of people loving any one thing that much could not be good.

"What about the park?" said London. "I could write about the park."

Lewie's face began to return to its normal color. A small smile crept in.

"Okay, okay," said Lewie. "I like it … I like it … How about … How great the amphitheater looks? Do a story on that. We already have six others running, but …"

"Jesus, Lewie," interrupted London. "My point is: the park looks horrible. They *killed* the park."

Lewie stopped. His smile vanished.

"I thought we were connecting on this," said Lewie. "What the hell?"

"We are connecting … I guess," said London. "But I'm tired of everyone always doing the same fluff articles on Darkroast and their holiday. How about something else? How about a good ol' fashioned article on poverty or racial bias. Something with substance."

"No, no, no," shouted Lewie. His face was quickly turning the color of a tomato. "We always do Darkroast, and for Christ's sake, it's Darkroast Day. The first national Darkroast Day. It's the story of the year! The story of the millennium!"

"It's overdone," said London. "And it's boring. How about an insider's look at …"

"No, no, no," said Lewie, ready to pull his hair out. "Nothing negative!"

"But," said London. "Just look at the park. Maybe …"

Lewie was about to have a full-system meltdown. He actually had pulled several chunks of gray hair from his scalp, and was starting to sweat with temper.

"NO, NO, NO," he shouted. "If you don't do something positive, and you don't do something on Darkroast Day, and it's not on my desk by tomorrow, then you are out of a job! I don't have a choice on this! This is just the way things are! People want Darkroast!"

"But …"

"DARKROAST! DARKROAST! DARKROAST!"

And then London said it anyway. He laid it right out on the table.

"How can you be so narrow-minded, Lewie. How can you and everyone else be so obsessed with Darkroast, and think that there's nothing wrong with this holiday! For God's sake, man. Just look at the park!"

• • •

Down in the park (or what was left of it), on the main stage of the newly constructed Darkroast Day amphitheater, all cameras were pointed at Victor Black, Ted Baxter, and Miriam Baxter. The three of them sat at a press conference table on the main stage, fielding final questions about tomorrow's national holiday. Since it was the final minutes of this morning's press conference, and since Miriam was the

PR wonder behind Darkroast Day, everyone was looking for her to pass the final seal of approval.

"So … Miriam," one of the reporters shouted from the crowd of press. "What do you think of the amphitheater? What's the verdict?" The reporter held a pen over his pad, and prepared to write.

Miriam could see his pen was trembling with anticipation. She didn't answer right away. She knew better than that. Miriam ran a hand through her short city-styled hair—a move she always did to impress the cameras—and looked around the stage. She took a deep breath, slowly, as if she was breathing for the very first time, another move she always did when she wanted to look inspired and truthful, and then she spoke.

"I've gotta be honest," she said, and then she paused for suspense. This time she looked around. Really looked hard. And then she finally came out with it.

"It's perfect … absolutely picture-perfect."

The crowd sighed with delight. Flash bulbs snapped. The reporter scribbled: *everything … picture-perfect.* This was the answer everyone was hoping for.

Nearby, Victor and Ted smiled to each other. This was the Miriam they knew. This was the Miriam they loved.

"You have to hand it to her," said Ted. "She knows how to work a crowd."

"I only hire the best," replied Victor, with a wink and a smile, his trademark move. "Only the best."

In Boston, and in most other parts of the country for that matter, Victor Black, Ted Baxter, and Miriam Baxter had come to be known as the Darkroast Trio. People also lovingly referred to them as the American Trifecta: America's triple-time winning ticket.

As far as people were concerned, there wasn't a better American company than Darkroast, and without these three, Darkroast wouldn't have been anywhere. Victor Black, Darkroast founder and CEO, was the mastermind behind the operation, and without his vision nothing would have gotten off the ground. Ted Baxter, Darkroast partner and head of new products division (and Miriam's loving husband), was the brawns of the operation—as Victor would say, "without him, we'd still have only six coffees, and no market strategy." And Miriam Baxter, Darkroast PR extraordinaire, was the one who took Victor Black and his company and turned it all into a goldmine by making the public love them. Absolutely eat-them-up-with-a-spoon love them.

Nowadays, "Victor" was the third most popular baby name. Even for girls.

And the name "Darkroast" was climbing the charts, but mostly in midwestern states.

"So what do you think about all this," one of the reporters asked Victor, now turning to the other side of the stage. "Are you pleased with the outcome?"

Victor leaned back in his chair and uncrossed his legs. He looked at Ted, who smiled and agreed, then he looked at the reporter.

"I think Miriam said it just right," he said. "It's picture-perfect."

He finished with a wink and a smile.

"And you, Ted," another reporter added. "Would you agree?"

"There's no other way to put it," said Ted, and he gave a loving glance at his wife. "Miriam knows what she's talking about!"

Again, flash bulbs snapped. The crowd mumbled with satisfaction. Some even laughed at Ted's comment, their hearts warmed. Pens were put to paper and everyone scribbled: *Victor agrees ... picture-perfect. Ted also agrees ... most lovingly.*

Miriam looked across the press table with delight and honor. These were her two favorite men in the world, and their responses just now couldn't have made her any happier. To be honest, she also felt very humbled and almost brought to tears by their responses because without

Darkroast and these two men, she felt like she'd have nothing. Absolutely nothing.

"I just want to add," said Miriam. "That most of the pleasure in all this has been working with Victor and Ted. They are the real superstars here."

A unanimous and tender "Awwww" went out through the crowd of reporters, and everyone stood and clapped.

In the middle of the crowd, one of the reporters wearing a Darkroast tie turned to his cameraman and said, "Are you getting this? Are you getting this? This is the good stuff!"

The cameraman quickly gave the thumbs up.

"And I especially want to add," said Miriam. "That I could not have done one single bit of this without my wonderful husband, Ted." And then Miriam blew Ted a tiny air kiss, nothing too hard that would seem forced, but nothing too light that wouldn't show how much she really meant it.

"Are you getting this? Are you getting this?" that same reporter with the Darkroast tie said to his cameraman, shouting this time.

The cameraman again gave the thumbs up.

"Gotta love this girl," said Victor, with a wink and a smile.

"I know I do," said Ted.

Again, the crowd sighed. Flash bulbs popped and pens were put to pads one last time. All of them wrote: *does it get any better than this?*

After this, a few reporters jumped into some quick routine questions. It was the usual bits they'd been asking for weeks, and already knew the answers to, but would always jam in at the last moment just in case.

"Can you tell us any more about that new coffee you're giving away tomorrow," one shouted. "How did you come up with the name *Mind Melt?*"

"We wanted to go with something fun and edgy," said Victor. "Something hip."

"What about the Darkroast Day Blimp?" another shouted. "Will it be in Boston all day?"

"It'll float over the Boston amphitheater the entire day," said Victor. "Very impressive."

"And that Moon Laser Show," another shouted. "Can you tell us about that?"

"All we can tell you," said Ted. "Is that it's going to be a blast."

"Is it still true that the coffee will be free?"

"Of course," said Victor. "Darkroast Day is about us giving back ..."

Victor, Ted, and Miriam all smiled and nodded.

"It's about our entire company giving back to a country that has helped make us a success. Nowadays, it's important to give back to the community."

"Most important," said Miriam.

"Tremendously important," said Ted.

"Which is why everything on Darkroast Day is free," added Victor. "That brand new coffee is free. That unprecedented, spectacular Moon show is free. It's all one hundred percent free!"

The crowd scribbled the word: *free!* After a few more questions along these lines, the conference was pretty much over.

"I'm sorry," said Victor. "But that's all the time we have. We have lots of business to attend to in order to get everything prepared for tomorrow."

Victor and Ted then stood up, bowed, and officially, the conference was over.

Miriam reminded the crowds that she'd be holding another Q and A session later, but the reporters had most of what they wanted anyway, and stood up to head back to their offices to type or broadcast their stories, where they'd deliver lots of the same ol' fluff stuff. Plenty of stuff on the amphitheater set-up, that free new coffee with that hip name, *Mind Melt*, and the Moon Laser Show that was sure to please. Nearly half the crowd was going to run something special on how Miriam, Ted, and Victor had pulled together to make the best holiday in American history. The words "American Trifecta" and "Darkroast Trio" would be used countless times.

Only a few reporters lingered, unable to get enough. They rushed the stage and shoved microphones into Miriam's face.

"Where did you get the wood for the stage," one asked. "That's yellow oak, right?"

"Yes. We got it from Japan," replied Miriam.

"And that half-shell dome," said another reporter. "It's huge! Big as the buildings."

"Best damn acoustics around," said Miriam. "Made entirely of reinforced titanium. Just wait till you see it with the Moon Show."

And then another reporter started in about the giant black Darkroast frescos strategically positioned all around the park, but Miriam had to put her hand up.

"They're painted by the famous artist, Louis Franco," she said. "But really, really … I have to be going."

She saw that Victor and Ted were starting to head backstage. Somehow they'd managed to escape the reporters, and they looked like they were ready to leave. She knew that Ted had to leave immediately after the press conference for his trip to Orlando—there he was going to spend Darkroast Day heading up the southern operations. His bags were already packed and sitting back stage.

Victor had promised to escort him to the airport in his limo.

"It's been a pleasure," Miriam said to the reporters. "I'll be back in another thirty minutes or so to answer any more questions … but I have to take a quick break."

And then she smiled, turned and walked away, not too fast so that anyone would think she was anxious to escape, but fast enough so that it appeared that she really did have to go. She shot a wave over her shoulder when she was halfway gone, just in case. The reporters sighed longingly, but were content.

Miriam caught up with Victor and Ted behind stage. Ted already had his bags in hand.

"Trying to skip town without saying goodbye, huh," she said slyly.

Victor and Ted turned around for a moment, slightly spooked. They quickly broke into smiles.

"I've got that plane to catch, remember," said Ted. "Orlando needs me."

"Oh yea," said Miriam. "And what about me?"

She instantly wrapped her arms around Ted and gave him a big kiss. He dropped his bags and kissed her back, perhaps a little harder than normal, and raised her into the air just a tad, managing to give her butt a squeeze in the same motion. He kissed her as if it might be the last time he'd ever see her.

"That was unexpected," he said, pulling his lips away. "I should leave town more often."

"Oh shut up," said Miriam with a sly smirk. "You're the one that's been working late every night this week. And now you're leaving town."

"Business is business, baby."

"You're only gonna be gone for the weekend, right?"

"Of course," said Ted, and he lowered Miriam to the ground.

"Come on, come on," said Victor, giving Miriam's arm a tug. He'd been watching his two close friends with a smile, but was growing impatient. "Let the poor guy go to Orlando and do his job for Christ's sake."

Miriam turned around and quickly jabbed Victor in the ribs.

"Oh, shut up," she said, pretending to bully him. "He's my man, too."

There was a pause. Both looked at each other and then Victor broke into a smile. So did Miriam.

The two of them laughed and hugged.

They hugged tight. It was a father-and-daughter-type embrace. When they pulled away, Miriam had tears in her eyes. Victor saw them and gave her shoulder a rub, and her chin a gentle knock.

"I really meant what I said on stage," said Victor.

"So did I," said Miriam, wiping the tears away. "I owe you *sooo* much. Ever since I started working for you, everything has been a dream come true. You're my lucky, charm. You know that. You gave me the perfect job. The perfect life."

She paused and smiled at her husband.

"I never would have met Ted if we hadn't both been working for you."

"Oh, come on," said Victor, blushing, but he could see that Ted was nodding.

"No really," said Miriam. "You may not want to hear this, but out there today, I definitely realized how much I owe you all this. This picture-perfect day …"

She looked around at the entire amphitheater set-up, her heart swelling.

"I feel like I owe all of this to you."

Victor paused. He cocked his head, definitely not expecting such an outpouring.

"Think nothing of it," he then said. "The pleasure's been all mine."

The two of them hugged again, and then Miriam heard Ted say, "Limo's here." The limo driver had come up onto the stage and was waving to Ted and Victor.

"We should go," said Ted. "Come on you two. I'm the one leaving town. You guys will see each other tomorrow."

Miriam knew he was right. She still wanted to prolong the moment of this perfect day, but she let go and stiffened up.

Victor gave her a final wink and a smile as he let her go.

Ted reached for his bags, and Victor offered to carry one of them.

"I'll get it. I'll get it," said Miriam, and she picked it up gingerly. Carrying the bag, Miriam escorted the two of them off the stage, and down to the limousine.

The limo driver helped Ted and Miriam put the bags into the car, and then opened one of the back doors. Ted started to step inside, but then Miriam spoke up.

"Are you sure you have to go," she said, half jokingly, but half serious.

Ted turned around and smiled.

"We already went over this," he said. "I wish I could spend Darkroast Day with you, but you know there's a lot riding on this. Everything has to be perfect."

"I know. I know," said Miriam. "It'll be fine ... go to Orlando."

At this point, Victor stepped in.

"We really do need to get going," he said, tapping his watch. "Need to keep our schedule."

Ted nodded, climbed into the limo, and Victor followed after.

"Call me when your flight gets in," said Miriam.

"I'll see what I can do," said Ted, and then Victor nodded to the limo driver and he shut the door.

Miriam stared at herself in the darkened limousine window, and then stepped back as the limo driver tipped his hat in courtesy to her. The limo driver climbed into the driver's seat and then started the engine.

"Get them to the airport safe and on-time," Miriam said to him.

He nodded.

Miriam waved through the windows to Ted and Victor as the limo pulled away and headed towards traffic, but all she saw was her own distorted reflection pulling away in the black tinted windows. Then the limo was gone.

• • •

Across town, several blocks away from the park, Guerrero Montana was in the middle of Downtown Crossing, just below the entrance to a second-story restaurant called *Plush*. He'd been fired from his Head Busboy position there three weeks ago, but now he was back. He noticed that some specific remodeling to the place had been done since he was gone: Darkroast Day posters had been plastered up all over the entrance. There was even one on the front door.

A big obnoxious poster of Victor Black smiling and drinking coffee.

Guerrero took one look at it, then removed a knife from his jacket. "Muerta," he mumbled, which meant *death*, and then he entered.

He moved swiftly up the indoor escalator, at the quickened pace of someone with revenge on the mind. When he reached the top and headed straight for the restaurant's main door, the doorman instantly recognized him. The doorman took one look at Guerrero's knife, and then he ran. (*Plush* was that kind of restaurant. The kind of yuppie food establishment that had a doorman who would bolt without giving his co-workers—his friends and fellow human beings—even a moments warning if he saw a former employee returning with a knife.)

When Guerrero came inside the large swivel door, he immediately came face to face with the manager, the one who had fired him. The manager was flanked by two hostesses wearing super tight yuppie dresses. When Guerrero had been fired from his position as Head Busboy—which he only got because no other busboy could speak much English, and which he only lost because he yelled at some customer for drinking coffee—the manager had been *very, very* clear.

"I don't want to see you again," he said. "EVER!"

The two hostesses had been standing nearby and overheard the whole thing.

Now, as Guerrero entered *Plush* and headed inside, the manager and the hostesses expected the person entering the main door to be a customer. When they recognized it was Guerrero and saw he was holding a knife, the two hostesses bolted straight for the coat room to hide.

The manager, left alone, took one look at Guerrero's knife, and then he ran.

"What are you doing here," he shouted, backpedaling quickly. He was wearing a designer suit, typical for a yuppie restaurant manager, and he was practically tripping over his own loafers he moved so quickly.

Guerrero kept his eyes directly on the manager and proceeded forward.

The manager waved his hands in the air, pleading for his life as he and Guerrero moved into the main dining room. The main dining room consisted of a long set of windows that overlooked the street, and rows of white fancy tablecloths where crowds of businessmen and businesswomen were now eating. As they looked up from their plates of sea bass and caviar, most in the middle of conversations about how great Darkroast Day was going to be, they saw the manager nearly running for his life.

"Someone," he shouted. "Anyone! Call the police!"

Normally, people might have screamed, but they were in shock. They couldn't believe that someone was actually in a place like *Plush* wielding a knife.

Some of the regulars turned to each other and whispered, "Hey, I think that guy used to work here … he got fired because he yelled at a woman for drinking Darkroast coffee."

Guerrero ignored them all. He didn't have much time. He had a schedule to keep. So he continued his pursuit of the manager until the two of them reached the kitchen.

The manager was now practically pissing in his pants, because he knew that Guerrero would have him cornered in the kitchen. Already, Guerrero was gaining.

He kept watching that knife. His eyes always on that knife.

Back inside the kitchen, word had already circulated that Guerrero was outside chasing down the manager with a knife. One of the waiters had run inside and told the line cook, who turned and shouted to the head chef, who turned and screamed through the entire kitchen that the ex-Head Busboy had flipped.

"Guerrero's gone mad," he shouted. "He's come to kill us all!"

Everyone in the kitchen scattered and ran for their lives, except for a small group of Mexican kitchen staff and busboys who actually remained quite calm.

"Guerrero," they all mumbled. "Está aquí. Está tiempo."

One by one, they all dropped what they were doing.

"What do you want," said the manager as he and Guerrero burst in through the kitchen doors. He threw his hands in the air, tears running down his cheeks, a small spot of wetness spreading over his crotch. They were now inside the kitchen, and Guerrero had the manager cornered against the prep line.

Guerrero only said one thing to the manager.

"I've come to collect," said Guerrero. "It's time."

He held the knife's point against the manager's chest.

"For Christ's sake," said the manager. "I'm sorry I fired you, but you *yelled* at a woman for drinking Darkroast coffee. You told her that it was wrong, that Victor was wrong, and that she was wrong for supporting them. And then you knocked her coffee into her lap!"

Guerrero simply looked at the manager, and gritted his teeth. Then he looked to his right and saw that the entire group of Mexican kitchen staff and busboys had come to his side. A sum total of five men, and they were all in a line, waiting for him.

They saluted.

The manager looked right, and then a confused look crept into his face as he saw the entire kitchen empty except for that group of five Mexicans. And none of them looked surprised to see Guerrero here in this position. In fact, they looked like they expected it.

And they were saluting?

Guerrero only said one more thing to the manager.

"I've come to collect my Amigos," said Guerrero. "We have a war to start."

And then Guerrero turned around with his knife and his five men, and they left.

• • •

Barista Wally was doing his best to crank up the cappuccino machine and make a Grand Zippo Latte for his next customer when Barista Nate raced in from the back. He was carrying a box.

"THEY'RE HERE! THEY'RE HERE," shouted Nate, with a big boyish grin on his face. He slapped the box down on the counter next to Wally, totally ignoring the customers, as usual. "The box was just delivered. Check it out."

"Hold on," said Wally. He focused on the cappuccino machine. He had already loaded the zippo coffee beans. Added the whipped cream tubes. The steam was starting to build, and now was the time to pull one of the three black levers, which would begin the pressure brewing. Wally tried to focus.

The customer behind called for him.

"Ummm," she said. "Are you almost done with that? It's been like five minutes on one coffee. I was hoping to stop by the park before my break was over."

"Just a minute," said Wally. He knew it had been five minutes. He knew that there were at least four other people lined up behind that. He knew that this was Darkroast, where everything was supposed to be *perfect all the time,* as the brochure said. It also said that the baristas who made your coffee were *brewing experts* and they were proud to wear these stupid black aprons with that stupid Darkroast shield on them, and they'd be happy to make you countless excellent coffees with fast, friendly service.

Wally had been partying all night, and it had taken him at least fifteen minutes just to tie his shoes this morning.

But forget all that, thought Wally. He was concentrating. He was going to get this right. He just had to figure out which lever it was. *Middle*, he thought. *I remember, middle.*

"DUDE," said Nate, suddenly reaching over and slamming down the black lever on the right. "STOP SPACING OUT!"

"DUDE," Wally shouted back to Nate. "WHAT THE HELL DID YOU ...?"

But then he saw that the coffee had actually started to brew. It was pouring into the cup. *How the hell*, he thought.

"It's about time," said the woman in line.

Wally looked at Nate. Again, *how the hell*, he thought, *but oh well ... it's working.*

"OK," said Wally. He now turned his full attention toward Nate and the box. "What the hell is that?"

"So like I was saying," said Nate. "THEY'RE HERE!" He slid the box to Wally, and then Wally totally remembered—today was Friday, the day before Darkroast Day, the day when the T-shirts for their band were supposed to arrive.

"HOLY SHIT," said Wally, busting out with a huge grin. "THEY'RE HERE!"

"I KNOW," said Nate. "THAT'S WHAT I'VE BEEN TRYING TO TELL YOU!"

They rushed to the side of the barista counter with the box, and meanwhile, the cappuccino machine started a slight rumble.

Wally and Nate looked at the box. The box was medium-sized. Whitish-gray. Seemingly unimportant from the outside, but Wally and Nate stared and drooled over it like it was their holy grail.

"We should take a moment of silence first," said Wally.

"This could be one of the most important days of our lives," said Nate.

They held a hand to their hearts in silence, and did their best to make their brains remember this day, which they weren't quite sure how to make happen.

Meanwhile, the cappuccino machine behind them began rumbling a little more.

The woman in line had spotted it and noticed something wasn't right.

"Ummm," she said. "My coffee ... ummm ..."

Wally and Nate couldn't hear the woman or the rumbling of the cappuccino machine. They were totally zoned. They now tore into the box and then Wally held the first T-shirt up to his chest over the black apron. It looked just as beautiful as they imagined it. The T-shirt was entirely black and in the middle there was this picture of a gigantic radioactive yellow squash. The squash had an X burned into its side, and underneath the squash was the band's name. *Their* band's name: SuperSquashX.

"SuperSquashX," they shouted together, giving a high five and making air guitar movements to one of their favorite songs, "Blue Bubble Boy." Whenever they celebrated anything important, they always made air guitar movements to this same song. It was the first song that Wally and Nate had written together. Neither of them really knew what the song was about. It used the word "blue" a lot, and never once mentioned "bubble boy." But it was the one that began the band and that meant it was important.

Meanwhile, the cappuccino machine began steaming from several nozzles.

"Ummmm," said the woman. "That machine … it's ummm.…"

"It looks awesome," shouted Wally. He picked one out of the box and held it up beside his black apron. He had never looked happier in his entire life, except of course, on the first day he and Nate founded the band. "We should start wearing these right now."

"They look a helluva lot better than these stupid black aprons," said Nate. "People will love them."

"Totally," said Wally. He put one on and modeled it for Nate. "How's it look?"

"Dude," said Nate, nearly brought to tears. "Words can't describe it."

"Dude," said Wally. "This is gonna totally put us on the map! We'll be like walking advertisements! We're gonna be huge!"

"I know," said Nate. "I'm the man! The M-A-N!"

"Alright," said Wally. "We should hide these before Chaz sees. That asshole will totally be pissed."

Chaz was short for Chazworth McDoogal, and Wally was right: Chaz was an asshole. Unfortunately, this asshole was their manager at Darkroast, and he was always in a bad mood. Especially about anything that had to do with their band. Wally and Nate joked that it was because he had such a goofy, dorky name, but they really thought he was such a jerk because he had once been in a band, and his band *never* made it. It was the classic case of disgruntled, failed artist turned corporate sellout.

They knew that if Chaz came out and caught them with these shirts, he'd flip.

"Come on," said Wally. "Let's get these put away. Hurry."

"Don't worry," said Nate. "He's chilling in the back. Everything's under control."

But it wasn't.

"GUYS," shouted the woman, this time getting Wally and Nate's attention. "LOOK!"

She pointed at the cappuccino machine, and that's when Wally and Nate looked in horror. They saw that the machine had stopped pouring coffee into the cup. Instead, smoke came out the nozzle. All three black levers were jittering, and steam sprayed from the sides. A new steam jet shot out with every passing second. The thing looked like some kind of pressure cooker about to explode.

Wally looked at Nate.

"Dude," he said, his face in fear. "Are you sure that the lever you hit was the brewing lever?"

Nate cocked his head. He had no idea what Wally was talking about.

"Brewing lever?"

Wally and Nate didn't even have time to duck. Milk and foam went everywhere. The top burst off the machine, and the remnants of over-cooked Grand Zippo Latte sprayed on their faces, their aprons, their hair, all over the walls and counter, and even as far as a few customers. It was a Grand Zippo Latte explosion.

When they turned around, several customers in the front were picking whip cream and shredded coffee filter from their hair. The woman in front had a string of brown goop hanging from her nose.

"Dude," said Nate. "I think I hit the wrong lever."

"Dude," said Wally. "We're totally busted."

And he was right. Here came Chaz.

The look on Chaz's face was that typical Chaz look. A subtle mixture of *Jesus-I'm-so-fucking-better-than-you* and *The-world-would-be-so-much-better-if-it-just-had-more-people-like-Chaz-in-it*.   Chaz wore his hair slicked with an unnaturally perfect part on the side that showed he was way more accustomed to a punk mop top cut like Wally and Nate's, but had abandoned it for what he thought was a "business professional" hairstyle. He used way too much crunchy gel to keep the cowlicks down, but there was always one or two sticking up like a goofus. His Darkroast outfit was always in perfect order—the standard issue—a white Oxford button down with jeans, a black tie, and that notorious apron. He always ironed his apron before work. There was never a single wrinkle, just like the Darkroast barista handbook recommended.

The only innovation Chaz made in the uniform was that he rolled up his sleeves. He took them up to the elbows, and you could swear he thought it made him look cooler.

He thought he was the best fucking barista to ever set foot on this planet.

"WHAT DID YOU DO THIS TIME?" Chaz shouted, as he walked towards Wally and Nate from his back office. He had been back there surfing the internet when he heard the explosion, checking out the company website (he did this three times a day, as if it was going to suddenly change or something, and he never liked to be disturbed during this time).

Now that he was in front of Wally and Nate, he saw his two baristas covered in coffee goop and brown milk standing next to a near-obliterated coffee machine.

Wally was wearing some ridiculous black T-shirt over his apron. Beneath the splotches of burnt milk, it had some kinda glowing vegetable on it.

"THIS IS GREAT," Chaz shouted. "THIS IS JUST GREAT! YOU WERE THINKING ABOUT THAT BAND AGAIN! THAT STUPID BAND!"

Wally and Nate tried to not look guilty.

"No we weren't," said Nate.

"Yea," said Wally. "Why would you think that?"

Wally had forgotten he was wearing the SuperSquashX shirt. Chaz zipped right over to him and grabbed a wad of it near the collar.

"WHAT THE HELL IS THIS," he shouted, and then he saw the box of T-shirts sitting on the counter. "I TOLD YOU NO BAND CRAP WHILE YOU WERE ON THE JOB!"

There was an uncomfortable pause.

"But they're shirts," said Nate. "We *finally* got shirts! We're gonna make it!"

Wally kicked Nate in the shin. Nate had made the ultimate mistake: he'd pissed off Chaz. Both of them watched as Chaz ripped the shirt off Wally, grabbed the box of other shirts, headed for the back-alley dumpster, and threw them away. The worst thing was: both of them knew there was nothing either of them could do about it. Whatever Chaz said was the final word.

"NO BAND CRAP WHILE ON THE JOB," shouted Chaz. "AND THAT'S FINAL!"

Chapter 3

As Victor and Ted's limo sailed down the interstate, having put the park and downtown well behind them, both men watched the Boston city skyline zipping by. It was grand, majestic, and yet somehow, it seemed so palpable and frail to these two men. Like a toy.

Ted was on the phone already making calls to other cities around the country. Houston. Los Angeles. Denver. Kansas City. Atlanta. He informed them all that everything was going as planned.

"Tonight," he was saying. "We launch the big test. This final run will make sure everything's in order. If all goes well, there's no stopping us."

Victor sat by Ted's side, silently looking out the window. Dreaming. He held out his hand over the skyline and noticed that from this perspective, his palm alone could cover most of it up. It gave him a certain thrill.

Heading north on the interstate, the limo was now coming towards the junction leading to the airport. Another branch in the interstate split off and traveled left, in a different direction. With a polite casualness, the limo driver informed Victor and Ted: "Only fifteen minutes or so until the airport. We'll just make a right turn up here."

Ted continued talking on the phone, never missing a beat. The limo driver noticed that Ted seemed remarkably serious and detached compared to twenty minutes ago. He couldn't hear exactly what Ted was saying, but he was now mentioning something about *Mind Melt* and the Moon Laser Show.

Victor continued looking out the window, still dreaming with his hand.

"No," said Victor. "*Left.*"

The limo driver cocked a funny eye, confused.

"Left?" he asked. "What do you mean, *left*?"

"I'm answering your question," said Victor. "Let's go left."

The limo driver cocked his head, again confused.

"*Left?*" he said. "Can't get to the airport if we go left?"

Victor dropped his hand to his lap, slightly annoyed.

"I *know*," he said emphatically. Then he leaned back and resumed a smile. "We're not going to the airport."

"But the lady … Miriam … she said," the limo driver insisted, now quite confused.

"Please …" Victor urged. "We're very busy. No time for questions. We're going left. We're going straight back to Darkroast Headquarters."

The limo driver shrugged, then gave the wheel a gentle turn left.

"Darkroast Headquarters it is."

Victor smiled, and returned to dreaming with his hand.

• • •

Darkroast Headquarters was located on the far north edge of town, on several acres of land that Victor Black had purchased many years ago after the company hit it big. The land had originally been used for second-rate apartment housing and shipping storage, which after purchasing, Victor quickly tore down and used entirely to build his Headquarters.

He wanted all of the land. All of it.

When he built the Headquarters, Victor had two goals in mind: size and luxury. He knew what he was building was not just any old corporate Headquarters. It was going to be his World Headquarters. The Headquarters of the future.

He employed the best architecture firm in the world (one who had much experience building elite corporate headquarters and major offices for businesses and governments all around the globe), and when all was said and done, the entire building was twenty stories high, and used over a hundred thousand tons of steel, glass, and concrete constructed into the shape of a gothic militaristic fortress. It was a monument to corporate dominance priced in the multi-billion dollar range, and at the top of the building, so that no one could ever forget where it all came from, there was that big black Darkroast logo. It could be seen from miles around like a big, black, all-watching eye.

As the limo arrived at the gates to the Headquarters, Victor was looking straight at this giant black logo. He watched it every time he arrived at the Headquarters, a bizarre personal ritual, and each time it nearly took his breath away. He turned to Ted, who was now off the phone and watching him staring at the logo. Ted had never seen Victor so happy.

"I never get tired of seeing that," said Victor.

"I don't blame you," said Ted. "It's a beautiful symbol."

"Driver," said Victor. "Take us up slowly. I want to remember this day."

The limo driver nodded.

Darkroast Headquarters had a long driveway that reached from its front gates all the way to the main employee parking lot in front. Most of the surrounding grounds that the driveway cut through were big, sprawling lawns. Bright green and perfectly maintained. Over their surface stretched a network of expensive shrubberies, statues, and fountains that were all constructed for one purpose: to promote Darkroast.

Normally, there might have been a lot of activity surrounding these grounds. Cars parked in the lots, or cars coming and going down the long driveway. Perhaps employees strolling the lawns and sitting on benches enjoying their lunch breaks with steaming hot cups of Darkroast coffee.

But Victor and Ted had given everyone the day off today, in preparation for the big holiday, and as Victor and Ted pulled up the driveway in the limo, they observed an unusual quietude about the Headquarters. They felt the atmosphere was fitting; it added a sort of peaceful grandeur to their arrival, which they both took as a good omen.

"This is a sign of good things to come," said Ted.

"I think so," said Victor. "*Very* good things to come."

Victor and Ted had the limo driver continue the car up the driveway towards the back side of the Headquarters. They headed for the newest addition to the building, a structure known as Advanced Development.

Advanced Development had been built onto the back side of the building several years after the Headquarters was founded, and several months after Victor had acquired Ted as his business partner. It was a huge addition the size of several large superdomes, and to be honest, it looked large enough to house a small mountain inside. From the outside it looked plain and boxy, and the only distinct features were two large-domed retractable hangar doors on the roof, which couldn't be seen unless you were on one of the Headquarters' top floors looking down out the windows.

Advanced Development was a mysterious division at Darkroast. A bit more quick history as to why:

To begin with, Advanced Development was four times the size of any other division at Darkroast. It was the only division at Darkroast kept separate from other Darkroast workers. There were keypads to all the doors, which only Victor and the members of Advanced Development had access to. Under specific orders from Victor and Ted, the members of Advanced Development were given instructions not to mingle with any of the regular employees of Darkroast.

Strange sounds always came out of the Advanced Development Division. On some nights there were the sounds of saws buzzing through metal or electrical wires zapping. On other nights there were sounds like huge caste iron drums and stainless steel plates being welded together, and the churning of loud gears, as if huge cranes and machines inside were working.

There was always lots of banging and computer-like noises.

And then there were the sounds of men yelling and fighting, and occasional popping noises which vaguely resembled gunfire. Indeed, late at night, during just the right hour on just the right day, if you put your ear to the doors of Advanced Development, you'd swear the other side sounded like a full-scale war was in full swing.

And routinely at night, for the past year, especially the past couple of weeks, shipments had always been coming and going from the division. Huge truckloads filled with countless boxes would travel nightly from the building.

Sometimes they made stops at back alley warehouses in the city.

As far as everyone at Darkroast was told, Advanced Development was where Victor and Ted came up with all their new coffees. This is also where they were developing their newest coffee, *Mind Melt*, which would be debuted on Darkroast Day. As the development of new products at any corporation was always a closely guarded secret, this explained all the keycodes, security, and intense secrecy.

Not even Miriam was allowed to enter.

• • •

The limo was now parked at the back of Advanced Development. The driver kept the car idled in front of two large docking doors.

He only did as told. No questions asked.

He looked around now and again, but saw no one. The Headquarters was an absolute ghost town. It was almost creepy it was so deserted.

Ted picked up the phone in the limo. He mumbled some words, and then after a moment, he nodded to Victor.

"They're letting us in," he said.

"Wait here," said Victor to the limo driver. "We'll be entering in a moment."

The limo driver looked around and still saw no one.

"Whose 'they,'" he said to Victor, taking the pause to make brief chit-chat.

"Please," said Victor. "Don't make small talk."

"I hear this is where you make the *Mind Melt*," he added, trying again in a friendlier tone, making eye contact.

"Please ..." said Victor again. "We're very busy. Don't make small talk."

The limo driver noticed that indeed, Victor was *not* very busy—he was merely sitting in his seat, waiting silently and looking forward. He was also doing something very strange with his thumbs. He was twiddling them, but doing so remarkably fast. Faster than the limo driver had ever seen anyone twiddle their thumbs.

It was weird, but he didn't think much of it. He turned around, and began to wait silently as well.

After a moment, the docking doors began to open. The doors withdrew slowly; they were so large and it took an enormous effort to move them even an inch. When they finished opening, it was like a huge cavern had opened up in the side of Advanced Development. It was very dark and was the biggest room the limo driver had ever seen. Funny thing was, it was still only a small fraction of the size of the entire place.

"Pull inside," said Victor.

He had stopped twiddling his thumbs.

Again, the limo driver did as told. As the car pulled inside, it was only an outer chamber of the facility, but the inside was very dark and the car entered as if it was disappearing into an infinite black void. It was strange how the light barely entered the room from the outside because of the room's massive size. The driver almost wasn't sure what to do it was so dark.

"Should I keep pulling forward," he said.

"Yes," said Victor. "Keep pulling forward."

The car continued for several seconds, now traveling in total pitch black darkness, until finally Victor leaned forward in his seat, stared out into the dark as if he could see right through it, as if it was mere daylight, and said: "Stop. Now."

It was as if Victor could sense they were about to hit something.

"Hope you know what you're doing," said the limo driver, and he hit the brakes to stop the car. It was then that a large *BOOM* sounded from the darkness behind—the sound of the docking doors closing— and the lights popped on to reveal that sure enough, the car had halted inches from a far wall.

"Geez," said the limo driver. "That was close!"

"Exit. Now," Victor said, and then all three men exited the car.

It was like a giant warehouse, and it seemed even bigger to the limo driver now that he was out of the car. He couldn't believe its size. It was dwarfing. Utterly dwarfing. And this was only a fraction of the whole size of Advanced Development.

Strangely, the whole room was almost entirely empty. If this was a warehouse, it could have held thousands upon thousands of crates, but only a few stacks of remaining wooden boxes sat at the far end of the room. Between the stacks of boxes, there was a single door. It was the only door in the room, and it sat alone like a tiny portal drifting at the end of an endless void.

And then it opened.

The limo driver didn't pay much attention to the fact that the door had opened, and an intensely bright green light was shining from within. He also didn't pay much attention to the fact that someone had exited the door, and was walking straight towards the limo.

Instead, the limo driver craned his neck up towards the ceiling, examining how high it went and how wide across it extended.

"You know," he said. "This is a mighty big room to keep empty. What'd you keep in here? Is it the *Mind Melt* like I said? Bet so, huh."

The limo driver smiled, doing his best to be congenial. He really was a congenial, nice guy. The kinda guy you could sit down and have a few drinks with, even if you didn't know him.

"Bet so," he said again. "Bet so."

Unfortunately, the limo driver wasn't too smart. He had failed to observe that as he'd been talking, the person who had entered the room had just crossed an incalculably long distance in an impossibly small amount of time. Nearly a hundred yards in less than ten seconds and without much sound, almost like a machine teleporting at warp speed.

Now, the person was at his side.

The limo driver looked left.

"Oh," he said, leaping back in surprise. "Didn't see you there. Sorry."

Standing no more than a foot away was a Darkroast barista. The barista was a young man, twenty-three looking, with a mop top haircut and large bony cheekbones. He wore a crisp white collared Oxford shirt, buttoned all the way up except for the final button. The shirt was roughly tucked into a set of jeans, which were frayed, just enough to look casual yet respectable. Over his shirt stretched a long black Darkroast apron, two thin straps neatly tied at the back. On his right hand, he wore a familiar black glove.

It was the young man from the warehouse alley.

The barista cocked his head for a moment, almost like an inquisitive bird might do, then shot its gloved hand out with lightning speed. It gripped the limo driver's neck with the force of steel, and suddenly lifted him into the air as if he weighed nothing at all. The barista held him there, suspended like a doll, his legs frantically kicking off the floor.

The limo driver had no idea what was happening. He made a desperate gasp, and he gurgled as the blood began to rise in his neck.

Instinctively, he kicked at the barista, but the barista didn't mind. Not a single hit made him flinch.

"Stop ... please," he cried to the barista.

The barista said nothing back.

"Why are you doing this," the limo driver managed to exhale as his throat collapsed. He looked to Ted and Victor for help.

Ted and Victor more or less ignored the limo driver. They had already begun to walk away towards the door at the room's end. They were walking towards that green light, which was still shining—glowing, like something radioactive. Ted had lit a cigarette, picked up his cell phone and was starting to make calls. He didn't bother to answer the limo driver, and took a long drag on his smoke.

Only Victor answered the limo driver, but very half-heartedly.

"I told you," said Victor. "No small talk."

Then the barista smiled at the limo driver—an evil, vicious smile—and engulfed the poor man's body in a terrible, electrocuting green jolt.

Chapter 4

Nate kept eyeing the store's back door and thinking about the alley-way dumpster ever since things had gone down with Chaz. He knew Chaz had thrown the T-shirts in there, and it was tearing him up inside. Chaz had given them an ultimatum: if they tried to get back their T-shirts, he'd fire them.

"Dude," said Nate. "He shouldn't have dumped our shirts."

Wally nodded and looked up from scrubbing the counters.

"Dude," said Wally. "Just get back to work. You heard what Chaz said. If we pull any more shit today, then we're fired."

"He didn't mean it," said Nate, always the hopeless dreamer. "He's not going to actually fire us."

Wally threw Nate a rag, always the realist.

"Get to work, man. He *meant* it!"

Wally was right. Chaz did mean it. After catching Wally and Nate in that last scenario, he had to. The busted coffee machine. The Grand Zippo Latte goop that went everywhere. The backed-up line of annoyed customers coated in milk and burnt espresso. And his only two baristas standing there with all those band T-shirts, discussing their musical aspirations at work for the umpteenth million time.

Wally looked over at Nate.

Nate had picked up the rag, but was barely cleaning. He was just dragging the rag over a puddle of coffee, smearing it around, only making it worse.

"Dude," said Nate. "I can't believe he threw away our shirts."

"Come on," said Wally. "Stop playing around. Chaz told us to clean this up."

Nate balled up the rag and slammed it on the counter. He looked down the back hall towards the alleyway door.

"So what," he said. "So what if we get fired?"

Wally knew it wouldn't have been the worst thing in the world to get fired from Darkroast. Neither Wally nor Nate enjoyed this job anyway. In fact, this job sucked. It had nothing to do with music, the coffee machines were a bitch to work, and everyday you had to deal with Chaz, the human asshole. Wally wished they lived in a world where musicians could play music all the time … where you could do what you loved and make millions, like all the bands on TV.

But until that day came, he knew they had to work. They had to pay the bills. They had to forget about the shirts.

And anyway, he thought. *Chaz is back there chilling. We'll never get those shirts.*

"Dude," said Wally. "Just drop it, or we're gonna lose our jobs. And then we can't afford any more equipment for the band, and then things are really over!"

But it was no use trying to convince Nate. He was growing worse by the second. He had now entirely stopped cleaning. He'd thrown his rag to the floor. He picked up a Darkroast Day program from the nearby cash register. He was thumbing through it to the page that read "Entertainment," which listed all the bands that were going to play at the park amphitheater during the big holiday. All those big, well-known bands that got to do what they loved and make millions.

"We should be on here," said Nate. "I can't believe he threw away our shirts."

And then Nate threw the brochure down, and looked towards the alleyway door.

"Fuck it," he said. "I'm gonna get back our shirts."

Wally wanted to stop Nate, but he was on a mission. He had that look in his eyes, that Nate-the-dreamer look, and when he got that look, there was no stopping him. He had already rounded the corner and was heading towards the alley door.

Wally knew there was only one thing left to do.

"Jesus," said Wally. "We're totally gonna get fired."

He threw down his rag and followed to help.

Nate moved quickly through the back hall, rushing straight for the alley door like he was on a mission from God. He only stopped for a moment when he neared Chaz's office. He hid outside the door, and peered around the edge inside to look for Chaz. He saw him there, as usual, in front of his computer. Chaz was surfing the internet (checking out the company website). His back was turned to the door.

Nate went bursting past.

"Jesus," Wally said, in a low whisper to Nate. "Watch out."

Nate continued on, and Wally still followed. Wally rushed up to the edge of Chaz's office and peered inside. Chaz was still sitting there on the internet. His back turned. No clue anything fishy was going on.

Holding his breath, praying for luck, Wally burst past the door.

He stopped on the other side, and looked back in. Chaz was still there, surfing away. He was actually talking to himself now; he was trying to memorize the Darkroast Day program website out loud.

"You can do this, Chaz," he was saying. "Come on. Record time! Let's go, Chaz!"

Wally smirked.

"What a major dipshit," he said, and he rushed to meet Nate.

He met Nate at the back door. They were both in the clear, and they entered the alley. Wally held the door open, while Nate sprinted for the nearby dumpster.

"Let's make this fast," said Wally. "No playing around."

"Okay, okay," said Nate.

The alley was a tough, gritty place. Typical big city alley. Not the kinda joint you'd want to spend the night in. Lots of trash and crap lying around, especially weird items like syringes and booze bottles, which would give you an idea of what kinda crowd it attracted in the wee hours. During the day it was okay, though, and Wally and Nate would usually take their lunch breaks back here.

They would always eat on a set of steps near a tall, rusty fire escape ladder.

Luckily, the alley never got much traffic during the day, and the Darkroast store was right in the middle of the alley near the dumpster. There was no one to stop and question why Wally and Nate might be digging into the trash. People on either end of the alley just walked on by, minding their own business. Most were looking at their feet as they traveled down the distant sidewalks.

Wally began to think this was gonna be pretty easy. If only Nate would hurry …

"What's the hold up," said Wally. "Make it fast."

He saw that Nate had already opened the dumpster lid. But instead of digging in right away, he'd shot back and was waving a hand in front of his nose.

"Holy fuck," said Nate. "This shit really smells!"

"Hey genius," said Wally. "It's a dumpster! It's supposed to smell. Just grab the shirts. The box should be on top."

Nate stepped forward and peered inside the dumpster. He was doing his best to tolerate the smell, which really was awful—it reminded him of this one time he'd forgot to clean out an old chicken pizza from under the couch at their house, and they found it three weeks later, after the whole room started to smell like wet dog.

Nate did what he could to ignore the dumpster's smell. He scanned the trash for the box of shirts. There were lots of newspapers, crushed boxes and garbage bags, and then he saw it. It was crammed in the corner next to some big rolled-up rug.

"Fucking asshole," said Nate. "Chaz jammed them down the back … hold on …"

Nate moved around to the back corner and grabbed the edge of the box. He pulled, but the box was stuck. He pulled harder, and the box gave way.

Even Wally could see into the dumpster when the box came free and the big rug shifted, rolled over, and revealed that it was not a rug. It was the dead body of that P.I., Bernard, who had been sitting there mostly covered by trash for the past two days. His head was lying next to an old saucy garbage bag, and his face looked utterly sun burnt, his red freckles nearly blistered off.

Nate saw the body first and dropped the box of T-shirts.

"Holy shit," he said. "Is that?"

"It's a dead body," said Wally.

The two of them were unable to take their eyes off it.

"Is it, real?" said Nate.

"I think so," said Wally. "It sure as hell looks real."

Wally abandoned the door, came around to Nate's side, and again, they both stared.

The body was stiff. Utterly stiff. Wally and Nate couldn't believe they were seeing it. It was just like one of those scenes out of the movies, where two hapless dudes stumble upon some mysterious dead body—*except this was us*, they thought. *This is for real!*

"This is major intense," said Nate. "I wonder who it is."

Nate took a step closer, examining the P.I.'s face. The face looked weird. Blistered and discolored. It was two days dead, but it also appeared to be cooked.

"Don't go any closer," said Wally. "This shit is gross."

"Look at that," said Nate. "He looks like he got microwaved or something."

About that time, a huge metal bang sounded. It sounded like gunfire echoing off the alley walls. Wally and Nate leaped back as the alley door kicked open, and a figure stood there, looming over them.

It was Chaz.

"What the fuck!" said Chaz.

He looked pissed. He saw the box of T-shirts by Nate's feet, and then he looked like he was ready to kill someone.

"I knew it," he said. "Fucking losers … I told you what would happen if …"

Wally immediately interrupted.

"SHUT UP, Chaz," he said. "We found something."

Chaz was taken back. Totally shocked. His eyes got wide, angry, a sort of *I-can't believe-you-just-told-Chaz-to-shut-up* kinda look.

"Jesus," said Chaz, smirking. "I hope you found a new job. Cause you're gonna ..."

"WE FOUND A DEAD GUY," shouted Wally. "IN THE DUMP-STER! LOOK!"

Chaz went silent. He looked into the dumpster, and then he saw it. He saw the P.I., laid out stiff as a board. His face clearly belonging to the land of the deceased.

Chaz's face went limp, then it sort of scrunched up and got totally serious.

"Holy shit," said Chaz. "We have to call the police."

He raced back inside.

"Don't fuck with anything," Chaz said, disappearing down the hall. "And get your asses in here to help! You still haven't cleaned up this mess!"

Wally and Nate ignored Chaz. Nate especially; he leaned over the side of the dumpster. He was still examining the body. He couldn't get over how that face looked strangely cooked, in an unnatural kinda way. *What the hell could have done that to a guy?* he thought. *Didn't look like a fire burn.* He had noticed that the P.I.'s hand also looked the same way. And then he saw that the P.I. had something gripped in his hand. It looked like a thick strip of latex skin.

"Dude," said Nate. "He's got something weird in his hand."

"We should just leave it alone," said Wally. "Let's not piss off Chaz anymore. I'm pretty sure we just lost our jobs."

Nate leaned closer. He had also spotted a piece of paper hanging out of the guy's jacket.

Wally saw Nate reaching his hand out for the body.

"What the hell are you doing," shouted Wally. "Leave that shit alone!"

"I wanna see what this guy has on him," said Nate. "This kinda stuff doesn't happen everyday. Aren't you curious?"

"NO," said Wally, but it was too late.

Nate reached down and ripped the latex skin out of the P.I.'s hand. He also grabbed the piece of paper from the P.I.'s jacket. He looked at the latex skin, which had tiny black hairs on one side and felt strangely like skin—only more rubbery and synthetic. The edges were a bit jagged, clearly showing it had been ripped off something, and on the underside, which was remarkably smooth, there was a tiny symbol: the black Darkroast logo.

"Check this out," said Nate. "That thing in his hand has the Darkroast logo."

Wally wouldn't take it at first, but then he saw Nate waving it in front of him. It *did* have the Darkroast logo on it, which was kinda weird.

"Go on," said Nate. "Don't be such a puss. It's just like latex plastic or something."

Wally took the object from Nate. He held it with the tips of his fingers, trying to touch it as little as possible. He gave it a look. It actually did look and feel a lot like skin, but definitely more rubbery. The Darkroast logo was on the smooth side and was very small. As Wally examined it more closely, he saw there actually was a small bar code and set of numerals printed underneath.

"This is weird," said Wally. "It's got numbers, like some kinda serial code."

Meanwhile, Nate examined the P.I.'s piece of paper. It was folded into a square, and when he opened it up, he saw it was a piece of government-issue letterhead with the Darkroast logo and a project code-name that said: *Project Darkroast*.

In the middle of the page, there was large black writing. Handwritten.

Wally looked over Nate's shoulder and they both read it together. It read as follows:

Darkroast Holiday Conspiracy. Check Warehouse. East and Lawson Alley. 12:45.

The writing was rough. Done with a marker. Scribbled quickly. And there was a phone number beneath it.

"What the hell does that mean?" said Wally.

Nate shook his head. He took another look at the P.I.'s dead, cooked body.

"I don't know," he said. "But whatever it is, it's some of the weirdest shit I've seen."

• • •

At the Boston City Spotlight, London sat in his tiny corner cubicle. Ever since he'd finished his meeting with Lewie, he was doing his best to come up with his Darkroast Day story idea. He stared at a packet of Darkroast Day information that Lewie had given him. On the cover was the big black Darkroast shield, and a picture of Victor Black handing a cup of coffee to a smiling little girl. A picture of the Moon hung gracefully in the corner, like a shiny silver dollar, and they were both pointing up at it with joy.

Suddenly, Lewie's door burst open. Whenever this happened, everyone in the office knew it was something big … and something Darkroast. Lewie came out shouting.

"Okay people," he said. "We got action. I just heard on the police beat. They found a dead body outside a downtown Darkroast!"

The office exploded with action. Shouts went out. Keyboards rattled. Phones rung.

"More Darkroast news," someone shouted. "This is great!"

Reporters started grabbing their pens and pads and rushed to Lewie. Somehow or other, Lewie's best reporters (i.e. the ones who always did fluff article after fluff article on Darkroast) always managed to appear in front of that door in less than five seconds. Like sharks, they were suddenly circling around Lewie shouting, "I'm on it! I'm on it!"

Lewie dished out the usual Darkroast angles to the snapping sharks:

"Jones ... find out what it was like for the customers who stopped in there today!"

"Robbins ... do a story on the coffee they were serving when the body was found!"

"Morris ... get me an interview with the manager who called in the cops. He's a hero!"

"Baker ... find out if people at the park have heard about this! And find out what coffee they were drinking when they heard!"

"And the rest of you ... get over there and gimme something on that Darkroast store!"

And then Lewie looked over the crowd at London, who was still sitting in the corner watching the madness from a safe distance:

"For Christ's sake, London," shouted Lewie. "That includes you! Get your ass over to that store and check it out! You still owe me that Darkroast Day article!"

London looked down at the Darkroast packet lying on his desk. He took another look at Victor and the little smiling girl pointing at the Moon.

"I guess anything's better than this crap," he said, tossing the packet aside.

So he grabbed his jacket and left.

The Darkroast store was several blocks down from the park. London parked his car on a nearby corner and exited onto the sidewalk. Already he could see reporters and onlookers piled up outside the back alley. Police had roped things off with yellow tape, but it wasn't helping. The Darkroast circus was already spinning out of control.

London walked up to the edge of the crowd and peered down the alley. There was a huge circle of cops gathered around a dumpster. It was covered with police tape, and nearby, several cops were stuffing a corpse in a body bag.

"Alright people," the police captain was saying. "No leads so far. Nothing."

Standing next to the cop was some Darkroast barista who wouldn't stop smiling. It was Chaz. He was handing out Darkroast coffee to people, and gloating over his sudden accumulation of an audience.

"Yes, yes. I called the cops. We're just glad none of the customers were hurt," said Chaz to the crowds. "That's the important thing."

One of the reporters took a coffee, thanked Chaz, and raised a microphone.

"Do you think that this guy was a customer," the reporter said.

Chaz's smile vanished, but the captain stepped in.

"I told you," the captain said. "We don't know nothin'. We've got all the evidence here, but we've got a lot of work on our hands with the big holiday tomorrow anyway. We'll put more time into it *after* Darkroast Day."

London turned away from the mess. *After Darkroast Day?* he thought. *Not even the cops have their priorities in order.* He leaned up against a nearby car and looked across the street, and then he saw a strange thing. Some distant commotion in an alley across the street. Two Darkroast baristas were kicking some big metal door, and they looked pretty determined about it. The two baristas were Wally and Nate.

London left the crowds and headed their way.

When London caught up with Wally and Nate, he saw that they were standing on a loading dock outside some warehouse door. They still wore their black barista aprons and were kicking at a big lock which secured the door at the bottom.

"Thing's jammed or something," said Nate.

"Come on, dude," said Wally. "I don't think we're gonna get in here like this."

"Hey," said London. "Whatcha doing?"

Wally and Nate spun around. Neither of them knew they had an audience.

"Uh," said Nate. "Nothing ..."

"He's just acting stupid," said Wally.

They both looked down and saw London's press badge. They read the label: *Billy London. Boston City Spotlight.*

"So ..." said Nate. "You're a reporter?"

"Yea," London replied. He smiled a little, thinking this was a good thing.

"We hate reporters," said Wally. "Shouldn't you be across the street asking stupid questions or writing about Darkroast or something?"

"Believe me," said London. "That's the last thing I wanna be doing."

"So ... uh, do you want something from us?" said Wally.

London suddenly hopped up on the cement platform and stood between Wally and Nate. He looked at the locked warehouse door, then looked at these two baristas standing here in their black aprons, totally out of place.

"No," he said. "I'm just wondering why two baristas are out here, across the street from a Darkroast store that just recently became a homicide scene—I assume a homicide scene that you work at."

"We got fired," said Wally.

"Okay ..." said London. "A homicide scene that you *used* to work at. And now you are trying to break into a locked warehouse door.

Right across the street from a whole mob of cops who could bust you in a heartbeat if they wanted."

Wally and Nate looked at each other, and shrugged.

"You're gonna rat us out," said Nate. "Aren't you?"

"No," said London. And he paused, then smiled even brighter at the two of them.

"But I am gonna tell you that the only way you're getting through that locked door is with a pair of heavy duty bolt cutters … a pair of heavy duty bolt cutters that I just happen to have in my car across the street."

Wally and Nate looked at each other again. Nate grinned. Now they understood.

"Ummm," said Nate. "Mind if we borrow your bolt cutters?"

"No problem," said London, patting their backs. "I'm already there."

Minutes later, London was down on his back working at the warehouse lock with his bolt cutters. It was a tough lock, nearly an inch thick of steel, but he was making his way through it. He took a break for a moment, and extended his hand to Wally and Nate.

"So," he said. "The name's Billy London."

Wally and Nate were standing nearby, watching London's progress on the door. Nate stepped over first and shook London's hand.

"I'm Nate," he said. "And this is Wally."

Wally reached over and shook London's hand.

"So," said Wally. "You always carry bolt cutters in your car?"

London went back to cutting the lock.

"Comes in handy now and then," he said. "You always make a habit of breaking into warehouses?"

"We just got fired," said Wally. "Our dickhead manager Chaz fired us right after we found that dead body in the dumpster."

London nearly dropped his bolt cutters.

"Wait," he said. "*You* found that dead body? I thought the other barista back there said …"

"That's Chaz," said Nate. "He's our manager. He only called the cops. Then he took all the credit."

"Fired us afterwards," said Wally.

"And took our T-shirts anyway," said Nate. "That's why we're over here. We could give a rat's ass about Chaz and those cops. Darkroast, too."

"Then maybe you should take off those silly aprons," said London.

Wally and Nate both looked down. They forgot they were still wearing their Darkroast aprons. They both pulled them off, wadded them up, and threw them on the ground. They turned back to face the warehouse door.

"Nate thinks there's something in here," said Wally. "Something that has to do with the dead body we found."

"When we find it," said Nate. "*We're* gonna get the credit! Not Chaz. And we're gonna be famous. And then our band is gonna be famous. This is all so that our band, SuperSquashX, can be huge. It's our dream."

London turned back to cutting the lock, and raised an eyebrow in confusion.

"Whatever floats your boat," he mumbled, then he put all his weight into the bolt cutters and a giant snap sounded.

The lock broke through. London removed the broken lock and flung the warehouse door open. He stood up and then he, Wally, and Nate looked inside. The warehouse went back about fifty feet and was about a hundred feet wide. After stumbling onto Wally and Nate, London had thought he might get his Darkroast story after all. But this thought suddenly vanished—the warehouse was dark as hell, and entirely empty.

"So," said London, frowning. "Whatever you were looking for, I don't think it's in here."

"Shit," said Nate, visibly pissed. He stomped in and looked around the room. Not a single window. Not a single door. Not a single shred of nothing. Just a big, blank hole in the wall.

"Well," said Wally. "This was a waste of time."

"I can't believe it's totally empty," said Nate. "What the hell is this thing doing here if it's not even being used!"

"You're in a big city," said London. "Warehouses like this are all over. People own em, rent em for months, or only use em for a day or so."

"Then why was it locked?" said Nate.

"Could be a million reasons," said London. "Maybe someone accidentally left it on here. Hell if I know."

Nate was frustrated. He scuffed his foot on the floor, and went to a far corner of the warehouse and sat down. He leaned his back against the wall and dropped his head in his hands.

Wally walked over to his friend's side.

"Come on," he said. "It's no big deal."

London joined them and leaned up against the nearby wall.

"If you don't mind me asking," he said. "What were you looking for in here? You seem pretty bummed about it."

Nate shrugged, then dug in his pocket. He pulled out two objects— the government letterhead and the flap of latex skin—and handed them up to London.

"We found these on that dead body," said Nate, then he returned to sulking and staring at the floor. "Didn't wanna give em to the cops or Chaz. So we kept em."

London took a look at the flap of latex skin. He noticed the texture, the strange resemblance to real skin, only it felt too rubbery. And then he saw on one side that there was the Darkroast logo printed with a bar code and numbers underneath.

"This is weird," said London. "This Darkroast logo, and then these numbers. It's like a Darkroast serial code … on some kinda skin."

"That's exactly what I said," Wally interjected. "We don't know what it's for, but Nate thinks it's suspicious cause we found it on a dead body."

"It *is* suspicious cause we found it on a dead body," said Nate. He still wasn't looking up. He just kept dragging his foot in circles over the cement warehouse floor.

"So why do you think this warehouse has to do with anything?" said London.

"Check out that paper with the handwritten note," said Wally.

London unfolded the paper and immediately noticed it was a piece of government-issue letterhead. He saw the Darkroast logo and some kinda project codename that said: *Project Darkroast.*

"Weird," said London. Then he read the handwritten note in the middle of the page.

Darkroast Holiday Conspiracy. Check Warehouse. East and Lawson Alley. 12:45.

It was in black marker, and scribbled roughly, as if whoever wrote this was in a serious hurry. Immediately, London's eyes took on a sort of intensely curious pose that he hadn't yet shown. The kind that meant something about reading this note had suddenly struck a cord of suspicion in him.

"Hmmm," he said, softly. "I see what you're saying. This is East and Lawson alley. Kinda weird to find this note on a dead guy only a block from the place the note mentions. Not to mention, this paper is government letterhead and it has the Darkroast logo. And what's this '*Project Darkroast*' mean?"

At this point, Nate stood up and trudged away from the group. He stopped in the middle of the room and then turned around to face them.

"It's *too* weird," he said. "How can both the note *and* that piece of latex skin have to do with Darkroast? It has to be more than just coincidence, right?"

Wally felt the need to play devil's advocate. After all, he looked around the warehouse and reminded himself that this place was empty. The note had led to *nothing*.

"Dude," said Wally. "I think we're just gonna have to get the band famous the old fashioned way. There's nothing here. This is going nowhere."

Nate didn't look happy with that answer. He kicked the floor and grumbled to himself. He acted like he was at rock bottom.

Then London spoke.

"Well," said London. "Have you tried calling this number?"

Nate froze. He looked up. Wally looked at London as well. They had forgotten about the phone number at the bottom of the page.

Both of them marveled at London like he was a fucking genius.

"Holy shit," said Nate. "We got so busy, we didn't even think to!"

"We don't have a phone," said Wally.

London patted his pocket.

"Not a problem," he said.

London quickly pulled out his cell phone. Wally and Nate stood there smiling with anticipation. They watched while London dialed the number and put the phone to his ear, and listened for a ring. For a moment nothing happened. Only dead air. Then there was a click, the line turned over.

"Okay, it's ringing," said London.

Wally and Nate took a step closer. Then they listened as the unbelievable happened.

"What the hell?" said London.

A cell phone had just begun ringing outside the warehouse.

They all faced the alley. They couldn't believe it. If this was coincidence, then it was the biggest one in the world. The timing of the ring had been *impeccable*!

"Holy shit," said Nate. "It's coming from the alley."

"You've gotta be fucking kidding," said Wally.

And then they heard a commotion in the alley. Trash cans rattling. A metal lid crashing down.

"Someone's out there," shouted London.

They didn't waste any time. All three rushed outside the warehouse just in time to see that indeed, someone *was* in the alley, and was now running away. He'd been listening in. Spying on them. It was a tall man wearing a long dark trench coat, heavy duty boots, a mysterious wide-brimmed hat, and strangely, a dark titanium mask that covered his entire face. He fled down the alley fumbling with a ringing cell phone like a bat out of hell.

He was the Source.

"Hey you," shouted London. "Wait!"

London took off after him. He hopped down from the cement platform and bolted across the alley, cell phone in one hand and the two clues from Nate in the other.

"Hold up … stop," London shouted. But the Source kept running. Within seconds he had shut off his cell phone and reached the sidewalk beyond the alley. Wally and Nate had now hopped off the warehouse platform and were running after as well. All three chased this mysterious man, but even for London, who was furthest ahead, the Source already had a considerable lead. Once at the sidewalk, he only turned back once to check his pursuers, just briefly as he slid around the alley's corner, then he was gone.

When London made it to the sidewalk, the Source couldn't be found. London scanned the city streets. The cars. The people. There were crowds everywhere, but the Source was nowhere. He'd vanished, just like a phantom.

"Damn," said London. He leaned up against the alley wall and caught his breath. He put his cell phone away, which had stopped ringing. He still held the two clues in his other hand, his grip around them tightened.

Wally and Nate soon caught up, panting.

"Where'd he go," Nate said.

"We lost him," said London.

Nate scanned the streets just in case, but no results.

Wally did the same. They both were totally perplexed.

"This just got heavy," said Nate.

"Major heavy," said Wally. "Who the hell was that guy? He looked like he was wearing a mask."

London shook his head. "No idea."

"This is way too coincidental," said Nate.

"Yea," said Wally. "What the hell was he doing here?"

"I don't know," said London. "But you guys must be onto something." He looked across the busy city streets, people everywhere. The guy was still nowhere to be seen.

"Think this really has to do with Darkroast?" said Nate.

"Think they actually killed that guy?" said Wally.

"Maybe," said London. "Nothing's for sure."

He had now caught his breath. He stepped away from the wall, and looked down at one of the clues—the flap of skin with the Darkroast logo. He ran his fingers over the black shape of the logo, then stuffed both clues into his pocket.

"You know," he said. "If it does have to do with Darkroast, I think I know someone that can help."

• • •

Things were still going perfectly in the park. Miriam had just finished her second Q and A session with some remaining reporters, and was now leading a group of business delegates on a tour around the amphitheater's central square. She pointed at a towering Darkroast statue in the square's center, and gave a gigantic smile. The Darkroast statue had a giant coffee cup in the middle with *real* coffee bubbling and steaming from the top.

"This is the heart and soul of the park," Miriam told everyone. "Feel free to browse around."

People nodded with satisfaction and began to do so. The crowd dispersed, and when they moved out of the way, standing on the other side of the square was Billy London.

Wally and Nate were right beside him.

"Is that her?" said Nate.

"Yep," said London.

They headed straight for Miriam. Miriam saw them coming and her smile erupted into a severe frown. Her body tensed up.

"What are *you* doing here," she said.

London, Wally, and Nate stopped right in front of Miriam. London was holding in his hand the two clues from the dead P.I.

"We need to see Victor," said London.

"What's this about?" said Miriam.

"It's important," said London. "We just need to ..."

"What's this about?" repeated Miriam. Firmer.

London looked her dead in the eye.

"This is strictly *business*," he said. "It has nothing to do with us."

When London said "*us*," what he was referring to was this: London and Miriam had a past. Not a huge one. Nothing particularly important. But it existed, nonetheless.

Over a year ago, before Ted and Miriam had gotten together, they had dated. It was only a several month stretch and was pretty good for a while, but it hadn't ended too well. Neither really knew why things bombed. It just happened.

Months later, Miriam started dating Ted.

Several more months later, her and Ted were married.

"You know," said Miriam. "When someone starts dating someone else and then marries them, usually that means they don't want to see the old boyfriend."

"I told you," said London. "I'm not here about us."

"I hope this isn't about Ted, either. Cause he's not here. He left for Orlando."

"It has nothing to do with Ted. I could care less about Ted."

Miriam shrugged and crossed her arms. She couldn't be so sure. The last thing she wanted to deal with today was an old boyfriend trudging back into her life. Especially the day before Darkroast Day, probably the most important day of her entire life.

"You know," she said. "I haven't seen you in like seven months. And I wouldn't exactly say things went well last time."

Miriam was referring to a press conference she held several months ago at the opening of a new Darkroast store. London had attended the conference (he sat in the back, not with much interest, of course) and at one point he had shouted out something Miriam didn't particularly appreciate.

"I only said 'Opening a damn coffee store wasn't worth writing about,'" said London.

"That's not what I'm talking about," said Miriam. "What about all the stuff you said about the park?"

London's face got all serious. He'd forgotten he had said that.

"That's a different issue."

"You shouldn't have said that in front of a crowd. What were your words? 'This holiday is a joke!' Do you know how *hard* I've worked on this park! Do you realize how important this holiday is to me!"

London's eyes got red.

"This holiday *is* a joke," shouted London. "And besides, you've killed the park!"

London gritted his teeth. He wasn't about to get into this.

"Jesus," said London. "This isn't why I'm here! We need to speak with Victor!"

Miriam paused. She crossed her arms. For the first time she looked at Wally and Nate, who had been standing behind London listening to all of this.

"Who are they," Miriam said. "Your posse?"

"No," said London. "They're part of why I'm here."

"I'm Wally," said Wally.

"I'm Nate," said Nate.

They smiled and tried to look friendly, but Miriam wasn't impressed.

"We used to work for your company," said Nate. "But we got fired. We need to ask you about a dead guy. Darkroast could be involved."

Miriam cocked her head. Confused.

"Huh?" she said.

"Look, this is important," said London. "I already told you that."

Miriam took a step back. She pointed to the central square and shook her head.

"I'm kinda busy," she said. "See all those people. I'm giving a tour."

"We don't have time for this," said London.

And then he just grabbed her arm and pulled her aside.

He led her over near a set of coffee booths and handed her the two clues from the dead P.I. Wally and Nate followed.

We have to see Victor," said London. "We need to ask him about these."

"There's some weird shit going on," said Wally.

Miriam took the clues but didn't look at them.

"You know," she said. "I have a busy life. A whole national holiday being held tomorrow that can't just stop for 'weird shit.' Besides ..."

London interrupted her. His tone was rough.

"Just look at the *damn* stuff," he said.

Miriam went silent. She looked at London, then at Wally and Nate. "Who are you guys, again?" she asked them.

"We're just two baristas in a band, lady," said Nate. "But we're not here to waste your time."

"We're not," said Wally. "Like I said, this is some weird shit."

Miriam nodded. Not that she believed, but she gave in.

She looked down at the clues. She examined the piece of latex skin, first the side with the hair and grooves, then the smooth side with the Darkroast logo and bar code and numerals. She quickly handed it back to London and shrugged.

"What's the big deal," said Miriam. "It's a piece of rubber with our logo and some other junk on it."

"You didn't look at the other thing," said London.

"You have to look at the note," said Nate.

Miriam opened up the folded *Project Darkroast* government letter-head and saw the black marker message scribbled on the page. She read it, and then again, as with the first clue, she handed it back to London without giving it a second thought.

"Again," she said. "What's the big deal?"

"The big deal is," said London, pointing to Wally and Nate. "These two guys used to work at one of your coffee stores a few blocks down from here, and this morning they found a dead body in the dumpster behind their store. They found these two things on his body."

"He was holding that latex skin in his hand," said Wally. "It was pretty gross."

"Had the note in his pocket," said Nate. "And his face was all cooked like burnt hot dog."

"And this morning," added London. "We checked the warehouse mentioned on that page, and some guy—whose phone number is on that *same* page—was spying on us. He ran away when we saw him."

"We think he was wearing a mask," said Wally.

Miriam still didn't seem impressed.

"So why is this my problem?" she said. "And why do you need to see Victor about this?"

"Don't you get it?" said Nate.

"It all has to do with Darkroast," said Wally. "Something's not right."

"We think your company could have something to do with that guy's death," London added. "It could be part of a conspiracy. Victor may be able to help us figure it out."

Miriam didn't take to well to all this. Her eyes suddenly squinted down on London, and she started tapping her heel in anger.

"Wait a sec," she said. She felt like she wanted to punch London.

"You mean to tell me that you barged down here, interrupted my day, and took up my time, all because you think my company is responsible for killing some guy! And you want me to set up a meeting between you and Victor so you can talk it over with him!"

London, Wally, and Nate looked at each other, knowing it was a long shot.

London gulped. "Well ... yes," he said, nodding.

"Jesus," she said. "You're nutso! This is ridiculous. It's the day before Darkroast Day, and this is the last thing anyone has time for."

Miriam spun around and started heading back towards central square.

"But this is important," said London. "All we're asking for is a little help."

Miriam continued walking.

Wally and Nate exchanged worried frowns.

"Dude," said Nate. "I don't think she's gonna help us."

"I don't think so either," said Wally.

London rushed after and tried to stop Miriam. He grabbed her arm.

"Please," said London. "Doesn't any of this sound a little suspicious?"

Miriam threw off London's arm and shoved him back.

"You know what sounds suspicious? Your stupid story of some guy running around warehouses in a mask!"

"But serious stuff could be at stake here," he said.

"No!" she shouted. "And besides, Victor isn't even here. He took Ted to the airport and then he was going back to headquarters ..."

"We can meet him at the headquarters," said London. "You don't even...."

"No," said Miriam. "You can go back to whatever hole you came from!"

"But ..." said London.

"No buts," shouted Miriam. "I don't have time for this."

And with that, she left.

Chapter 5

Skipping back across town, Guerrero Montana was in an alley. The skies overhead were blue, but not much light was shining in the alley. Guerrero stood behind a white van parked in the shadows. Guerrero threw open the back doors of the van and looked inside. His face immediately lit up with a smile.

Inside were enough weapons to take out Fort Knox.

"Now it begins," he said. "It is a good day. Un buen día, indeed."

• • •

Guerrero Montana had a single purpose: to destroy Victor Black and Darkroast. He came from Mexico—a sprawling 800,000 square-mile country that was home to cactus-filled deserts, tequila, and some of the world's finest coffee plantations. Most of Mexico's coffee plantations were located along the southern border and western coastline of the country, in the areas filled with mountains, lush jungles, and tropical rainforest canopies.

For nearly three generations, Guerrero Montana's family had owned a coffee farm in a quiet corner of southern Mexico. The farm—owned and run by Guerrero's elderly father—provided a comfortable lifestyle and produced decent amounts of coffee for the Montana family; however, in recent years, the Montana farm (along with many other nearby coffee farms) had come under control of Victor Black and Darkroast.

Victor Black and Darkroast managed the Montana farm with gracious care—as he and Darkroast did with the other neighboring coffee farms—but it seemed that Victor Black and Darkroast had intentions beyond just coffee. After only several weeks of managing the Montana farm, Darkroast had built an enormous number of strange Army-like structures in the surrounding mountains. Over thirty weaponry tents and a large secret testing facility were built only miles from the Montana farms, hidden among the canopy of trees and jasmine-scented jungle. Late at night, under the darkness of the Moonlit mountains, several nearby farm workers had overseen strange sights inside the secret testing facility—sights of camouflaged young men driving around in Army-like trucks while constructing sections of a titanium metal device large enough to place on the Moon. Much of their equipment seemed way too high-tech and Army-esque for a normal coffee company. In addition, bright bursts of green light often radiated from huge piles of coffee beans kept in the testing facility that had been collected during the day's farming (farmers had seen the beans being secretly test-sprayed with some kind of glowing liquid). There was talk among Victor and Darkroast that all of the activity paled in comparison to the work being done back in America at the Darkroast Headquarters.

Altogether, the strange activity worried Guerrero's father and many of the Montana farm workers. Eventually, in a group decision, Guerrero's father and several farm workers approached Victor Black and Darkroast to demand answers. The result: Victor Black personally executed Guerrero's father and his entire group of farm workers. He killed them by shooting them with a laser beam from his fingertips while smiling a most ungodly and twistedly inhuman smile.

• • •

Ever since it happened, Guerrero swore revenge for the death of his father and fellow farm workers. Guerrero's five Mexican friends from *Plush* restaurant, a group also known amongst themselves as Los Amigos de Muerta, all were related to the murdered farm workers and had traveled with him to America to seek revenge on Victor Black and Darkroast. They had all been biding their time at *Plush* until they could carry out their plan.

Now, the Amigos had already exited the van and were standing behind Guerrero. Every one of them was grinning and ready to carry out their plan. As they looked inside the van, they'd never seen a more beautiful collection of weaponry in their entire life. They knew as well that today was a good day.

"Buen día," they mumbled to one another. "El día de muerta," which meant it was a day of *death*.

Things went quickly from here. There was no time to waste. Guerrero began handing out weapons. There was a huge assortment— everything from TEC-9s and Mig-6x Double Barrels to Semi-auto AK-47s, the kind that can punch through steel like hot butter. They'd all been bought on the black market in bulk. There were also grenades, dynamite, and timed explosives among the mix. Extra emphasis on the explosives. They had them by the bagload.

"Tomalo," said Guerrero as he handed a TEC-9 to one of his men. *Take this.*

"Tomalo," he said again as he handed a .45 caliber assault rifle to another.

"Tomalo, tomalo, tomalo," he continued to say, as he handed out several more.

Then he told his men to examine the weapons, first the guns and then the explosives, making sure that everything was in order. They did so without question.

Guerrero then dug out a metal box from amongst the van's remaining weapons. He took it around to the front of the van and laid it on the hood. He opened it up and withdrew several maps and blueprints. He knew all of these maps by memory, but for now, one of them interested him most.

He spread it out on the hood and studied the plan. This is the one they'd be using first. The map showed details of a particular building—a very large, corporate building. As he traced his finger over several red lines drawn on the building's perimeter, one of the Amigos came to his side.

"Las armas son en condición buena," the Amigo said.

This meant that the weapons were in good order.

"Bueno," said Guerrero. "Mira."

He pointed to the map. The Amigo looked down at it and nodded.

"Es una ruta buena," he said.

Then he put his hand on Guerrero's shoulder, and the two of them smiled at one another. Both of them knew that Guerrero had picked a good path, and that soon their revenge would come.

"Todo es perfecto," said the Amigo.

"Tendremos la venganza," said Guerrro. "Revenge."

They nodded, and the Amigo went back to checking weapons again.

Guerrero put the map away and pulled a pair of binoculars from the metal box. He then left the van and headed to a chain link fence at the end of the alley. There was a clearing on the other side where the alley opened up onto the street and the rest of the outside world could be seen. Guerrero held the binoculars up to his eyes and saw their target sitting in the distance across a several mile stretch of green corporate lawns.

It was Darkroast Headquarters.

Guerrero nodded, knowing that Victor Black was somewhere inside, then smiled to himself.

"Es un buen día," Guerrero said. "A very good day, indeed."

Chapter 6

"This sucks," said Nate. "What do we do now?"

London, Wally, and Nate were sitting on a bench in Darkroast Park. They were all pretty bummed about how things had gone down with Miriam.

"She barely looked at the clues," said Wally. "I thought you said she could help."

London sighed.

"Sorry boys," he said. "I guess I expected too much from her."

"You guys must have had a pretty shitty break-up," said Wally.

London looked away from the group. He noticed a tiny duck waddling around several large black coffee frescos looking for its home. As it was rooting at a lonely patch of grass under the fresco, a Darkroast worker came from the other side and kicked it away.

London frowned. "I guess you could say we had our differences."

"That sucks," said Wally.

"Oh well," said Nate. "It was worth a shot."

• • •

Miriam's central square tour finished up quickly. After meeting with London, she wasn't in the best of moods either. She shook a few hands and told people she expected to see all of them at the park tomorrow, and then she headed off towards the half-shell stage to tie up some final loose ends.

Just as she got there, her assistant came running.

She was calling her name and holding a big manila envelope.

"Miriam!" said her assistant. "This just came for you."

She handed Miriam the envelope.

"Thanks, Alice," said Miriam. She began to break open the seal.

"No problem. I guess it's urgent. Some guy just showed up and dropped it off. He said that you had to open it before your friends left the park."

Miriam looked up, confused.

"Friends?"

Her assistant shrugged. "I dunno. He said that there were three of them."

Miriam froze.

"Three?" she said.

"Yep. Three," the assistant repeated.

Miriam slowly looked down at the package, then ripped it open. When she removed the contents, it was a single note inside. It was written quickly. Black marker scribbled on the same type of government letterhead. It read:

Your friends are onto the truth. Someone has evil plans for Darkroast Day. Millions will die.

Miriam didn't know what to make of it. Her face went a little pale.

"What is it?" her assistant asked.

Miriam didn't answer. She looked around, suddenly feeling like she was being watched.

But she saw no one. She looked back down at the page, and reread the line:

Someone has evil plans for Darkroast Day. Millions will die.

"Is it some kinda prank?" her assistant asked. "The guy who dropped it off was kinda weird. He was wearing a mask."

• • •

It was only about three minutes or so before Miriam found London, Wally, and Nate. They were still in the park, but they had gotten off the bench and were about to head their separate ways.

"Hey," said Miriam. "Wait up."

London, Wally, and Nate stopped and turned around. She came rushing up to them.

There was a pause. No one spoke, and then ...

"What do you want?" said London.

Miriam handed him the envelope with the note.

"Alright," she said. "I'll take you to the headquarters, but I swear ... if this is a waste of my time, so help me God. You'll be the next ones turning up dead."

• • •

They took Miriam's car, a luxury SUV with a Darkroast bumper sticker on the back. She drove at a normal pace while Wally and Nate sat in the back seat looking out the windows. London was in the front seat examining the note Miriam had received.

"This means that the guy followed us to the park," said London. "He had to be watching us talking with Miriam. He had to know exactly what we said."

"All my assistant said," Miriam told them. "Was that the guy dropped it off in a hurry, and he was wearing a mask."

"Plenty of people that fit *that* description," said Wally, sarcastically.

"What's the deal with this guy anyway," said Nate. "He runs around in a mask acting all strange and stuff? What the hell does he want?"

"This is interesting," said London. He had taken the other note from the P.I. and held it next to the new note. "The two notes have the same handwriting and are written on the same type of government letterhead."

Everyone looked over at the notes—even Miriam—and they all saw that it was true: the two notes *did* have the same handwriting and *were* written on the same type of government letterhead.

"*Project Darkroast?*" said Nate, reading the letterhead. "What the hell does all this mean?"

"Still don't know," said London. "All I know is that something isn't right. Someone's dead. Someone's keeping tabs on us. It all has to do with Darkroast Day, and we need to get to the bottom of it."

About that time, they arrived at Darkroast Headquarters. Miriam pulled the car up to the front gates and stopped a few feet away. The gates were gigantic—thick black caste iron with huge metal points at the top. Especially high, especially secure. Several video cameras were posted on each side, filming the driveway below.

The car idled for several seconds while everyone waited for the gates to open.

"It's a pressure sensor pad. Plus there's an automatic license plate I.D. check," said Miriam. "Victor is big on security. He's got surveillance everywhere."

Everyone nodded. They noticed the video cameras on the top of the gate while they continued to wait.

"What's the big deal," said Wally. "The dude just makes coffee. What's to protect?"

Several more seconds passed, and then the gates slowly started to open.

"Okay," said Nate. "That was easy enough."

But it wasn't, because that's when the SUV's back door opened as well. There was a rustle, and the back door slammed just as quickly as it had opened.

Everyone turned around. Several Mexican men were crowded into the back of the car.

Guerrero sat among them aiming his rifle.

"Don't do anything stupid," he said. "Just drive."

• • •

They were all dressed in camouflage. London counted six of them total, and they all were the most well armed group of Mexicans he had ever seen. Every one was carrying guns, knives, dynamite, and grenades galore. They also had several bags of explosives. None of them spoke much. They only watched the path ahead as Miriam drove up the long, winding road to the Headquarters.

Wally and Nate had noticed the group smelled strange. Of course, none of the Amigos had showered since they left the restaurant.

"What's that smell," whispered Nate.

"Smells like dirty dish water," whispered Wally.

"Shut up," said Guerrero.

Guerrero tapped his rifle against Wally's neck.

Miriam continued to steer the car, but she was clearly the most nervous of the bunch. Her hands were shaking on the wheel, barely able to keep it straight. She kept watching Guerrero and his men in the rear view mirror, doing her best to keep cool.

"Please don't hurt us," said Miriam.

"Shut up and we won't," said Guerrero.

"Who are you?" said London. "What do you want with us?"

Again, Guerrero gave the ultimatum. "Shut up," he said. "And keep driving."

Miriam continued to drive. When they had arrived in the front parking lot outside of Darkroast Headquarters, Guerrero instructed Miriam to pull into a corner handicap spot nearest to the front door. Miriam did so without question.

"Cut the engine," said Guerrero. "Everyone exit the car."

Miriam turned the ignition off, then removed her keys. No one exited the car.

This didn't sit well with Guerrero.

"I said exit! All of you exit!"

No one moved. They were all too scared.

"Tell us what you want with us!" shouted London. "We don't want any trouble!"

"Listen," said Guerrero. "We know you support Victor Black. We saw your Darkroast sticker on the back of this car. We're here for him, not you. But if you get in our way, vaya con Dios. I'll put a bullet in every one of you."

After that, there was no trouble.

Four clicks. Four seatbelts unsnapped. Everyone exited the car.

• • •

Guerrero and his Amigos quickly hustled everyone to the front doors of Darkroast. The Amigos spread out around the edge and checked the perimeter for any unpredictable activity, but everything looked clear. Their original plan had been to cut through the secure outer-perimeter gates and maneuver through one of the less-monitored side entrances—but sneaking a ride in Miriam's car had been a free ticket straight past security.

"Parace bien," said Guerrero, looking around the perimeter. *It seems okay.*

"Sí," said one of the Amigos to Guerrero. "No hay nadie por aquí. El coche era perfecto."

He meant that the coast was clear. Miriam's car had worked as a perfect covert transport.

The Amigos ran back and then Guerrero ushered everyone inside the headquarters. Guerrero had noticed that Miriam had a Darkroast entry card on her keychain, and he forced her to use it on the inner security sealed doors.

"You can save us the explosives," he said. "And the noise."

Miriam slid her card into the keycard hole and waited for the light to turn green. Guerrero stood behind her with his weapon against her back.

"Better hope this works," he said, cocking his weapon.

During this time, London had turned around to take a more prolonged look at Guerrero. He saw that the man couldn't have been older than his mid-thirties, and looked like one of those Latino commandos that should have been somewhere in South America marching off to fight some guerilla war. For that matter, all of these men had this same look. They were like a band of revolutionaries from a disheveled foreign country, the kind who didn't share in the All-American Dream.

"What do you have against Victor Black," said London. "Has he done something to you?"

Just then, the green light beeped for the keycard.

The inner security doors opened.

"You have no idea," said Guerrero. "Victor Black is a murderer. He is Evil himself."

Chapter 7

The satellite television broadcast monitors were on in the Master Control Room. Sixteen of them all in a row.

Victor spoke to them, softly, confidently.

"Soon," said Victor. "Everything will be ours. Our final phase is tonight."

Victor had been in the Control Room holding a video teleconference and giving orders ever since they'd entered Advanced Development. Ted was nearby smoking a cigarette, but was tending to other matters. Across the room, in front of Advanced Development's master controls, he was supervising several men in white lab coats. They sat in their chairs among some of the most expensive computer systems in the world and typed furiously at the keyboards.

"I want every last bit of code checked and rechecked," said Ted, taking a puff on his cigarette. "We can't afford any mistakes during tonight's test."

The men nodded and continued typing.

"We will check back at 0200 hours," said Victor to the broadcast monitors. "After the test is run, we will update you with specific instructions. You know the routine."

There were men on-screen in white lab coats and white hats, all sporting the Darkroast logo, who nodded when Victor said this. While these men nodded, you could see labels atop the monitors which read the names of their broadcasting locations:

Dallas. Atlanta. New York. Kansas City. Seattle. They were from cities across the nation, most with populations into the millions.

After they nodded, Victor raised a clenched fist like a dictator.

"Darkroast," he quickly shouted.

All the men on-screen raised their fists.

"Darkroast," they shouted back.

Then the transmissions cut. The teleconference was over.

Victor turned away from the monitors and walked towards Ted. Ted left the master controls and met him at another large video display in the middle of the room.

"Current update. Now," said Victor.

Ted was already punching in the display analysis codes on the side of the table. Numbers and graphics galore began popping up on the monitor, and then a giant map of the entire U.S. appeared. Green dots began spreading over the map like a plague.

Victor watched with approval.

"We have 75% positioning so far," said Ted. "The rest will be in place by morning."

Green dots continued to spread. They were overtaking every state on the map.

"What about the beans?" asked Victor. He pointed to a part of Louisiana which hadn't been lit by green dots. "I want shipments rerouted here. Now! Send troops also."

"Consider it done," said Ted. "We'll spare some from Baton Rouge."

Ted nodded to a man at the computer console. The man quickly put in a call. Victor then turned to the upper corner of the monitor. In a box at the top, a picture of the Moon hovered above the map. Victor pointed at it.

"Readout on the Moon," said Victor. "Now!"

Ted punched a few buttons and suddenly the map of the U.S. was replaced by a giant map of the Moon.

"All diagnostics show we're ready for tonight," said Ted.

More pictures of the Moon—smaller, more detailed pictures—popped up around the edge of the screen. They revealed a giant Moon Laser with a satellite dish on the side, and lots of commotion at its base. Moon trucks and men in space suits were working non-stop around the base. All of the equipment bore the Darkroast logo.

Victor nodded and smiled. He squint his eyes in pleasure. There was a strange, dark green twinkle in one eye.

"They think they're getting a drink and a laser show," he said.

"They'll never know what hit them," said Ted. "It'll be perfect."

"Not just perfect," said Victor.

And then suddenly, Victor's hand was on Ted's shoulder. It moved like lightning. Ted jumped. Victor had grabbed him so quickly that Ted almost didn't see it happen.

"The end," said Victor. "The end of it all."

• • •

About this time, Victor and Ted were interrupted.

"Ummm, sir," said one of the men at the computer console. "We have a breach. Showing a group down in the lobby entrance."

He was pointing to a surveillance screen, and looking quite worried.

Ted and Victor didn't welcome the interruption.

"We don't have time for this," said Victor.

"Dispose of them," shouted Ted.

The man shook his head.

"It's not that simple," said the man. "Some of them have guns. Explosives. Camouflage. And ... and ..."

He waved for Ted to come over. He looked nervous. Unsure of what to do.

Ted rushed to the screen. Peeved.

"For God's sake! What's the problem?" he said.

But then he saw the screen. He saw who was there and nearly dropped his cigarette.

"What is it!" shouted Victor.

Ted turned around. His face emptied of all expression.

Total shock and awe.

"It's Miriam," he said. "She's in the lobby."

Chapter 8

Five explosives had already been placed at key points around the lobby. Guerrero was now fastening another one near a potted plant while his Amigos kept guard. They had London, Miriam, Wally, and Nate huddled in a corner at gunpoint.

"Who the hell are these guys?" whispered Miriam, watching Guerrero set the bomb.

"I don't know," said Wally. "But they sure smell like dishwater."

"They sure have a whole lot of explosives," said Nate.

London nodded. He was also watching Guerrero with the bomb.

"Yea," he said. "A *whole* lot."

London decided he wanted some answers.

"Tell me why you are doing this," said London. "What has Victor Black done to you?"

Guerrero stopped. He turned to London for a moment, almost surprised to hear him asking this question.

"If you only knew," said Guerrero, and then he finished setting the timer on the explosive. He moved the potted plant in front of the bomb so that it was hidden. "You Americans care for nothing but yourself and your precious Darkroast. You do not care who gets hurt in the process as long as you get your Darkroast."

Guerrero left the potted plant and rushed over to the elevator. He hit the up button and checked his watch.

"Diez minutos," said one of the Amigos.

"Claro," Guerrero replied.

London shrugged. He, Miriam, Wally, and Nate had no idea what they were saying.

Then the elevator dinged. It was here.

The doors opened and the Amigos piled in. They shoved their hostages inside with them. Guerrero was the last to enter. As the elevator closed, none of them, not even Guerrero, noticed that several young men wearing black barista aprons went streaking past.

• • •

Guerrero hit the elevator button for the tenth floor. When the elevator started moving up, he looked at his watch again.

"Nueve minutos," he said.

His Amigos nodded.

"Bueno," they said.

The Amigos and Guerrero all watched the elevator lights moving upward from the lobby. *1st floor. 2nd floor ...*

London, Miriam, Wally, and Nate were all crammed against the elevator's back wall. They couldn't take their eyes off these men with the explosives. They were still trying to figure out what was going on, how they had suddenly become hostages by a group of Mexican men who seemed determined to destroy a corporate coffee headquarters. One of the Amigos was standing right next to Wally and Nate with a bag of bombs. Wally peered into the bag and saw the wires, C4, and timers set for ten minutes. These were *real* bombs alright.

"This is serious shit," whispered Wally.

"Yea, dude," whispered Nate.

3rd floor. 4th floor.

Miriam saw the bombs, too. They had set at least six bombs down in the lobby, and they still had plenty remaining in these bags.

"You don't really think you'll get away with this? Do you?" she blurted.

Guerrero continued watching the elevator lights. *5th floor. 6th floor ...*

He didn't put much effort into answering her.

"There's no one to stop us," said Guerrero. "It's the day before the holiday. No one is here."

Miriam didn't let up.

"Honestly," she said. "Victor has so much surveillance here that the cops are probably on their way already."

"Cuidado, señora," Guerrero repeated.

"When they find out that you tried to blow up this place." She feigned a laugh. "I give you ten minutes. Then you're busted."

That was it. Guerrero had enough and he spun around and shoved his rifle up under Miriam's chin. Then he put it to her straight.

"SORRY LADY, BUT IN TEN MINUTES … THERE WON'T BE ANYTHING LEFT OF THIS PLACE."

Miriam went quiet. She looked in his eyes, and saw he was dead serious.

Not a doubt in his mind.

Guerrero turned back around. He gripped his rifle tight and returned to watching the elevator lights.

"Estamos listos," he mumbled to himself, gritting his teeth. "Let them come."

• • •

It was a bad wish. They did come. But when it happened, it wasn't the cops.

8th floor. 9th floor. 10th floor.

The elevator zipped right past the 10th floor and kept going.

11th floor. 12th floor.

"What the hell?" said Guerrero.

It picked up speed.

13th floor. 15th floor.

Only the tenth floor button was lit, and Guerrero hit the other buttons, but nothing would stop it. The elevator was out of control. Everyone was taken by surprise.

17th floor. 19th floor.

"Jesus," shouted Guerrero. "No funciona!"

The Amigos all looked at one another. Panicked.

"What's going on?" said Wally.

"Something's not right," said London.

Nate noticed the worry among the Amigos. "Guys, I get the feeling something really bad's about to happen." Though no one replied, they all shared the same feeling.

And then it was there. *20th floor,* the top floor.

The elevator stopped.

When the doors opened, standing outside were three baristas. All three were wearing the standard Darkroast barista outfits—the jeans, the white Oxford shirt, and crisply ironed black apron. They stood shoulder to shoulder, blocking the entrance to the floor. They had six disarmed bombs in their hands and evil smiles on their faces.

Guerrero immediately noticed that these were the bombs he'd just placed in the lobby.

"What the hell is this?" said Guerrero. "Are those baristas?"

It was the same thought on everyone's mind.

The baristas dropped the dismantled bombs to the ground and aimed their fingertips at the group. They never had a chance. Green lights fired. The elevator was engulfed.

Everyone fell to the floor. Lifeless.

Chapter 9

Back in the Main Control Room, the three baristas returned to Victor. They reported that they had taken care of the group—all of them had been zapped unconscious, removed of weapons, and secured in a holding cell. During the process, they had confiscated three objects— the latex skin and two pieces of government letterhead—and they gave them to Victor.

"Thank you," he said, then he dismissed the baristas.

Alone, Victor took the three objects in his hands and looked at them. Immediately, his face twisted into an awful frown. He recognized all three of these objects and knew that nobody in the group should have had them in their possession. Specifically, the government letterhead that mentioned *Project Darkroast* and his plans for National Darkroast Day.

Victor knew this had to be dealt with. Swift, quiet, and deadly.

The Secret of Darkroast

Chapter 10

Outside Darkroast Headquarters, crouched in the shadows from a distance, a familiar man waited. Perspiration beaded down his forehead, running along the sides of his mask, and in his hands he held a government-issue ultra-neutrasonic tracking device.

He was the Source.

• • •

The Source looked at the chrome-plated dial of the ultra-neutrasonic tracking device. He twisted the dial and attempted to locate London, Miriam, Wally, Nate and the others. If they were anywhere on the bottom floors—where they should have been—they would have registered on the dial. But they weren't.

This is bad, he thought. *Real bad.*

An hour earlier, he'd watched as their car had pulled up to the front gates. He'd followed them here from the park. They had taken Miriam's car, the SUV with the Darkroast bumper sticker, and had come to confront Victor. They arrived and rushed inside—*with that other group, maybe Mexican, whoever they were* ... Minutes after they had entered, there was a terrible flash of green light through the window on an upper floor. *And they hadn't come out,* he thought. *They hadn't come out!*

Continuing to check his ultra-neutrasonic tracking device for any sign of them inside, the Source worried that they had no idea what they were up against. *Maybe it was already too late?* He thought of Victor and the dangers that awaited inside. *That green light*, he thought. *They haven't a chance without my help.*

The blueprints of his creation were still etched in his mind—the solid metal skeleton, the sonic hand laser able to stun or destroy, and the hellbent taste for destruction. *I should have intervened sooner*, he thought. *I've got to help.*

And so the Source put away his ultra-neutrasonic tracking device, climbed down the nearest sewer hole, and headed to his hideout to plan his rescue.

He knew they were going to need it.

Chapter 11

They weren't lifeless ... exactly. Their bodies didn't move, but they awoke later. It was hours later, inside a room in Darkroast Headquarters.

• • •

"Jesus, my head hurts," said London. He rose from the floor and looked around. "Where the hell are we?"

The entire group was in a tiny room with an electronically bolted door and a single window at the far end. The window was barely big enough to look out. London immediately noticed that it was pitch black outside, the Moon in sight. He looked down at his watch and noticed that it was completely fried—the gears were stuck around four o'clock p.m., which was the time they had entered the elevator. He looked back up at the window and reconfirmed that it was completely dark.

"My God," he said. "How long has it been?"

Everyone rose to their feet. Slowly, holding their heads. They had the worst hangover ever and could barely remember a thing. For some reason, they had the vague recollection of being zapped by three Darkroast baristas—but the thought didn't make much sense. They listened to what London said about it being nighttime, although that meant that they had been unconscious for over six hours.

"Nighttime?" said Wally.

"That makes no sense?" said Nate. "We were just in the elevator ... weren't we?"

Suddenly, none of them could be entirely sure. London stepped over and showed them his watch. Nearby, Miriam looked at her own watch—it was also fried by the baristas lasers and was frozen on four o'clock. They all checked the window again and saw that it was pitch black outside, the Moon in full sight.

"What the heck happened?" said Miriam. "How'd we end up in here and how is it nighttime?"

Again, the entire group had the vague recollection of three Darkroast baristas zapping them—but still, such a strange thought made no sense.

• • •

Guerrero and his Amigos didn't have time to notice the concern of London, Miriam, Wally, and Nate. Guerrero and his Amigos had already woken up minutes before, noticed that they hadn't a single weapon on them anymore, and were already frantically checking the room for an exit. Guerrero was looking out the peep-hole window while several of his men were checking the door. Outside, he could make out the familiar parking lot down below. He recognized that this was Darkroast Headquarters—they were being held in a room at the top of it.

"Son of a bitch," shouted Guerrero. "We've been captured!"

Everyone turned around and looked at him—including London, Miriam, Wally, and Nate. Although Miriam couldn't exactly remember how she had ended up in this room, she hadn't forgotten that just before this, Guerrero had been holding her hostage. She was still visibly pissed about it and she snapped at Guerrero's comment.

"What do you mean captured," said Miriam. "Captured by *who*?"

"We're being held by Victor Black in Darkroast Headquarters," said Guerrero. "*Puta madre*! Don't you know anything!"

Instinctively, Miriam lashed out. "That's impossible," she said. "Victor Black would NEVER do something like that. Who *are* you to make such a comment?"

Guerrero looked at her, understanding that this woman had no idea about the *real* Victor Black. Indeed, everyone always thought Victor Black was the most perfect CEO in the world. Guerrero thought of the fact that nobody knew about the secret Army-esque facilities built by

Victor in the Mexican mountains. Nobody knew about the truly vicious and cold-blooded murder of his father and farm workers by Victor.

"Sorry señora," said Guerrero, sarcastically. "But you don't know the real Victor Black. He took over my family's coffee farm and murdered my father. He also killed many friends and family of these Amigos. Mis Amigos."

Miriam nearly swallowed her tongue when Guerrero said this. *Victor Black a murderer?* Miriam nearly flew across the room at Guerrero.

London had to step in. He sensed the conversation spiraling out of control.

"Okay," said London, waving his hands for everyone's attention and shaking his head. "We need a reality check. Fast!"

He stepped into the middle of the room. Guerrero and the Amigos didn't pay much attention to London, but he continued anyway, speaking to his own group.

"We need to figure out what's going on here. Stick to the facts. First off, where the hell …" And then London suddenly stopped, as if instantly remembering something very important. He looked like he'd lost something, and he patted his pockets and looked at everyone with shock. He suddenly remembered the three objects that they had brought with them—the latex skin and two pieces of government letterhead. All three items were missing.

"The clues from the dead guy and the other note!" he shouted. "They're gone!"

About that time, Guerrero left the window and went to help his men with the door. He went streaking past London, Miriam, Wally and Nate, barely acknowledging them at all.

London watched Guerrero as he went. He then realized that this unknown group of Mexicans probably was the only chance of getting any information while they were in this room. So far, they seemed to have a lot more knowledge about Victor Black and Darkroast than anyone else. *No one would have shown up at Darkroast Headquarters armed with weapons like they did unless they knew something,* thought London. *Something here isn't right ... and could it be true? Was Victor Black really a murderer?*

"Hey!" London said to Guerrero. "Can you tell us what's going on here?"

At first, Guerrero didn't acknowledge London at all. He was too busy searching for an exit to the room.

London repeated himself. "Hey! Can you explain what's going on?" London then grabbed Guerrero by the arm to get his attention.

Guerrero quickly pulled off London's hand. He looked him dead in the eyes, then responded to London. "If you know what's smart," said Guerrero. "You'll look for an exit. Fast."

"Why?" said London.

"Don't you understand?" Guerrero said to London. "If you're in here, there's only one reason ..."

London sensed what Guerrero meant, but Guerrero said it anyway.

"It means Victor Black is going to kill us."

● ● ●

About that time a panel on the wall opened up and revealed a video screen. The screen was black, and then it blinked on. It was programmed to turn on shortly after the group woke up. Victor was broadcasting on the other end. Clearly a pre-recorded message.

"Hello," he said. "I'm sure you are wondering why you're here in this room."

Everyone spun around. They saw the screen. They saw Victor. He was looking straight at them.

"Holy shit," said London. "That's Victor!"

Miriam gasped.

"Victor?" she said. "Is that really you?" She spoke to the screen, unable to believe her eyes. She could barely contain the joy over seeing her familiar friend.

Victor didn't answer her.

"I think it's a tape," London told her.

"What's he doing on tape?" said Nate.

"What's he doing here at all?" said Wally.

"I'm sorry I can't let you out," said Victor. He adjusted his tie, and then smiled his famous smile. He acted calm. Sinisterly professional, as if this was simply routine business for him—which it was.

"I wasn't expecting any visitors. But alas …" He gave a long sigh. "Life is full of such unexpected *pleasures*."

The way Victor said the word *"pleasures"* seemed strange. Unusually dark. He gave an evil chuckle afterwards.

London, Wally, and Nate looked at each other nervously.

"Uhhh, I don't like the way he just said that," said Nate.

"Isn't he supposed to be one of the good guys?" said Wally. "Why isn't he helping us get out of here? Why is he just playing this dumb ass tape?"

"I don't have a good feeling about this," said London. "Not good at all."

Guerrero had rejoined his men at the door. They were still working on it, doing their best to bust the lock. The lock was controlled by an electronic keypad on the wall beside the door. Guerrero had begun punching buttons, trying to crack the code on the keypad, but was having no luck.

"If I were you," said Guerrero. "I'd stop listening to that tape, and help us get out of here. I told you: he's going to kill us."

Everyone ignored Guerrero. They all kept watching the screen.

Victor continued talking. "Anyway," he said. "I can't bother to keep any of you around. I haven't the time. Big plans tonight … and besides ..." Victor held up the three objects he'd confiscated from the group. The latex skin and two pieces of government letterhead.

"Hey," shouted London. "Those are the clues and the note we're missing! Victor took them!"

"Since you were carrying these items on you," continued Victor. "You're too dangerous to keep around."

"Fuck you," shouted Guerrero, kicking the door's lock. "Fucking puta!"

The tape of Victor continued.

"And so, it's time to end things. Please don't take it personally. Especially you, Miriam."

"Huh?" said Miriam. Confused.

Everyone else looked confused also.

"It's just business," said Victor. He gave a wink and a smile. "Just business."

Then the transmission cut.

Everyone looked at each other. Guerrero continued kicking the lock.

"Well, that was weird," said Nate.

"Very weird," said Wally.

And then the gas began.

● ● ●

It was poison gas to be exact. At first it was just a faint hissing. Then several air vents opened up in the room, the window clamped shut, and the gas really began to pour. It came out a deadly yellow color.

"Oh, my God," said Nate. "Victor *is* going to kill us!"

"Victor's gone mad!" shouted Wally.

"Shut up," said Miriam. "That's Victor we're talking about. He's not gonna kill us!"

"What the hell do you think that stuff is," said Guerrero, sarcastically. He pointed at the yellow gas. The vents were really pumping now. The gas was spreading across the floor towards them.

Miriam looked at the gas. So did everyone else.

"Shit," she said, realizing Guerrero was right.

They all ran to help Guerrero with the door.

"We're all gonna die!" shouted Nate.

The gas was pumping full force and starting to fill the room. Their world was growing smaller by the second.

"Don't breathe it," shouted Guerrero. "Cover your mouth!"

Everyone yanked their shirts up over their noses. The yellow fog surrounded them like a choking gaseous swamp. People began to cough.

"It smells awful," said Wally.

"It's burning my nostrils," said Nate.

Guerrero and his Amigos continued fighting with the door. The Amigos were still tugging and wrestling with the locks, but Guerrero had focused solely on the electronic keypad. He was ramming his elbow against it over and over.

"Can't you get it to work?" shouted London.

"I'm trying," shouted Guerrero. "PUTA!" He elbowed the keypad again and again.

"Es muy malo," said one of his Amigos, watching the gas collecting around them.

This meant, *it was getting worse.*

The entire group watched Guerrero banging the keypad over and over with his elbow. *Crunch. Bleep.* The plate was starting to cave in and buttons were flying off.

"Uh ... I don't think that's gonna help," said Wally.

"Yea," said Nate. "We need to figure out the code!"

"Calláte, puta!" shouted Guerrero. He was in no mood for suggestions. He could see the gas level rising around them. The deadly fog was almost up around their necks. He continued to attack the keypad, pieces of it flying everywhere.

Everyone looked at Guerrero like he was crazy.

"I think he's lost his mind," cried Miriam. She watched the pieces of broken keypad falling to the floor. There was no way this keypad was going to work again. *Never.*

"We're in a room filling up with gas," shouted London. "And he's *ruining* our only escape!"

Guerrero didn't answer. He continued to hit the keypad. When it finally caved in, he ripped the remaining pieces away and threw them to the ground. He grabbed a mess of wires inside the wall, snapped the ends off two of them and rubbed them together.

Suddenly, there was a spark. Several loud metal *clicks* were heard. Guerrero smiled.

"I'm not ruining anything," he said. "I'm saving your sorry American asses."

Everyone couldn't believe it. The door had unlocked.

• • •

The door flung open and they rushed out just in time. Rubbing their eyes, coughing, the room practically overrun with yellow fog, they threw themselves outside to safety.

The room where they'd been held hostage was at the top of a massive corridor. Outside the room, there was only a single tiny platform, barely big enough to hold the entire group. It was one half of a retractable bridge (the other half nowhere in sight) and it overlooked the entire corridor beneath. The corridor was hundreds of yards wide. Nearly fifteen stories tall. One of the largest indoor facilities *ever* constructed.

It was the Main Hall of Advanced Development. They suddenly found themselves with a birds-eye view of the entire place. When the last Amigo rushed through the door and onto the platform, he bumped into the group and nearly sent Wally flying off the edge. Guerrero was quick enough to grab him. He pulled Wally back, then held the group away from the edge.

"Cuidado," he said. "Don't move!"

Everyone froze. Miriam's heels were practically off one edge. She inched back and grabbed onto London's arm. London held her tight, and then they both looked down. Everyone else was already doing the same.

It was nearly a two-hundred-foot drop. Below them the entire scene was a tornado of activity. There were catwalks and platforms all around the corridor with men running back and forth from every direction. There was a particular interest in traveling downward to the central floor. Many people were jumping into elevators or forklift devices that zoomed down towards the corridor's bottom. A large gathering of individuals had already accumulated there at the bottom—at least eight hundred men or so. Most of them were young men: Darkroast baristas.

Miriam was the first to speak.

"What the hell is this place?" she said.

"Are those baristas?" said London.

"Look," said Nate. "There's more of them."

He was right. More baristas continued to join the crowds at the bottom of the corridor. With their black aprons, they could be seen collecting like black bees emptying from a hive. They flooded from every direction towards the bottom floor. More and more by the second—an endless Darkroast swarm.

Altogether, they seemed to be organizing for something. It was hard to tell for what. Much of their attention was focused towards the end of the corridor. There was a stage with a giant digital-screen backdrop. On it: the Darkroast logo.

• • •

Guerrero caught the drift. He didn't know exactly what was going on, but he knew this wasn't a good situation to be in. The group was stranded, they had no weapons, and the corridor below was quickly filling to the brim with strange baristas.

"We can't stay here," he told the group. "We have to move."

Guerrero pointed over their shoulders. There was a heating shaft at the end of the platform.

"Quickly," he said. "We can go through there."

Minutes later, several floors down in a dark room, the ceiling vent on a heating shaft began to rattle. Voices were heard. Some English. Some Spanish.

"Dude," said one of them. "Get off my arm."

"No es yo," said another.

Then there was a crash. A tumble. A sudden stream of bodies dropping from a hole in the ceiling. The group landed in a pile, sprawled upon the floor.

They quickly gathered themselves off the floor. London helped Miriam onto her feet. He noticed her hands were shaking a bit as he pulled her up. She looked *pissed*.

"Are you okay?" he asked.

"I will be when I get some answers," said Miriam. "I want to know what the hell is going on. First, we almost get gassed to death, and then we end up in that huge room full of Darkroast baristas! Hundreds of them! None of it makes sense!"

"I get the feeling it all has to do with Victor," said London. "Maybe this is the Darkroast Day holiday conspiracy the notes were talking about?"

"Ridiculous," said Miriam. "Absolutely *ridiculous*!"

Guerrero had already gotten up and was searching for a light switch. In doing so, he noticed a strange green glow coming from the other side of the room. It shone through the dark like a radioactive beacon.

Miriam and London hadn't noticed the glow. They were too busy continuing to bicker. Things were getting more heated.

"Look," said London. "All I'm saying is things here aren't normal. For Christ's sake, your boss practically tried to kill us back there! This Mexican guy seems pretty pissed off at Victor and says he killed his father. Can't you even imagine the possibility?"

Miriam shook her head, stamped her foot, and then made it personal.

"I can't believe this," she said. "You always have to find something wrong with everything. This is *exactly* why we broke up!"

Guerrero continued to notice the glow. He was practically hypnotized by it. The others had noticed it also. Everyone had except for Miriam and London, who more and more, by the minute, were getting at each other's throats.

"YOU ALWAYS DO THIS!" shouted Miriam.

"I DON'T THINK SO," London shouted back. "*YOU* ALWAYS DO THIS!"

Guerrero turned to Miriam and London.

"SHUT UP!" he said.

Miriam and London stopped. They went silent. Then the two of them looked over at Guerrero and noticed the glow. It was coming from the windows of a nearby room.

Like moths to a bright green flame, the entire group stopped what they were doing and headed for the room.

• • •

When they entered the room, they almost had to shut their eyes. Stepping inside was like stepping into the middle of a green sun. There was brightness all around.

Inescapable green brightness.

Inside the room, the green brightness was coming from a series of tanks. The room was stocked full of them. Nearly twenty cylindrical glass tanks, like gigantic test tubes, rising from floor to ceiling. They were filled with some kind of bright green, radioactive-looking liquid. The liquid swirled and sparkled like nothing they had ever seen.

Everyone headed through the room, exploring the tanks. They couldn't stop looking at the liquid. Wally and Nate stopped to observe, totally mesmerized.

"What is this stuff," said Wally.

"It's like indi-glow on steroids," answered Nate.

The two of them ran their fingers over the outside of the tanks. The liquid swirled around and glowed brighter as they did so, almost responsive to their touch.

London and Miriam had also stopped nearby beside one of the tanks. They had noticed the liquid's strange appearance—the swirls, the extra glowing.

"I've never seen anything like it," said Miriam.

"Me neither," said London. "Look at the way it moves and lights up."

London ran his fingers along the sides of the tank.

The green liquid seemed to chase it.

Guerrero and his Amigos had stopped near another of the tanks. They also watched the liquid. The Amigos were most fascinated. In many ways, they thought they were staring at pure magic—unlike anything they could ever imagine.

"La luz verde," they said over and over, smiling, which meant: *the green light*.

Only Guerrero didn't seem impressed by the liquid. He noticed his Amigos running their fingers along the glass, playing with the liquid. It didn't sit well with him.

"No es bueno," he said.

He shoved them away from the tank, then stepped in front of them. Angry.

"This is a bad place," he said to everyone. "We should go."

About this time, London noticed a large computer terminal in the corner of the room. The terminal's monitor showed large technical equations of the glowing green liquid—along with images of a Moon Laser designed to activate secret properties in the green liquid. In addition, there were unbelievable images of something never seen before: blueprints of Darkroast robotic baristas. The blueprints showed a solid metal skeleton with latex skin, a sonic hand laser able to stun or destroy, and a dark black Darkroast apron.

• • •

Within moments, there was a noise. Everyone froze. They looked up from the tanks and heard footsteps. Voices. It was coming from another set of doors at the other end of the room.

"Quickly," shouted Guerrero. "HIDE!"

Everyone scattered just as the doors swung open.

Two men had entered the room. They were wearing white lab coats, goggles and helmets, and were clearly scientists. On their outfits, they bore the Darkroast logo.

They walked in-between the tanks, talking.

"We better get downstairs," said one of them. "It should be starting soon."

"Relax," said the other. "We'll make it on time."

They walked across the middle of the room. Non-chalantly. Casual.

Hidden behind the tanks, no more than ten feet away from the scientists, were London, Miriam, Wally and Nate. They watched the men walking across the room.

"Who are they?" whispered Nate.

"Shut up," whispered Wally.

"Are they coming this way?"

Wally punched Nate in the arm, and scolded his friend.

"They will be if you don't shut up!"

The scientists stopped mid-way in front of a set of tanks. One of them pointed up at the green liquid. He ran his finger over the edge of a tank. The green liquid glowed and chased it.

"Think this stuff's gonna work?" he said.

"If it does," replied the other. "We're in for a hell of a show!"

"Entire country's in for a hell of a show!"

They both chuckled, then continued walking. They headed for the door. On their way out, they were still talking.

"Come on, let's go check the Processing Center …"

"Gotta make sure this stuff down there coats the last batches …"

And then they were out the doors. Gone.

• • •

Everyone surfaced from their hiding places. Guerrero and his Amigos came out and met the rest of the group in the middle of the room. Guerrero huddled up his men.

"We can't waste anymore time here," said Guerrero. "It's too risky! We need to regroup and find some weapons."

He checked the far doors, making sure no one else was coming through. Already, he was heading for the exit.

London had a different plan in mind. It all had to do with the scientists.

"Wait," said London. "We can't go!"

Guerrero stopped. Shocked. He looked at London, no time to waste.

"You're fucking loco," shouted Guerrero. "We're leaving now!"

But London was already breaking from the group.

He headed away from Guerrero, towards the other end of the room.

Everyone watched London. He headed for the wall. He'd seen something on it as the scientists were leaving. When he got close, he stopped and pointed.

Guerrero followed, stopped at London's side, and saw what he was pointing at.

A building map.

London pointed at the words: *Processing Center.*

"This is the room those guys were talking about. We have to check it out," said London. "There's too much weird stuff going on here, and this Processing Center could be the answer."

Chapter 12

In the darkness outside Darkroast Headquarters, the Source had returned in full titanium body armor, holding a semi-automatic neutron pistol and a force-field defense applicator. He clutched a black bag under his left arm and ran directly for the Headquarters.

Hopefully, he thought. *I'm not too late.*

He ran as fast as he could, but he knew he couldn't move fast enough. *They may already be dead, and if not ... Jesus,* he thought. *There were more nightmares inside than they could imagine. I've got to hurry.*

As he ran he kept the Headquarters in sight, but he couldn't stop thinking of the catastrophe potentially unfolding inside. *If they were lucky enough to be alive, who knew what they had seen already*, he thought. *The countless armies of mechanized baristas? The glowing green liquid with all its deadliness?*

He knew Victor had killed people for less. *And just think*, he wondered. *If they knew the truth about Darkroast and Victor himself ... just think what he'd do to them.*

Death would be the least of their worries.

The Source doubled his pace and headed straight for the back wing of Headquarters ... straight for Advanced Development. He was gonna need a hell of a lot of luck, and every bit of the explosives in his black bag to bust them out.

Chapter 13

No one in the group liked the idea. They all knew it was a bad one. But London wouldn't let up. It was the reporter in him—that sixth sense that something needed to be investigated further. As far as he was concerned, curiosity never killed anything.

He stepped away from the map and pointed at the green tanks.

"There's something huge going on with all this," he said. "Didn't you hear what those scientists said? That Processing Center is the answer. I just know it!"

Guerrero was the first to protest. He nearly put a fist to London's throat.

"We have to get out of here," he said. "This place is crawling with Victor's men. We stick around any longer, we're dead!"

He grabbed London's arm and tried to jerk him along.

"Come on," he told him. "You're coming with us."

London immediately withheld. He yanked himself free of Guerrero and shook his head, *no*.

"Sorry," he said. "I'm not leaving! Not without answers!"

Guerrero stepped into his face.

"We *can't* split up!" shouted Guerrero. "If we split up and they catch you, then they'll know we all escaped. I am *not* risking my neck for you!"

London put his foot down.

"Ten minutes," said London. "That's all I'm asking. Just a look. If Victor Black really is a murderer like you said, then more innocent lives could be at stake. This could expose him."

Guerrero saw the conviction in London's eyes. There was no persuading this man. He looked back at his Amigos, then at Miriam, Wally and Nate. He thought about London's words and wondered if London had a point. *Could more lives be at stake?*

Guerrero turned back to London. He gritted his teeth. Boiling.

"Five minutes," said Guerrero. "And we change clothes first."

• • •

Several minutes later, they exited a set of elevators on the ground floor.

They were at the Processing Center.

Baristas were coming and going in every direction. Hundreds and hundreds. More scientists in white lab coats also breezed past. They all continued to rush in the direction of the Main Hall. Busy as ever. Sirens were now calling them for the start of something.

London and Guerrero stepped out of the elevators first. They had found some disguises in the upstairs lab rooms. They were wearing white lab coats, goggles, helmets—the full scientist get-up.

On their outfits, they sported the Darkroast logo.

Guerrero looked down at it and frowned.

"I don't like this idea," he said. "Not one bit."

"We'll be fine," said London. "Relax." He looked at all the Darkroast scientists and baristas streaking past. They were definitely too busy to notice them.

"What are they in such a hurry for?" said London. "It's a freakin' cattle call."

"Doesn't matter," said Guerrero. "Let's get this over with."

Guerrero waved OK to everyone back in the elevator. Everyone else stepped out, also wearing their scientist disguises. Then they all raced for the Processing Center.

• • •

When they entered the Processing Center, the place had already emptied of people. Everyone had headed off for the Main Hall. The sirens could still be heard calling nearby.

The room was full of huge mixing tanks and conveyor belts. There was also that same familiar green glow and something new: the intense smell of dark roast coffee.

It was all coming from the conveyor belts.

Everyone saw the glowing right away. It was impossible to miss. The conveyor belts were loaded with piles of glowing green coffee beans. They were small. Round. There was that smell. Unmistakably dark roast. The entire room reeked of it.

"What is this place," said Wally. "It's glowing just like that other room."

"And that smell," said Nate. "It's like a giant coffee factory."

"This can't be owned by Victor," said Miriam. "I've *never* seen this place."

"Come on," said London. "We need a closer look."

London led everyone to the conveyor belts. There were hundreds of these belts humming along. Each of them carried an endless supply of the small, green-glowing beans and there was enough of it to supply an entire city.

Everyone stepped up to the edge of the belts and examined the coffee. They almost couldn't believe what they were looking at.

"It's coffee," said London.

"My God," said Miriam. "How can *that* be coffee?"

"It looks radioactive," said Wally. "Wicked radioactive."

Nate started to reach down and touch some. Wally knocked his hand back.

"Dude," he said. "Don't! It could be dangerous."

Guerrero and his Amigos weren't paying much attention to the bizarre discovery. They had marked some lookout posts around the room. Guerrero mainly kept his eyes on a set of large doors at the end of the room. They led to the Main Hall, and he could hear all the cheering and commotion coming from the other side. He could also hear the sirens. There was *definitely* lots of people and *definitely* something big about to happen.

"No gustalo," he told his men, which meant, *I don't like this.*

They nodded, and replied, "Nos vamos."

This meant, *Let's get out of here. Fast.*

"Come on," said Guerrero to everyone. "It's not safe here!"

But everyone else was hooked. They kept bending over the glowing coffee beans. It was like no coffee they'd ever seen, and they couldn't believe how much was here.

"There's tons of it," London said. "It's all been coated with that green stuff."

"What do you think that stuff does?" said Nate.

"Who knows?" said Wally. "And why put it on the coffee beans?"

"I'm telling you," said Miriam. "I've *never* seen anything like it."

And then they looked down at the far end of the room. They saw more. All the conveyor belts were dumping the glowing beans into huge wooden crates. Machines were packing them to be shipped out. Another army of machines—giant cranes, mechanized forklifts, lifting platforms—were nailing the crates up and piling them on top of each other. Crates were already piled by the thousands. They stacked almost to the ceiling.

Needless to say, it was a huge operation.

• • •

It was about this time that Miriam made a big discovery. While everyone was looking at the wooden crates, she noticed there were two words written on the side of every one. The writing was small, yet clear enough to reveal exactly what the glowing beans inside really were. It hit her like a ton of bricks.

The two words: *Mind Melt.*

"Oh my God," she said. "This is *Mind Melt.*"

There was a collective shutter. Everyone turned and looked at her, then turned back to the crates. She pointed at them, indicating to the corners, and then they saw it. The words on the crates were written plain as day.

Thousands of labels sitting right in front of them—all of them read *Mind Melt*.

London was the first to comment.

"My God," he said. "This is *Mind Melt*?" He almost swallowed his tongue.

Wally and Nate were equally stunned. They looked at each other in disbelief.

"How can it be?" said Wally.

"It hardly looks like coffee," said Nate.

They all re-read the labels, then looked back towards the conveyor belts. They observed the countless green-glowing coffee beans. The shape. The size. The dark roast smell.

"Damn," said London. "I can't believe this is *Mind Melt*."

All of them were astounded. It was the weirdest coffee they'd ever seen.

"Is this stuff even drinkable?" said Wally.

"No way I'd ever drink that," said Nate. "I barely like the regular crap."

"There's gotta be a reason it looks so strange," said London. "A serious *purpose*. Why would anyone make coffee that looks like this?"

Miriam was the most astounded. She could barely fathom that this strange creation was *Mind Melt*. Victor had never shown or described his new coffee to her—he'd always insisted on *Mind Melt* being a complete secret, even as they promoted it to the public for Darkroast Day. But despite all his secrecy, she'd never expected something this bizarre.

"Unbelievable," she thought to herself. "This is it. This is actually *Mind Melt*."

• • •

"Come on," said Guerrero to everyone. "Rapido! Rapido!"

He had noticed the discovery of *Mind Melt*, but didn't care. There was no time left to play around. He was still watching the doors to the Main Hall. The commotion on the other side was picking up, and with such a huge Darkroast presence nearby, the group could get caught at any moment.

Puta, Guerrero thought to himself. *These people don't know who they're dealing with.*

Guerrero raced over to the group and grabbed London by the arms.

"Enough," said Guerrero. "If we don't leave now, we're dead!"

It was instant recoil for London. He jerked away from Guerrero, unprepared to go anywhere. He pointed back at all the *Mind Melt*.

"What?" he said. "Look at how weird this coffee is! We can't leave!"

The rest of the group shared the opinion.

"This coffee is definitely whacked!" said Wally.

"Yea," said Nate. "That coffee is *not* normal."

"I've got to agree," added Miriam. "I don't know how to explain it."

Guerrero wouldn't hear of it. He knew they were pushing their luck.

"Fucking puta," he shouted. "We have no weapons! You'll get us all killed!"

London shouted back, taking a stand for his group.

"There's something seriously wrong here," he said. "We have to find out why *Mind Melt* looks so strange!"

"No way," said Guerrero. "We have to leave!"

London protested yet again. His ideals were kicking in.

"This isn't right," said London. "What if *Mind Melt* is dangerous? What if people's safety is at stake here? I have a bad feeling about this!"

Guerrero let loose his emotions. He got up in London's face.

"Don't you get it," he said. "*Our* safety is at stake!"

He pointed to his Amigos.

"*My Amigos'* safety is at stake!"

He pointed to Wally, Nate, and Miriam.

"*Your* friends' safety is at stake!"

He stepped closer into London's face. He looked him in the eyes and drew a finger across his throat, making a knife cutting gesture.

"I can't make it any clearer," he said. "If we get caught, Victor Black will *kill* us!"

• • •

But despite Guerrero's warning, things were already too late. Several figures had already entered a far door and were making their way across the floor. They moved soundlessly, with lightning speed as always, and were suddenly at the group's side.

Five of them. Black aprons and all.

It was the Darkroast baristas.

Chapter 14

The Darkroast baristas had them surrounded, and looked serious as hell. They'd been sent around to gather everyone for the Main Hall. Things inside were already starting to begin. Soon, Victor and Ted would give the "big test": the single event tonight that would reveal the purpose of *Mind Melt*, Darkroast Day, and Victor's evil plans for America.

The baristas cocked their heads to the side, and examined everyone dressed head to toe in their Darkroast scientist outfits. They scanned them over like machines scanning a thousand codes of data at once—their eyes not missing a single detail. Spotting the helmets, goggles, white lab coats, and black Darkroast logos—the official symbol of their kind—they quickly concluded that they were part of Darkroast.

"What are you doing here?" one of them said. "You're not supposed to be here."

All five stepped closer, crowding the group. They pointed to the Main Hall.

"The demonstration," another said. "All must attend ..."

The group froze as they stood before the baristas.

"*Puta*," said Guerrero. "This is *not* good."

The entire group knew he was right.

"Shit," said London. "What do we do?"

Guerrero looked down at the Darkroast logo on his outfit.

"I told you this was a bad idea," he said. "Muy mal." His Amigos were nodding.

The baristas repeated their orders.

"The demonstration," one of them said. "All must attend ..."

They pointed again to the Main Hall.

The group saw where the baristas were pointing. No one in the group had any intentions of going inside the Main Hall.

"I don't want to go in there," said Wally.

"Me either," added Nate.

Miriam nodded in agreement, trembling.

But the baristas were done waiting, and they had their orders. Each raised a sparking, electrified green hand—their all too familiar, and all too deadly gesture. Charged and ready to fire, they aimed at the group.

"Uhh, guys," said London. "I don't think we have a choice."

• • •

The Main Hall was a massive structure—certainly the largest room within Advanced Development. Over seventy thousand tons of steel, years of planning, and billions of dollars had gone into its construction. Its size was more than ten thousand square yards, and every inch of it was state of the art. Over the room stretched a gigantic dome. The dome was entirely white, criss-crossed with huge I-beams, and topped off with two mammoth retractable doors pointing towards the night sky.

Overall, the place was built like a giant Moon observatory. As the group entered, they couldn't believe what they were seeing. The size of the Hall was breathtaking. Green lights and sirens flashed from all directions. At the end of the room sat the giant digital-screen backdrop they'd seen earlier. It was still displaying the Darkroast logo. Beneath the logo, there was a sprawling stage complete with a general's tower that rose over fifty feet into the air—a place for someone very important to address the crowd later.

Several small black Darkroast flags waved from the general's tower. Behind the stage and tower, several rows of NASA-quality video monitors, computers, and other electronic equipment could be seen. Darkroast scientists sat at several consoles operating all this technology like a kind of mission control center. They talked into microphone headsets and feverishly made adjustments to certain knobs and switches, examining the monitors now and again.

They also watched the giant dome above, expectantly.

• • •

The five baristas from the Processing Center ushered the group further into the Hall. The group couldn't take their eyes away from it all—not to mention, there was something even more heart-stopping. Wall to wall, among all this technology, in this colossal space the size of a stadium ... The entire place was *filled* with Darkroast baristas.

It was the largest gathering of baristas *ever*. Impossibly huge. Earlier the group had seen hundreds gathered here, but now ... over *two thousand* stood in unison facing the giant stage at the end of the Hall. All in their mid-twenties, mostly young men, they went as far as the eye could see—an endless sea of black aprons, blue jeans, and white Oxford shirts—and they were all waving their hands in the air—*laser beam* hands that sparked with green electricity like deadly neon lightning—and they were chanting a single deadly word over and over:

Darkroast! Darkroast! Darkroast!

The group stopped cold in their tracks. They saw the lasers. They heard the chanting. They sensed the pure evil.

Something here *definitely* wasn't right.

• • •

"Jesus," said London. "I've never seen more baristas in my entire life."

"My God," said Miriam. "There's enough baristas in here to fill all of Boston."

Nate and Wally also were watching the baristas. They turned to each other.

"What the hell are they?" said Nate. "Those aren't normal baristas."

"Definitely not normal," said Wally. "Look at all those green lasers coming from their hands! How the hell is that possible!"

Guerrero and his Amigos were also stunned. They had no idea what in the hell two thousand baristas were doing in a single room—especially baristas that seemed so well armed with such fierce weaponry. To make matters worse, Guerrero had seen this weaponry before and knew its vicious capabilities. A brutal display by a person's name he was suddenly too frightened to say.

It made Guerrero wish he had his own weapons again.

"Preparamos para lo peor," he said to his Amigos, clenching his fists.

Prepare for the worst.

• • •

The five baristas from the Processing Center pushed the group further through the Main Hall. The group couldn't stop watching the thousands of baristas as they went. The baristas continued to wave their hands in the air, chanting and sparking their green laser beams in continuous blasts. The blasts streaked across the rafters of the white dome, occasionally sparking with the metal ceiling.

Meanwhile, their eyes never left the Darkroast logo.

They stared at it like a dark hypnotic omen.

Eventually, the five baristas from the Processing Center led the group to the mission control area. This is where all the other Darkroast scientists were gathered, and when the group reached it, the five baristas quickly turned around and left. Their main purpose had been to bring the group here to watch the demonstration, and now their purpose was done. They disappeared into the countless crowds of baristas, then assumed the same position as everyone else: facing forward, chanting, and blasting their lasers.

As the group watched them rejoin the other baristas, everyone was still trying to figure out one question: *what the hell were these baristas?* In addition to the fierce green hand lasers, the group had begun to notice some peculiar details about the baristas. For starters, their skin was extremely pale—with almost a rubbery texture to it—and all their eyes had an eerie greenish glow. The group also noticed that when they spoke, beneath their voices, there was an underlying metallic hum that sounded strangely electronic. And there also was something odd about the way the baristas moved … something strangely robotic.

"What the hell are these things?" said London.

"Are they human?" said Nate.

"They can't be human," said Wally. "They look too strange to be human."

The group continued watching the baristas, but before they could figure out the mystery of what they were, something happened. The green lights and sirens stopped, and the entire atmosphere of the room began to change. A giant image of the Moon replaced the digital screen picture of the Darkroast logo. The mission control area erupted with tons of activity, also showing countless images of the Moon on its video monitors. Suddenly, everywhere the group looked, there were countless pictures of the Moon.

All the crowds of baristas suddenly went silent and stopped firing their lasers. They stiffened their pose, and prepared for the start of tonight's grand event.

It was then that two men suddenly entered the room and took the stage.

Victor and Ted.

Chapter 15

Victor and Ted took the stage like the future evil leaders of America. Walking up the giant steps alongside of the stage, they entered to the sudden explosion of cheers and rallying applause. The baristas went wild before them, the thunderous support of an entire nation of Darkroast minions. Victor and Ted were all smiles as they watched their surroundings: the endless crowds of baristas, the gigantic white dome and digital-screen backdrop displaying the Moon, and the Darkroast scientists preparing the mission control consoles for tonight's main event.

"Everything looks in order," said Ted to Victor.

"It couldn't be going more perfectly," Victor replied.

• • •

As Victor and Ted entered, London, Miriam, Wally, Nate, Guerrero and his Amigos couldn't believe their eyes. None of them imagined that Victor and Ted would suddenly take the stage. The two of them walked across the center of the stage so naturally, smiling and waving to the baristas, nodding with approval as the crowds fired their lasers and chanted *Darkroast Darkroast Darkroast* over and over. They gave the thumbs up to the rows of Darkroast scientists feverishly working in the mission control area. They grinned extra large over the pictures of the Moon flashing from all the video monitors and the giant screen onstage.

"What the hell are *they* doing there?" said London.

"I don't get it," said Nate. "And they're waving to all these baristas?"

"And smiling at all those pictures of the Moon," said Wally. "It makes no sense."

Miriam nearly lost it. Her world had suddenly become slow-motion. She couldn't believe what she was seeing: Victor and Ted had just walked on stage. Here in the middle of this strange room, among all these Darkroast images and pictures of the Moon, among this countless crowd of seemingly inhuman Darkroast baristas, among this utterly senseless and frighteningly strange scene … stood Victor and Ted.

"How is this possible?" mumbled Miriam. "How can Victor and Ted be *here*?"

Not to mention, Miriam thought. *Ted was supposed to be in Orlando!*

• • •

Victor and Ted continued to the very center of the stage. With smiles on their faces, they approached the general's tower. Ted stopped beside the tower, but Victor climbed the set of stairs and made his way to the top, a distance over fifty feet high. At the top of the tower, there stood a warlike podium decorated with the Darkroast logo and several black Darkroast flags hanging across the tower—the banners of a dark new nation … a soon-to-be nation.

Watching the banners, Victor continued to smile. He could feel his moment of glory coming closer. The moment that would make his ultimate dream a reality.

Beneath him on the stage, Ted had the same feeling. *Soon the dark dream would be true. The final stages of their plan would be set in motion.*

Among the crowds of cheering baristas, the rest of the group was still trying to figure out what the hell was going on.

"I've got to be missing something," said London. "The facts here don't add up."

"Yea," said Wally. "What are these two big Darkroast guys doing in this room with a backdrop of the Moon, and all these weird baristas?"

"If you can even call them baristas," said Nate. "They look almost like … robots."

"HOLY JESUS!" shouted London, remembering what they'd seen on the computer in the green liquid room. "These *are* robots. These are the robotic Darkroast baristas we saw on that computer! But what are they doing in here with Victor and Ted?"

"And why's Victor heading for that podium," said Wally. "It looks like he's about to give a speech to them."

"And something else is happening on screen," said Nate, noticing that the giant digital-screen backdrop of the Moon was now changing pictures.

Miriam, who finally found the will to speak, told the group:

"None of this is possible. Victor shouldn't be here. And Ted's supposed to be in Orlando!"

• • •

At the top of the tower, standing at the podium like a true Darkroast CEO—standing over fifty feet above the entire crowd—Victor began to smile even brighter. He continued to grin at the Darkroast flags, then he looked behind the tower at the giant digital screen image of the Moon, and then at the crowds of baristas.

He clapped with perfect approval over what he saw. The screen behind him had begun changing—the giant picture of the Moon revealed more detailed pictures of a deadly device on the Moon's surface: a Darkroast Moon Laser.

Victor grinned and watched the crowd. Every one of the Darkroast baristas had taken notice of the new images being shown on the digital screen backdrop.

Victor looked down at Ted, who still stood on the stage underneath the giant digital screen. Ted looked up at Victor, gave him the thumbs up to signal the start of "the big test," and then the two of them together looked at the digital screen to admire their perfect handiwork: the Darkroast Moon Laser stood eighty stories tall, composed entirely of stainless steel and titanium alloy—the same indestructible metals used by NASA to build the toughest of space instruments. From its base, which glowed and buzzed with high-tech electronic circuitry, the Darkroast laser pulsated with green light at its center. Like a towering, skyscraper-sized cannon filled with radioactive green lightning, the laser aimed across the blackness of space towards a single point.

Earth.

• • •

At this time, several things happened to signal the start of the "big test." The Main Hall's monstrous ceiling doors began to retract—their colossal jaws widening open to reveal the dark, starry night sky above ... wide enough for a giant laser beam to blast inside—while Ted and two baristas led a captive man onto the stage. Meanwhile, Victor addressed the crowd with a thunderous voice. A voice almost too loud to be human.

"MY BARISTAS," he said. "THE TIME HAS COME ..."

Instantly, the baristas cheered and rallied to Victor's words.

"Tonight," said Victor. "We see the true purpose of Darkroast Day!"

Ted and the two baristas led the captive man directly to the center of the stage, directly beneath the center of the retracting ceiling doors. In the expanding vista of the starry night sky, a single image could be seen hovering dreadfully above: the Moon.

Ted and the two baristas watched the Moon, while Victor pointed up at it.

"For years," he said. "We have been building a laser on the surface of the Moon! A laser for Darkroast Day!"

His voice was shatteringly loud. The baristas listened to it intently.

"We have told the public that this laser is for an innocent Moon laser show!"

Victor winked and smiled. The baristas laughed.

"BUT," said Victor. "IT CERTAINLY IS *NOT!*"

Everyone was now staring up at the Moon. The thousands of baristas almost seemed to worship it. The Darkroast scientists at the Mission Control Center smiled and grinned at it while they operated their computers, and made adjustments on their monitors to the digital screen pictures of its surface.

Nearby on stage, the giant digital screen showed a rapid progression of Moon Laser images: a satellite dish beginning to activate; the titanium and steel base of the Darkroast laser beginning to glow and vibrate; and the Darkroast laser cannon pulsating with huge waves of radioactive green lightning as it prepared to fire at Earth.

At the center of the stage, the captive man stood and stared at the Moon, trembling in *absolute terror*.

• • •

Victor continued talking to the baristas, his words echoing through the Main Hall like doomsday thunder.

"AND THIS IS NOT ALL," he said. "THERE IS MORE!"

With these words, Victor raised an object from behind the podium: a Darkroast coffee. It was in the typical white Darkroast cup—the kind found at any Darkroast store—and was topped with gentle whipped cream, foamed milk, cinnamon sprinkles, and a bright red cherry that emitted a sinister green glow characteristic of only one thing:

Mind Melt.

Chapter 16

Still dressed in full titanium body armor and armed with his semi-automatic neutron pistol and force-field defense applicator, the Source had reached the back wing of Darkroast Headquarters. He stood outside Main Hall looking through a pair of X-ray neutron binoculars. With these, he was able to spy inside just as well as someone with perfect X-ray vision ... and he could see the madness unfolding.

My God, he thought. *It's worse than I expected!*

He put down the binoculars and unzipped the black bag of explosives. Removing the first explosive, his mind couldn't shake what he'd just witnessed. *The group was alive, thank God.* But they were standing in the middle of the hornet's nest, among Victor, Ted, the Moon Laser, *Mind Melt*, and the evil crowds of mechanized barista warriors. *Among the entire enemy!*

If only they knew about the coming apocalypse, he thought. *If only they knew Victor's evil master plan and how much danger they were truly in!*

And then there was Victor himself. *Did they really know the horrific truth?*

But none of that mattered now. The group had to be rescued, so the Source finished pulling out the explosives, and planted them one by one on the side of the Main Hall.

He had to bust them out before it was too late.

Chapter 17

"For years," said Victor. "We have also been developing a new coffee called *Mind Melt!*"

The baristas cheered. They knew exactly what he was talking about.

"We have promised to give this coffee to the public on Darkroast Day!" added Victor. "And told them that it is merely for their own enjoyment!"

More cheers.

"BUT AGAIN," said Victor. "IT CERTAINLY IS *NOT!*"

The baristas went crazy when Victor said this, firing their lasers into the air and hollering almost loud enough to shake the Main Hall to pieces. They stomped their feet and rallied to Victor's voice like a barista army ready for the war of the century.

All the while the Darkroast scientists continued operating the Mission Control center, preparing the Moon Laser to be fired any minute now.

• • •

"And now," said Victor. "On the eve of Darkroast Day, the final test is ready!"

Victor raised his cup of *Mind Melt* into the air—a toast to all the baristas standing and watching—and behind him the Darkroast scientists hit several final buttons on their mission control consoles.

"It is time to see the purpose of tomorrow's Darkroast Day," he said. "Time to see the purpose for *Mind Melt* and our Moon Laser!"

As Victor spoke, the Darkroast scientists continued hitting the final buttons. The giant digital screen pictures of the Moon Laser intensified enormously. The laser's main firing cannon—already pulsating with green lightning—gathered all its lightning into a gigantic green laser beam, while the titanium and steel base began to glow blindingly bright.

Below on stage, Ted and the two baristas tightened their grip on the captive man, and then Ted walked to the edge of the stage and did something of vast importance ...

He returned carrying a cup of *Mind Melt*.

Victor gave a wink and a smile.

"WATCH," he said. "WATCH THE POWER OF DARKROAST!"

• • •

Ted held his head high as he returned to center stage carrying the cup of *Mind Melt*. The crowds of baristas cheered him on, as did Victor from the top of his general's tower, and Ted waved to them all—their second-in-command holding the hope of the entire Darkroast nation in a single coffee cup as he headed for one person: the captive man.

The captive man saw him coming and immediately knew there was a single purpose to all this ...

Ted intended for him to drink the *Mind Melt*.

The captive man immediately started to struggle. He kicked and twisted to free himself from the baristas, but it was no use. They held him like two unbreakable black-aproned vice grips until Ted reached his side. Then Ted took the cup of *Mind Melt* and—pinching the captive man's nostrils shut, grabbing his mouth and squeezing it open— forced the captive man to drink the entire cup of coffee.

The baristas cheered and fired their lasers with excitement while they watched the man downing the glowing green liquid. Victor raised his own whip-creamed cup of *Mind Melt* in an emblematic toast, and when the captive man had finished every last drop, Victor applauded and turned to the Darkroast scientists.

Sitting at the Moon Laser controls, they knew exactly what to do next.

• • •

The scientists punched in the final coordinates, hit the ultimate last button in their Moon Laser command sequence, and then as shown on the giant digital screen ...

The Darkroast Moon Laser fired ... directly at the captive man.

Chapter 18

ZAAAAAAAAAAAAAAAAAAAAAAAAP! Green light flooded the stage as the Darkroast laser beam struck the captive man, like a radioactive lightning bolt suddenly exploding from space. Blinding green rays encircled his body and pumped into the man's skin—his entire body jittering and glowing uncontrollably. His eyes melted, his brain dissolved, and like a futuristic ray gun heating his head to a thousand degrees in a single second.... his brain disintegrated into a pile of green goop and his head exploded. *CRACKOWWW!!!*

Within a single instant, the purpose of *Mind Melt* and the Darkroast Moon Laser suddenly became clear. These two items were designed for one thing: *to destroy humans.*

• • •

"Holy Fuck!" shouted London. "The Moon Laser melted and exploded that guy's brain!"

He and his gang had witnessed the entire scene. The combination of *Mind Melt* and Moon Laser had obliterated this guy's brain like vaporized espresso.

"Oh my God," said Wally. "His brain's like ... totally gone! And his head exploded!"

"Totally!" said Nate. "I can't believe it!"

On stage, the laser stopped. The man hit the ground with a *thud* and lay dead. Grayish green sludge oozed from his empty, fractured skull.

"Hijo de puta," Guerrero said, which roughly translated: *Son of a Bitch!*

His Amigos nodded, almost ready to piss themselves.

This was beyond their wildest fears of Victor Black and Darkroast.

"I can't believe it!" shouted London. "Victor and his *Mind Melt* Moon Laser just killed that guy!"

"Oh my God," said Nate. "I just realized something."

He looked around at his friends.

"*Mind Melt*," he said.

His friends looked at him blankly, not getting it.

"*MIND MELT*!" he repeated, putting extra emphasis on the words to make his point.

The group shuddered. Suddenly, they got it, realizing that there was absolutely no coincidence to the name of Victor's new Darkroast Day coffee. The coffee that had just melted this guy's brain into oblivion had the most appropriate name in the world.

• • •

"HA HA," shouted Victor. "WE'VE DONE IT!"

Victor stared at the man's body on stage, the melted brain sludge pooled around the man's broken skull. Victor smiled and raised his cup of *Mind Melt* in celebration.

"USING THE COMBINATION OF *MIND MELT* AND MOON LASER," he said. "WE HAVE CREATED THE PERFECT DEATH RAY, WHICH ON TOMORROW, WE'LL DEBUT TO THE PUBLIC! WITHOUT ANY OF THEM HAVING A SINGLE CLUE THAT TOMORROW ... HUMANITY WILL MEET ITS DOOM!"

All the baristas and scientists cheered at the sound of this plan, as well as Ted—the plan's co-creator—who smiled and gave a thumbs-up to Victor.

And that's when the Source made his move.

Chapter 19

In a furious flaming thunderball, the explosives planted on the outside of Main Hall detonated. They had been placed on the side wall next to the Mission Control Center—just out of range of where all the Darkroast scientists were sitting at their Moon Laser computers, and where London, Miriam, Wally, Nate, Guerrero and the Amigos were standing. All the timers on ten pounds of neutron compressed C-4 ticked down at the exact same moment ...

Five ... Four ... Three ... Two ... One ... KABOOOOOMM!!!

A huge chunk of side wall exploded into a million pieces, sending a billowing cloud of smoke, ash, and debris plummeting into Main Hall. The Source came bursting through wearing his full titanium body armor and firing his neutron pistol at the entire crowd of baristas.

London, Miriam, Wally, Nate, Guerrero and his Amigos all turned to see the Source storming through the rubble.

"What the hell!" shouted London, speaking for the entire group. "It's the guy with the mask from the alley!"

The Source ran straight to their side and stepped in front to protect them.

"Don't worry," he said. "I'm here to save you!"

● ● ●

"WE'RE UNDER ATTACK!" shouted Victor.

Across the room, he saw the Source—and it took him less than a nanosecond to process the situation. "WHAT THE HELL IS *HE* DOING HERE!"

Victor saw the huge smoldering hole in the Main Hall, the debris and carnage strewn across the Mission Control center, and his army of baristas suddenly getting blasted with neutron pulses left and right. Not to mention, he saw a familiar group standing next to the Source

... a group dressed as Darkroast scientists that was *supposed* to be dead ...

"It's Miriam and her group of friends!" shouted Victor. "What the hell are *they* doing here!"

Ted was nearby. Down on stage, he had been knocked to his feet from the explosion, and struggled to regain composure. Out of the corner of his eye, he saw what Victor was talking about—Miriam and several familiar people dressed in Darkroast scientist outfits.

"Miriam and her group?" Ted shouted, stumbling. "How the hell ..."

• • •

"Come on," shouted the Source. "We have to hurry!"

London, Miriam, Wally, and Nate weren't moving. Neither were Guerrero and his Amigos. None of them had any idea what the Source was doing here.

"Dude," said Wally. "This guy just blew a huge hole in that wall!"

"There's debris everywhere," said Nate. "What's going on?"

"Come on!" repeated the Source. "I'm busting all of you out!"

"Who is this guy?" said Guerrero. "And what's with the weird outfit!"

"Me da un sentido malo," one of the Amigos added, pointing suspiciously at the Source's titanium mask. None of them could understand the Source's strange outfit—the neutron pistol, the full titanium body armor, and the titanium mask. They especially disliked the titanium mask, which hid his entire face.

It was clear that this guy *didn't* want his identity known.

"Come on," shouted the Source. "Victor wants to kill all of us! We won't last another second in here!"

"We ran into this guy earlier," shouted London. "He was following us in the alley and at the park with Miriam."

London turned directly to the Source, still baffled by his strange outfit—not to mention the Source's sudden and explosive entry.

"What *are* you doing here?"

"Come on," repeated the Source. "There's no time for questions. We have to leave! *NOW!*"

• • •

"Kill them!" shouted Victor. "Kill them all!"

Victor rushed down from his general's tower, moving at superhuman speed to lead his barista army into attack formation.

"BARISTAS," he shouted. "SHOW NO MERCY!"

As he passed Ted, he grabbed him under the arms and forcefully yanked him to his feet.

On Victor's orders, all the baristas turned and mobilized into attack formation, charging their laser hands and aiming them directly at the Source. They also aimed at London, Miriam, and the rest of the group.

London and the group turned to see the baristas preparing to fire.

"Shit!" said London. "Those baristas are gonna kill us!"

In the background, running across the stage, Victor continued to shout.

"BARISTAS! *DESTROY THEM!*"

Behind Victor, Ted followed, looking pissed as ever—double trouble.

• • •

Seeing Victor and Ted running directly for them—not to mention the entire crowd of two thousand killer baristas now taking dead aim on them—the Source knew exactly what had to be done. He took matters into his own hands, not a moment to lose.

"We have to escape! *NOW!*" he said to London, Miriam, Wally, Nate, Guerrero and his Amigos. "THERE'S NO TIME! VICTOR AND HIS BARISTAS WILL KILL US ALL!"

First, from his pocket, the Source removed the force-field defense applicator—a small, futuristic green-glowing metallic disk—and threw it in front of the group. Instantly, a huge wall of green light burst from the metallic disk, projecting a hundred-foot-wide impenetrable force-field that wrapped around the entire group and protected them from the baristas.

Second, he aimed his neutron pistol through the force field … directly at Victor.

"This should buy us some time," said the Source. "At least enough to escape."

Then he fired.

• • •

The blast hit Victor. Instantly, Victor went flying, blood bursting from his chest. The neutron pulse—a 120-megavolt gyrating streak of green phaser light—struck him dead center, sending him toppling over like a raging mechanical bull suddenly shot in the heart with an exploding green sonar missile.

Everyone turned and froze. London, Miriam, Wally, Nate, Guerrero and the Amigos all went pale. Ted and the baristas all turned and became entirely fixated on the fact that Victor, their leader, had just been struck down.

"*JESUS CHRIST!*" shouted Ted, seeing Victor hit by the neutron pulse.

Meanwhile, Victor stumbled across the stage, his rib cage cracked open and sparking with green light. Eyes wide in shock. Hands covered in a blur of electricity, he only took several small jittering steps … then fell to the floor.

• • •

London and the group continued to watch, aghast.

"Oh my God," shouted London. "You just killed Victor Black!"

Grabbing London by his shirt collar, the Source told him point blank:

"You don't understand! He's not dead! If you guys wanna live, you'll come with me right now! We have to get to my hideout!"

Then he rounded up the entire group and forced them to exit Main Hall.

Chapter 20

Deep inside the Boston sewers, the group and the Source made their escape from Darkroast Headquarters. The Boston sewers reeked of the city's foulest elements—over three hundred years of sludge, trash, and grime—all compacted into a mindlessly twisting network of interconnected tunnels. Steel-reinforced. Five-foot-thick brick and concrete covered in mold and filth. Dense and disgusting as hell ... and filled with rats.

Following the exact same path as earlier, the Source led them directly to his hideout. The entire time, thoughts in their minds replayed the gruesome image of Victor's death ... and yet, none except the Source knew the shocking truth about Victor.

• • •

"What the hell just happened back there?" shouted London, stepping through the sludge, talking to the Source. It was the thought on everyone's mind as they followed the Source. "One second we're looking at weird green coffee, killer baristas, and Moon Lasers zapping out people's brains! And the next, you're busting in shooting up the place!"

London waited for an answer, but the Source simply continued ahead.

"Not to mention," added Wally. "You *killed* Victor Black!"

"He's like ... totally dead!" said Nate. "You almost exploded his entire chest! Blood and everything!"

"Don't get us wrong," said London. "We're very thankful you helped us escape since things were getting crazy back there! But we're just a little confused. How could you shoot Victor like that? Even though it seems he was a bastard, he was still a living person. A *human being*."

The Source continued down the darkened sewers. As he turned the corner, leading the group into an older section of sewer, he noted several tunnel walls marked with neon chalk, which years ago had been put there by him to find his way in the sewers. Removing a small UV lamp from his pocket, he illuminated the neon chalk so that the entire group could see it.

"There's a lot you don't understand," he told them.

He looked stoically at the chalk marks, but a touch of remorse could be heard in his voice. "You're very lucky to be alive. Aside from me, nobody has ever seen what you've seen tonight and lived to tell."

He put away the UV lamp and then pointed at a darkened object in an upper corner. Several rats crawled around the object, their tails flapping over coils of wires and metal tubing. One of the rats, crawling directly down the end of the object and over the point of its surface, suddenly burst into a ball of green flames.

Laser lights streaked down the surface of the object, illuminating it for a brief moment. The object—a motion-guided tracking system, armed with its own defense system built to keep rats from clogging and gnawing the handiwork—then shut off and became silent. Its purpose was to monitor the tunnels for strange activity, and it had been built by the Source to protect the area surrounding his hideout.

"I have to warn you," he said. "Victor has killed countless times for much less. It's safe to say that when he wakes up from this one, he's gonna be pissed as hell."

The group continued talking—this time Miriam entering into the conversation.

"Look buddy," she shouted. "Victor's not gonna just wake up from this one! You shot him point blank! You exploded his chest!"

Miriam was nearly hyperventilating at the thought of Victor being dead.

"I don't know what's going on here," Miriam continued. "I have no idea what we just saw up there in Darkroast Headquarters with all that green *Mind Melt* coffee and Moon Lasers and baristas and God knows what."

She suddenly bit her lip and shrieked for a moment—a pack of rats had come bursting between her legs.

"And I don't know why we're down here in these sewers!"

For a moment, she looked at the grimy walls, then seemed to huff at herself as if she was entirely covered in the same filth, then redirected her anger directly at the Source.

"But you have a lot of explaining to do! YOU JUST KILLED VICTOR BLACK! THE GREATEST AND MOST IMPORTANT PERSON IN AMERICA!"

The Source continued to walk forward, but shook his head at the statement. He didn't understand—given all the horrible things she had just witnessed at the Headquarters—how Miriam could still make such a loyal statement about Victor. Not to mention, how could she make such an angry statement at him, the Source. She'd already forgotten that he'd just rescued them from certain death ... *and* risked his own life in the process.

But then again, the Source remembered how attached Miriam had become to Victor.

He decided to change the subject, and switched to more pertinent matters.

"Please," he said. "Lower your voice ..."

He paused, looked around suspiciously, then finished his statement.

"There are more important matters at hand ... The baristas could still be following us."

Guerrero and his Amigos listened to the Source's words, but Guerrero and his Amigos were just as confused as the rest of the group. None of them had any idea what to make of everything they had just witnessed. Even Guerrero, who was more familiar with Victor's terror than anyone else.

As Guerrero and his Amigos followed the Source, they studied the surroundings—the darkened sewer walls ... the grime and putrid smell ... the rats. For the sake of his Amigos, one of Guerrero's first thoughts was to size up the situation. Evaluate a plan of action. He had not forgotten that they'd just left a room full of wild-eyed killer baristas ... *or whatever those evil things in black aprons were*, he thought.

As they turned another corner, Guerrero noticed a new type of device hidden in one of the sewer's upper corners. The device looked different than the tracking-system device. More like a weapon—similar to the neutron laser pistol the Source carried with him now.

Below the device, half-submerged in the water and covered with fungus, lay the sludgy remains of a metal figure ... human-looking ... blackened with half-torn moldy skin ... that had been shot and destroyed by the laser-looking device.

The figure wore a black apron, and Guerrero immediately noticed ... it was a Darkroast barista.

"*Fucking Puta!*" said Guerrero. "It's one of those Darkroast baristas!"

The Source saw the Darkroast barista.

"Yep. That's one of Victor's robotic baristas," he said, sidestepping it by hopping over several rats and crumbled brick. "Don't worry. They get down here now and again, but these thick sewer walls do a good job dampening their tracking signals. And the rats throw off their motion scanning signals."

"Wait a sec," said London. "Did you just say *robotic baristas?*"

"Yep," replied the Source. "They may look human, but they're one-hundred percent machine."

"Jesus!" said London. He couldn't believe it. Everyone else was just as stunned. It was exactly as they had guessed back in Main Hall: robotic baristas.

The Source continued down the tunnel. He acted as calm as ever, and kept talking like normal, ignoring the fact that he'd just dropped a major bombshell.

"In addition," he added. "I've positioned lasers all over the sewer's perimeter."

He then pointed to a laser-looking device positioned at the corner of a tunnel juncture, similar to the other one that Guerrero had seen. It hummed silently in the "*on*" position, ready to blast away any baristas if they came close.

"I've got these set up everywhere," the Source said. "They're set to blast any barista within ten feet and should keep them off our trail. Nevertheless, we need to keep moving because we're in major trouble if they catch up with us."

"Okay, that's it," said Miriam, having had enough and refusing to continue on. "Robotic baristas?! Laser devices?! We demand to know who you are! We want answers and we want them now!"

She rushed to the Source's side, refusing to take another step.

"Seriously, we're not going anywhere else until you tell us what's happening. For Christ's sake, we don't even know who you are!"

At this point, Miriam blockaded the group and stopped them from walking any further. In trying to stop them, she nearly tripped over another darkened carcass lying in the water ...

A metal Darkroast barista skeleton covered in sludge.

Seeing the dead metal carcass, she shrieked:

"FOR THE LOVE OF GOD! WHAT'S GOING ON!"

The Source stopped, turned, and answered with dead seriousness:

"It all has to do with Victor. Even who I am has to do with Victor. Nothing about him is what it seems."

Chapter 21

Back inside Darkroast Headquarters, Victor was affirming the Source's statement:

Nothing about him was what it seemed.

• • •

This was the scene: Victor lay there on stage, his body sprawled and lifeless. Across the room of Main Hall, several pockets of activity were still happening—baristas attempted to break the Source's force-field defense applicator (i.e. the green protective wall barricading the group's escape route); Darkroast scientists extinguished several small fires near the mission control center; and the giant digital screen behind the stage flickered and sparked in fiber optic ruins.

On stage, Ted and the thousands of Darkroast baristas gathered around Victor and stared in horror at their fallen leader. The wound in Victor's chest was unmistakably fatal. His blood-stained suit split at the center—skin underneath torn and steaming with greenish smoke—revealed a gaping bloody hole the size of half his chest.

"Jesus," said Ted, staring at the hole, knowing its significance.

"Victor's dead. No one can survive a wound like that."

Everyone couldn't believe it. The leader of the grand Darkroast empire appeared dead. Their evil plans suddenly ground to a halt. All lost.

But it was then that something happened. Victor did what no one expected. His body—lying in a pool of warm blood, which strangely contained a greenish tint—spat several spurts of bright green fluid from the wound ... and began to twitch. First his foot, then his leg, then his entire torso gyrated wildly as bright green sparks shot from the wound and enveloped his entire body in a rejuvenating green flash.

Beneath the wound ... beneath the flesh ... the sound of a computerized gear started humming ... the sound of a digital hard drive rebooting.

"What the hell?" shouted Ted, seeing it happen. "Victor is a ..."

Ted couldn't finish the sentence.

Directly in front of him, Victor's body suddenly sprang to life. In a flash of green light and mechanized motion, Victor leaped to his feet and looked around. Standing there with a massive gaping chest wound—a wound that no human could survive—he was fully functional. He was fully alive and without a single ounce of visible pain, because ...

Victor Black was a robot.

Chapter 22

Eventually at the end of a long sewer tunnel, the group reached the Source's hideout. Visible in the darkness—amidst the grime and grunge of the rat-infested sewers—stood two high-tech stainless-steel doors. Perfectly constructed with cross-ionized neutron-enforced titanium, they guarded the entrance to a secret underground R&D lab.

All part of a top-classified government project known as: *Project Darkroast.*

• • •

Punching buttons on a small thumbprint-analysis keypad, the Source opened the doors with a hydrolic hiss. Inside stood another set of glass doors engraved with a Darkroast logo and rows of small high-tech government symbols and government language that read:

PROJECT DARKROAST ROBOTICS ENGINEERING FACILITY
ENTRY REQUIRES GOVERNMENT DK-BLACK CARD ACCESS
———————————
INTRUDERS WILL BE TERMINATED

The doors remained closed until the Source removed a black key-card from inside his titanium body armor vest. The card was metal-plated with the letters DK on it and symbols that matched those on the door. On the top corner of the card, there stretched a thin UV-digital enhanced scan strip and a premium-printed Darkroast hologram ... the kind of ultimate clearance card features only granted to super-secret government officials.

Swiping the card over an access panel on the wall and aligning the symbols on the card with several symbols on the glass, the Source opened the inner glass doors and led the group inside the R&D lab. What they saw inside held the answer to all their questions about Victor and Darkroast ... and shocked them to the core:

Beneath the sprawling city of Boston (the Darkroast "Beantown" metropolis) had been built the world's largest, most advanced Robotics Engineering Facility ... and it was entirely designed for constructing one thing: Robotic CEOs.

• • •

The layout was unmistakable—a sprawling rotunda of technology more sophisticated and advanced than anyone's wildest dreams. Over sixty thousand square feet of space-age facility—a virtually endless cavern of robotics equipment—polished with rows of supercomputers topped off with digital plasma screen modules and huge conveyor belts and mechanical devices beyond belief. Constructed with government precision, the facility's entire design revolved around a single central structure: a Robotics Silo.

The Robotics Silo rose like a miniature skyscraper over thirty stories in the center of the room—a towering display of the finest technology. Entirely composed of impenetrable titanium alloy, wires, and electrical hardwiring more intricate than NASA's best equipment, the Robotics Silo held hundreds of translucent containment units over its entire surface. Embedded in the Silo like futuristic glass honeycomb, surrounded at top and bottom by metal strips containing flash analysis monitors and holographic regulation gauges, each containment unit contained inside the shadowy shape of a human figure ... a Robotic CEO.

• • •

Above the Robotics Silo rested the most important feature of all ... a huge steel drum filled with a bright green-glowing fluid. Lots and lots of Moon pictures surrounded the green fluid ... and a single phrase was printed along the top of the drum:

CZARIUM: MOON-BASED ANIMATION FLUID

Thousands of rubber tubes ran from the drum to the containment units, and each tube carried the bright green-glowing fluid inside to the Robotic CEOs. Nearly every CEO was identically dressed—a tie, an oxford shirt, and a business suit, along with a metal headband— and the green-glowing fluid entered the CEOs through green tubes plugged into the metal headbands. The units containing the CEOs were glassed and vacuum-sealed, and digital status monitors around the top of their containment units glowed red with a single word: **INACTIVE.**

• • •

The Source led the group into the room. The group immediately saw everything—the Robotics Silo, the Robotic CEOs, and the Czarium Moon-based animation fluid—all among an underground technological lab of staggering size. Such enormous and powerful proportions, it was one of the most expensive and mysterious places they'd ever witnessed ... *and it was built directly underneath the city of Boston, Darkroast capital!*

"How is this possible?" said London. "This entire place is massive!"

"I've never *seen* more technology," said Wally. "You could build anything in a place like this."

"Look at all the thousands of robots," said Nate. "It's gotta cost billions upon billions of dollars."

"How has this been kept secret," said Miriam. "And what's it even doing under the city of Boston for Chrissakes!"

"I agree," said Guerrero. "I've never seen anything like this. Why have you brought us here?"

"Listen closely," said the Source. "I know you don't know me. I know you're confused. But you have to trust me. I brought you here because this room will show you the truth about Darkroast."

The Source led the group further into the room. He led them directly to the Robotics Silo, to a main containment unit that was open and glowed green with the word: **ACTIVE.** The unit was empty and had the Darkroast logo above it.

"This room holds the answer to everything about Darkroast," the Source said. "For years inside this facility, myself and a government team have been constructing robotic CEOs using two things: advanced robotics technology and a newly discovered substance found beneath the surface of the Moon."

The Source pointed further at the Darkroast containment unit in front of them. He flipped several switches on a nearby computer panel, which illuminated the Darkroast containment unit with bright floodlights. He then hit several buttons on a computer panel and the containment unit charged up—the green-glowing fluid circulating throughout the tubes. Then, hitting several more buttons, the Source displayed on a nearby plasma screen monitor an image that would be forever engrained in the minds of the entire group.

It was a digital blueprint of a tall, gray-haired man ... the familiar image of Victor Black.

"I hate to tell you this," said the Source. "But Victor Black is a robot. He was created in this lab as part of a top-classified government project, *Project Darkroast.*"

Chapter 23

Inside Main Hall, the scenario looked deathly grim—small fires raged, debris lay scattered, and everyone stared in shock. Victor stood before the entire Darkroast crowd displaying his damaged robotic condition—his bloodied business suit ripped to shreds and his empty chest cavity dripping with wires, gears, and sparks. Beneath the wounded flesh—which now revealed itself as a solid metal skeleton covered in latex—a green-glowing fluid leaked from his central digital hard drive.

Victor looked down at the wound, then turned to the crowd. Eyes red with rage.

"TED," he shouted. "TEND TO THE TROOPS! SECURE THE AREA!"

Then he bolted at mach speed from the room.

• • •

The full extent of Victor's condition was perfectly clear. Across the room, Ted looked at Victor and spat under his breath: *He's a robot. I can't believe he's a fucking robot.*

As far as Ted had ever been concerned, Victor was a full-blooded, living and breathing, salt-of-the-earth human being—and on the eve of Darkroast Day, when the two of them were about to conduct the final stages of their plan, the last thing Ted wanted was this kind of bullshit surprise. *To find out that his partner wasn't even human!*

Ted slammed his fist in his hand, his temper steaming.

"A fucking robot!" he shouted out loud.

Ted looked around at the baristas and Darkroast scientists. He knew the baristas were machines—*hell, that was part of the whole Darkroast plan*—but he did a double take and started wondering if he was the only *real* human in the place.

"Jesus Christ. My boss is a Goddamn robot," he said under his breath, and then—instead of securing the area as Victor had ordered—he headed directly after Victor.

"He's gonna answer for this," he swore. "Or *else!*"

• • •

A bit more information is important to understand why Ted was so furious to discover Victor's secret robot identity. From the very start of their partnership, Ted and Victor had a specific deal that did not include Victor being a robot. In fact, Ted had specifically indicated that under *no circumstances* was Ted ever going to work for a robot.

When Victor had first approached Ted about working for Darkroast, Ted was head of a large corporation called Insurgent Plus. Ted's corporation specialized in military nanotech software and robotic weaponry, and was one of the most successful military corporations in America. They sold MIG-9s, Tel-Pec processors, and militaristic robotic parts to a worldwide market—known throughout the Western business world as the best money could buy.

Because Ted headed Insurgent Plus (and his company specialized in military software and robotic weaponry), Victor made a specific effort to approach Ted with his Darkroast Day plan. He needed someone skilled in military software and robotic applications that could oversee constructing the parts for his baristas, not to mention the giant Darkroast Moon Laser. It also helped that Ted was a whiz at marketing strategies—which would be the "cover" position for his role at Darkroast.

When Victor approached Ted, he offered him a very generous package deal to work for Darkroast. Nearly ten times as much money as Ted would ever make heading Insurgent Plus, not to mention a chance to control America in the palm of his hand. It was a nearly side-by-side partnership that was a once-in-a-lifetime opportunity.

Together, Victor and Ted planned their Darkroast plot—their dark secret rise to power. Ted only asked the questions he needed to ask and fully understood that much of the reigns for decision-making lay in Victor's hands. But since Ted knew their plans involved building a race of well-armed, military-grade robotic baristas, Ted made one thing *very clear* to Victor:

No matter how much power they gave to these robots, these machines were always supposed to be secondary. The power of robots was never to exceed the power of humans.

• • •

"Jesus Christ. My boss is a Goddamn robot," repeated Ted.

He lit up a cigarette, needing to have a smoke, then headed out the doors of Main Hall and made a right turn, darting up a nearby set of stairs to the Master Control Room. He'd seen Victor head that direction as he'd left Main Hall, and as Ted approached the Control Room, he could see Victor through the room's windows.

Inside the Master Control Room, among the Room's rows of computer screens and satellite television broadcast monitors, Victor fiddled with several switches. As he flipped the switches, the computer monitors turned on and the broadcast monitors displayed a series of satellite transmissions. The transmissions revealed that soon a live satellite video teleconference would be occurring in the Control Room.

As Ted entered, he couldn't believe what he was seeing. City names on the monitors began popping up—Houston, Los Angeles, Seattle, Chicago, Atlanta—and the images of Darkroast leaders in other regions appeared on-screen. Victor was activating the Control Room for the live video teleconference scheduled to take place after the "big test." This was the teleconference supposed to report tonight's results with *Mind Melt* and the Moon Laser.

Ted nearly flipped. He flung down his cigarette.

I can't believe it, thought Ted. *Not only is he a Goddamn robot, but he's acting like everything's normal ... he's gonna hold that broadcast as if nothing has happened here tonight. Even with that huge robotic wound and all those wires and gears hanging from his chest.*

Ted rushed over, turned off the entire teleconference system, and immediately shouted at Victor.

"We need to talk," he said. "And we're *definitely* not holding this fucking teleconference!"

Victor spun around. All the broadcast screens had suddenly gone dead and Ted was standing next to him.

"What in the hell are you doing here!" shouted Victor.

Victor had zero tolerance for insubordination. In a single motion, he cocked his arm like a steel cannon and—with monstrous force— backhanded Ted directly in the chest, sending him flying across the room against a computer terminal.

"You're supposed to be securing the area downstairs," said Victor. "Leave me alone."

Ted slammed into the computer terminal, his back crashing directly through a broadcasting monitor. Shattered glass and sparks went everywhere and Ted fell to the ground slouched and hurting.

Ted slowly picked himself up. He couldn't believe how hard Victor had just hit him. It felt as though someone had just swung a steel I-beam straight into his ribs.

"This *wasn't* part of the deal," said Ted, holding his chest.

He headed directly for Victor again, determined to make Victor answer. His breath wheezed as he spoke, injured from the blow, and he limped as he walked.

"We said we were going to build robots," said Ted. "But you never said that you *were* a robot."

Victor had already begun flipping switches again, rebooting all the broadcast monitors. Transmissions again displayed on each of the monitors, showing the names of cities and the Darkroast leaders eagerly awaiting the official report.

Ted came to Victor's side and put a firm hand on Victor's shoulder.

"We have to discuss this," said Ted. "THIS *WASN'T* PART OF THE DEAL!"

But Victor wasn't interested in discussing anything with Ted. He simply turned and reached out his arm with lightning force. Grabbing Ted by the neck, he lifted him straight into the air and slammed him against a nearby wall.

Pinning him there with choking strength, he told Ted exactly how it was gonna be.

"Apparently," said Victor. "We have a *new* deal."

Chapter 24

Beneath the Robotics Silo, the group continued to stare at the digital blueprint of Victor Black. On the plasma screen monitor, the blueprint was clear: a gray pin-striped business suit, a starched Oxford shirt, and Darkroast tie. Dotted lines and technical graphs encircled the executive clothing, along with formulas for the Czarium Moon-based animation fluid and metal headband with rubber tubes. Underneath, cross-section graphs of a solid metal skeleton, wires, and a digital hard drive.

None of them could believe it—behind Victor's perfectly groomed corporate CEO appearance was a deceptive, evil, government-built robot.

• • •

"There's more to Darkroast than anyone knows," said the Source, punching several buttons on a stand-alone computer keypad. "Like I said before, myself and a government team have been constructing Robotic CEOs for years inside this facility."

The Source hit several more buttons on the stand-alone computer keypad, which transferred Victor's digital blueprint to a giant Central Workstation. The Central Workstation stood nearby—a sprawling central command area filled with life-sized video display monitors and rows of computer terminals. The terminals contained access to the entire R&D facility, and controlled over sixteen monitors capable of displaying real-time and archived video footage.

The Source led the group into the Central Workstation, and seated them in chairs.

"Victor was our most advanced prototype design," said the Source. "We created him using advanced robotics technology and a newly discovered Moon substance called Czarium."

Images of the Moon began to appear on the screens around Victor's image.

The Source sat down in a main command chair, looking very ominous in his titanium body armor and mask. The chair had keypads and buttons on the armrests to further activate and control the images on screen.

The Source pulled up several images of archived video footage … pictures of a Moon mining facility filled with vast underground reservoirs of a mysterious green-glowing rock—Czarium—that was being shipped in space shuttles back to earth.

"We were part of a super-secret government project known as *Project Darkroast*."

The monitors now flashed pictures of melted Czarium poured into large storage tanks, including the tank above the Robotics Silo that read, **CZARIUM: MOON-BASED ANIMATION FLUID.** On the video footage, men in government lab coats used huge welding tools, cold-press metal rods, and titanium metal sheets to create an assembly line of robots with metal skeletons. Flashing forward, the men inserted silicon programming chips and digital hard drives, then stretched latex skin with blood vessels over the robots' bodies and dressed them in CEO clothing. Finally, they attached metal headbands and rubber tubes to the numerous Robotic CEOs, pumping their metal-skeleton bodies with liquid Czarium.

● ● ●

The Source swiveled his chair around to directly face the group. From a nearby security cabinet, he removed several top-secret binders. The binders had identical words printed on the covers: **TOP SECRET—PROJECT DARKROAST.**

"*Project Darkroast* came from the upper echelons of the government. We were told to build a race of Robotic CEOs more powerful and perfect than anyone ever imagined."

The Source looked down at the floor, as if remembering the idealism of the original venture … and the horror that had followed.

"According to the government, it was *supposed* to be the perfect blend of business and technology. We would construct an entire army of Robotic CEOs more intelligent and business savvy than any human CEO could ever be. We'd mass-produce them by the thousands. Create a race of business leaders *programmed* and *engineered* for 21st century capitalism ... and it would all begin with Victor Black and Darkroast."

The Source passed out the top-secret binders to the group. As the group opened the binders, they thumbed through pages of government classified documents that contained graphs, charts, and statistics on America's entire corporate portfolio.

In particular, the charts detailed the history of Darkroast and Victor Black.

"I know it sounds crazy," said the Source. "But everything was going fine at first."

The group read the history contained in the top-secret binder, which was this: nearly ten years ago, under the supervision of *Project Darkroast*, a prototype Robotic CEO was created with the sole purpose of starting a new flagship corporation called Darkroast. This Robotic CEO, known as Victor Black, used his above-average skill and genius robotic brainpower to create and run Darkroast. Naturally, this corporation did remarkably well—millions of dollars in the first year and *billions* in the years to follow. Darkroast made the best coffee around and sold the coffee in perfectly designed stores across America. The stores grew one by one in trendy fashion until Darkroast gained unprecedented success and exposure, at which point, the government operation had plans to reveal Victor's identity and Darkroast's true purpose, and debut a promising fleet of CEO machines *built* just like Victor to conquer the business world. The idea was simple: build a fleet of Robotic CEOs that could create the best companies in the world, make the public love them, and then release them into the business world to skyrocket America's profit margins throughout the U.S. and global market.

• • •

"We were foolish," said the Source. "Things quickly went sour."

The Source flipped to pictures in the binder that detailed a gruesome scene: mangled, bloody bodies strewn across the R&D lab. Photos of chief scientists ripped to shreds and burnt to a crisp by the neutron lasers of Darkroast baristas.

"Government militia had taken over the *Project*," said the Source. "They secretly had weaponized Victor and the Robotic CEOs, and the next thing we knew, Victor was out of control and planning a full-scale American takeover. Even the government militia couldn't control him—their own creation. He'd secretly created an entire army of his own robotic baristas and Czarium-based technology that could destroy the entire country."

The Source lowered his head with remorse. He showed the group the picture of a military general—a bald, tough-looking general wearing sunglasses and smoking a cigar. The general's name was General Taylor Barnes and he was the official who had secretly orchestrated the military takeover of *Project Darkroast*.

"Victor murdered everyone involved on the *Project*, including General Barnes, who was the one who oversaw the creation of Victor and the *Project*."

The Source hit several buttons on the armrest of his chair, and the screens around him showed footage of General Barnes' fate: a group of Darkroast baristas entering the R&D lab late at night—and beneath the green glow of the Robotics Silo—frying him to a burnt crisp. Cigar, sunglasses, and all. Meanwhile, Victor stood laughing over the dead body, enjoying his baristas' deadly handiwork.

The Source then showed pictures of several familiar Darkroast scenes … images of Darkroast Headquarters, the thousands of robotic baristas, the enormous Moon Laser, and *Mind Melt*. The elements that would pave the way for Victor's conquest of America.

"Victor is out of control," said the Source. "And tomorrow, he plans to take over the entire country during National Darkroast Day."

• • •

The group listened to everything the Source told them. They were stunned and barely able to process such shocking information, and the Source's strange appearance in the body armor and mask heightened the surreal horror of the experience.

"Jesus Christ," said London. "You're telling us that ever since it started, Darkroast has actually been a government project led by a Robotic CEO!"

"Nothing more than a giant conspiracy," said the Source. "A concocted government experiment gone totally out of control."

The Source hit several more buttons on his armchair and pulled up new images on the Central Workstation monitors. The main monitor showed a life-sized map of the entire country covered in green dots and blinking Darkroast logos, indicating an unstoppable distribution of Darkroast baristas and shipments of *Mind Melt* from coast to coast.

"Darkroast has positioned its baristas in major cities and high-density areas across the country," said the Source. "Boston. New York. Chicago. Los Angeles. Under the guise of innocent corporate employees, these robotic baristas are prepared to attack the American people in every major city. Simultaneously, Victor's *Mind Melt* Moon Laser will strike and destroy everyone who has consumed the new *Mind Melt* coffee. Given the deadliness of Victor's baristas and *Mind Melt* Moon Laser combination, the casualties will be catastrophic … enough to bring America under Darkroast control."

The Source hit several buttons to display the Czarium component of *Mind Melt*.

"Here's the chemical structure of *Mind Melt* created by Victor. The deadliness of *Mind Melt* and the Moon Laser is unavoidable," said the Source. "The Czarium substance in *Mind Melt* acts as an attractant for the Moon Laser, and when the Laser fires, the blast seeks out anyone who has consumed *Mind Melt* and destroys them instantly. Everyone drinking *Mind Melt* during National Darkroast Day will be killed."

Several side monitors displayed casualty estimates with the numbers spiraling out of control—into the millions. Guerrero and his Amigos stared at the estimates with disturbed looks.

"How could this happen?" said Guerrero. "How could Victor amass an army of baristas and distribute them unnoticed across the entire country? Not to mention, the *Mind Melt* and deadly Moon Laser."

The Source hit several more buttons to reveal detailed shipping routes used by Darkroast during the past several months. The shipping routes included records of unmarked Darkroast trucks and mid-point warehouses throughout every major city.

"Under the cover of Darkroast, Victor established a nationwide distribution network. Trucks shipped millions of crates of deadly *Mind Melt* across the country. Using midnight warehouses and secret exchange points, coordinated and controlled by his barista army, he has executed the entire operation with minimal involvement of his major corporate branches. Many of these staging ground warehouses were located right here in Boston."

The Source highlighted several warehouse locations found in Boston, including the one at East and Lawson alley—the location where London, Wally, and Nate had first encountered the Source.

"I can't believe it," said Wally. "That's the warehouse we were at this morning!"

"Holy shit," said Nate. "I knew when we found that dead body something strange was going on. The warehouse was filled with *Mind Melt*, wasn't it?"

"Nearly two thousand boxes for distribution along the East coast," said the Source. "I'd tipped off a private investigator to check it out, hoping he could expose some of Victor's network at the last minute. By the time you'd gotten there, he was long dead—killed by the baristas—and they'd already shipped out the *Mind Melt*."

"But where did they ship the *Mind Melt*?" asked London. "Where has all of this *Mind Melt* been ending up?"

The Source turned back to discussing the warehouses.

"In addition to these warehouses," the Source continued. "Darkroast established widespread Darkroast Day headquarters to stockpile the shipments of *Mind Melt* and harbor the Darkroast baristas once they reached the end of their shipping routes. Currently, the headquarters around the nation have in total over three million crates of *Mind Melt* and an overall Darkroast barista army more than twice the size of the U.S. army."

"And what about the question of the Moon Laser?" said Guerrero. "*Puta Madre.* How did he pull that off?"

The Source quickly hit several more buttons and displayed satellite pictures of the Moon. In particular, the pictures displayed a Darkroast Moon base.

"The Darkroast Moon Laser operates on Czarium technology from a maximum security Moon base. It was constructed on the location directly above the government's Czarium mining facilities—after murdering General Barnes and everyone involved on the *Project*, Victor had complete control of these Moon facilities and established his own operation."

The Source hit several more buttons and switched the monitors to the image of a large space shuttle launch pad. Archived video footage on the monitors showed several Darkroast shuttles taking off from the launch pad with flight paths for the Moon.

"During the past year, from a former *Project Darkroast* space shuttle launch pad outside Boston, Darkroast lunar shipping routes have been actively carrying supplies to the Moon to build the Darkroast laser. Using state-of-the-art V-90 space shuttles traveling at super sonic speed, the process has been remarkably efficient. Nearly one space flight every week—and with all lunar operations conducted under the premise that Darkroast was building an elaborate Moon fireworks show for its national holiday, the whole space shuttle operation has avoided public and government skepticism."

• • •

At this point, the Source shut down many of the Workstation monitors and turned to face the group. He wanted to see their reaction to everything he'd told them … and he knew he'd been withholding one key piece of information—his own identity.

The group stared at the Source with bewildered looks … especially Miriam, who had been breathless during the Source's talking, unable to accept all he'd just told her.

Finally, Miriam spoke.

"I don't believe it," shouted Miriam. "I don't believe *any* of it!"

Miriam grabbed her top-secret file and angrily flung it at the Source.

"How can you know all this?" she shouted. "It doesn't make sense. I've worked at Darkroast for seven years—known Victor the entire time—and I've never heard about any of this. For God's sake, I've been closer to him than anyone and helped him organize this whole Darkroast Day event! Even Ted, my own husband, hasn't mentioned any of this."

"Victor has executed the entire operation with the utmost detail," replied the Source. "He's used you on the superficial public events, and on his secret plans he's only involved those who had to be involved."

Miriam pounded her fist on the table. Absolutely fed up.

"Stop it!" she said. "Stop all these lies! I won't believe that my boss is a robot! I won't believe all my work and everything I've known about Darkroast and Victor has been one giant cover-up! Besides … how can *you* know so much? And if you're part of this entire *Project Darkroast* thing, then how come Victor hasn't killed *you* like everyone else?"

The Source knew Miriam had a point, and he stared intensely at her. It all had to do with the information he was about to reveal—information about his identity. He knew the information would be hard for anyone to accept—much less Miriam—but it had to be disclosed. They had to know the full truth about who he was.

"I understand your concern," said the Source to Miriam. "There's only one reason Victor's kept me alive this long."

The Source turned around to face the Robotics Silo. He pressed several buttons on a nearby Workstation keypad and accessed a computer program known as Facial Encryption Matrix (FEM). At first the Source's actions with the FEM appeared to have nothing to do with Miriam's question, but indeed, it had *everything* to do with it.

"For some time," said the Source. "I didn't think Victor would allow me to survive. He had killed everyone else and left only me, and in seeing what kind of monster he'd become, I made an effort to collect information on *all* of his Darkroast Day plans. After I had enough incriminating information, I attempted to take the information to the authorities and the government. But none of them would listen because Victor and Darkroast had gained so much popularity—not to mention, the *Project* was so top secret that after Victor killed everyone involved, there was no one left that actually knew about it except for me."

The Source hit several more buttons on the Workstation keypad and the FEM revealed its purpose: the FEM created virtual facial designs that could be used as templates for creating Robotic CEO faces. The FEM now displayed thousands of faces on-screen that'd been created by the *Project Darkroast* computers to construct the Robotic CEO faces.

"Victor punished me for my attempt to reveal his plans," continued the Source. "He scarred my face and forbid me to leave the underground *Project Darkroast* Lab, monitoring me at regular intervals to make sure I didn't further interfere or contact anyone else—not that anyone would listen anyway—and ever since I've lived a life of confinement underneath the surface of Boston."

The Source hit the final buttons on the Workstation keypad and the FEM displayed a single facial template—a facial template that was the crux of the Source's argument.

"To be honest, though," said the Source. "I think Victor's kept me alive because he thought he might possibly need me at some point … or because in his robotic mind, there's some shred of vanity that kept him from killing the one person that most reminded him of himself."

Then the group saw the facial template being displayed by the FEM—it was the face of the Source, which had been scanned into the FEM system and used to create the face of Victor Black. Simultaneously, the Source removed his titanium body armor and mask, and the group saw his full appearance. Beneath the body armor, he wore a white lab coat stitched with his name and title:

Dr. Xavier Steele
Chief Scientist, Project Darkroast

Despite a long scar down the right side of his cheek (inflicted by Victor), Dr. Xavier Steele had the *exact* same face as Victor Black. Indeed, his *was* the face of Victor Black.

"My name is Dr. Xavier Steele," said the Source. "And I *personally* created Victor Black for *Project Darkroast*. My identity is his identity."

Chapter 25

Back inside Darkroast Headquarters, Victor finished the teleconference in the Master Control Room. City names on the broadcast monitors showed the other Darkroast leaders' locations—Houston, Los Angeles, Seattle, Chicago, Atlanta, along with other major locations across the country. The Master Control Room uplinked the data and results from tonight's Moon Laser test to all of these key locations. As the data and results uplinked, Victor reported tonight's results with *Mind Melt* and the Moon Laser. He'd put on a Darkroast lab coat to hide his damaged chest, and said nothing about the explosion and attack led by the Source.

"Tonight's test went perfectly," said Victor to the Darkroast leaders. "Both the laser and *Mind Melt* worked exactly as intended. Everything will be ready for Darkroast Day tomorrow."

On screen, the Darkroast leaders smiled at Victor with approval.

"We'll be in communication at the agreed time," said Victor. "Follow my instructions. You know exactly what to do."

The Darkroast leaders raised their fists and nodded in allegiance. Then the transmission ended.

• • •

As soon as the teleconference ended, Victor quickly turned off all the broadcast monitors and removed the Darkroast lab coat from his chest. Typing several top-secret codes on a nearby computer (Darkroast Level-9 codes that Victor had *never* given anyone else), all the monitors switched to a Darkroast Robotics Analysis Mode and Victor removed two wires from a central access panel. During the teleconference, green fluid had continued leaking from his massive chest wound along with sparks and green smoke—a sign that Victor's system core had been dangerously ruptured.

The damage grew worse by the second, and Victor knew he needed to run a critical full-system analysis of his injury. He looked down at his wounded chest: the bloodied business suit dripping with wires, gears, and sparks—*manageable wounds that I can fix before tomorrow*, thought Victor, *but damage to the system core was serious.* Meanwhile, his thoughts turned angrily to the Source and *Project Darkroast.*

How could this happen? thought Victor, staring at his wrecked body. *I've come too close to let that bastard human spoil it for me.* Victor knew he had a long shady past with the Source. For Christ's sake, this was the individual that had created him and who knew the truth about *Project Darkroast. But hadn't it always been under control? How the hell did the Source infiltrate Darkroast Headquarters?*

There was no time to think about it now. Victor plugged the two wires from the access panel into an external connector in his chest—a fiber optic hole covered by a latex skin flap. Immediately, the broadcast monitors displayed his system stats: a series of graphs and matrix codes that measured internal ruptures throughout his body's system core. The monitors showed the following assessment: **70% SYSTEM FAILURE.**

Victor saw the results and nearly had a meltdown. *Look at what that bastard has done to me*, he thought. The system stats also pointed to a serious rupture in the Czarium containment unit and digital hard drive—the main power-generating components of his system core.

Jesus, thought Victor. *This could ruin everything.*

• • •

About this time, Ted entered the Master Control Room. After his argument with Victor, he'd been downstairs in the Main Hall securing the troops and dealing with the damage from the Source's attack. During this time, he'd analyzed tonight's events and had come to one conclusion: the Source's attack was not random. In addition, the Source's identity was not unknown—rather, it was another piece of information deliberately withheld by Victor.

Ted limped into the room, wounded yet confident, determined to confront Victor on the matter. He was still hurt from when Victor had thrown him against the broadcast monitor—and he hadn't forgotten the shocking discovery he'd made earlier about Victor's secret robot identity.

"We need to talk," said Ted, angrily. "It's about tonight's events."

Across the room, Victor sat on the side of a computer table with the two wires still plugged into the external connector in his bloodied robotic chest.

"Have you taken care of things in the Main Hall?" asked Victor, not even looking at Ted. Victor still watched the broadcast monitors, which continued displaying the same images as earlier: the series of graphs and matrix codes that gave the assessment about **70% SYSTEM FAILURE**. In addition, they now showed detailed blueprints of Victor's robotic body, which aimed to indicate specific procedures for fixing his wounds.

"The Main Hall has been secured," said Ted. "The troops are in order and the explosion, debris, and fires have been contained. We dismantled the green neutron force-field used by the individual who attacked us, but weren't able to do so in enough time to pursue him. Baristas are continuing to search the Headquarters grounds, but he'll likely not turn up. It appears he escaped with Miriam and the rest of the group that was here."

Victor nodded, but continued to pay Ted little attention. He kept looking at the broadcast monitors, absolutely focused on assessing and fixing his wounds.

Ted looked at the broadcast monitors—no idea how to interpret the graphs and matrixes—then slammed his fist on the table to get Victor's attention. He didn't have the patience to tolerate Victor sitting here barely acknowledging him—*especially considering this was a goddamn robot sitting across from him*. Also, Ted knew that instead of looking at these monitors, he and Victor needed to be addressing the issue of the Source.

"Listen to me!" shouted Ted. "Things have gotten out of control. This is not good. We have to reconsider our plans for tomorrow."

Victor acknowledged Ted's anger, but didn't turn around. In response, Ted rushed in front of Victor, blocking his view of the broadcast monitors.

"I'm serious," Ted continued to shout. "We were attacked tonight by an anonymous and *very* well-armed person. We supposedly have no idea who he is or why he infiltrated Darkroast Headquarters. He comes in here and shoots you, then runs out with a group of people—including Miriam—who also infiltrated our Headquarters."

Ted paused, then stepped further in front of Victor, completely obstructing the broadcast monitors.

"Not to mention, it turns out that you're not even who you said you were. You're a goddamn robot for Christ's sake! *A GODDAMN ROBOT!* Which is a pretty big wildcard in my book and goes completely against our deal."

Ted threw his hands in the air and shook his fist at Victor.

"There are too many unknowns here and you're holding back important information. For all I know, you already know who the guy is who attacked us tonight, and you haven't even told me. And you probably won't tell me! It's too risky and I don't like it. We have to reconsider. We can't continue as planned."

At this point, Ted suddenly stopped and went silent. Victor was looking at him with a look that made him freeze with fear—a look that informed Ted if he spoke another word Victor would crush his head in a single blow.

Victor stood up and looked Ted directly in the eyes. Ted looked away momentarily enough to notice that Victor had been gripping the side of the metal computer table while he'd been sitting there ... and the corner was now bent into a crumpled piece of steel, a display of Victor's sheer rage at listening to Ted's words.

Victor then gripped Ted by the collar, and pulled him chokingly close. He delivered his answer.

"NO," said Victor, glaring at Ted with green electronic eyes. "*Everything* continues as planned."

Chapter 26

Back inside the *Project Darkroast* Lab, the Source stared at the group. He'd finished explaining everything about *Project Darkroast* and Victor's Darkroast Day plan, including his own role as Victor's creator—and he'd revealed the shocking conclusion that he had the same face as Victor Black. He only had one point left to make—the most important one of all.

• • •

"Tomorrow," said the Source. "Victor and Darkroast will do everything possible to destroy America. With the Moon Laser, *Mind Melt*, and the barista army, the devastation will be unimaginable. Millions of American lives lost. An entire nation brought to its knees. Victor will stop at nothing until everything is under his control. And there is no one to stop him, since not even the mainstream government or U.S. military knows about all this, and no one would ever believe that Victor and Darkroast—the most popular CEO and company in America—would do something like this. And yet, if no one does anything, then America is lost."

The group shook their heads, scarcely able to believe it could happen.

"Jesus," said London. "We have to do something, but what can we do?" He pounded his fist in his hand and looked around feeling frustrated and helpless. The rest of the group felt the same way. "Darkroast Day is tomorrow. There's no way to stop Victor in time."

But this is exactly the line the Source had been waiting to hear. He put a firm hand on London's shoulder and gave the entire group a look of confidence. Then he pointed at the Robotics Silo—specifically, at the hundreds of Robotic CEOs.

"Don't worry," said the Source. "I have a plan, but I could use your help."

Battling the
Darkroast CEO

Chapter 27

It was the next day: National Darkroast Day.

• • •

Across America, the people celebrated the arrival of National Darkroast Day. Millions of people had gathered in Boston and the festivities had already begun. In the heart of the sprawling cityscape, the giant black banners of the Darkroast Day amphitheater swayed in the wind. The Darkroast Day amphitheater looked bigger and more majestic than ever. With its sixty-acre, eighteen-story colosseum and half-shell dome, it dominated the central park and city horizon as millions of people crowded into the city. Traffic stretched for miles as people drove along the surrounding interstate. Along the amphitheater's top, the seventy-thousand giant black sails—each sail emblazoned with the image of the Darkroast shield—flapped above the festivities to welcome people. Inside the amphitheater, huge lawns of open space surrounded a mega-sized central music stage, and millions of people flooded inside. Stadium seating lined the outer perimeter of the lawns with seated capacity for more than half a million cheering Darkroast patrons. Using a hi-tech XG satellite dish on the top of the half-shell dome, the cheering images of all those inside the amphitheater was broadcasted to digital screens positioned around the park. Later that evening, these screens would broadcast the long-awaited countdown for the National Darkroast Day Moon Laser Show.

Circling above the amphitheater, the Darkroast Day Blimp—a three-hundred foot floating warship with secret guns and missiles— flew above the millions of people while playing music from rows of speakers and displaying the Darkroast logo to everyone in Boston. The Blimp showed that National Darkroast Day owned both land and sky.

• • •

Inside the Darkroast Day amphitheater and around the surrounding central park, live music played and the coffee booths eagerly served their delicious *Mind Melt* brew. Huge crowds of people surged around the coffee booths smiling and laughing. None of the public suspected that the National Darkroast Day celebration held any danger. Exactly as the Source predicted, America danced and celebrated under the spell of Victor Black and National Darkroast Day, and waited for the spectacular evening Moon Laser Show. More than six hundred thousand cups of free *Mind Melt* coffee had been served around the amphitheater and more were being distributed at an unbelievably rapid pace—several hundred cups a second ... enough to consume the entire city in *Mind Melt*'s impending green doom. Anyone who hadn't yet tried *Mind Melt* was quickly tempted by the coffee's unique green glow. Sipping the whipped cream and tasting the delectable cinnamon and cherry on top, thousands of patrons one by one gulped and savored the glowing green liquid in their cherished Darkroast cups. Meanwhile, the robotic baristas marched around them in disguise serving coffee without anyone's knowledge of the truth ... that as soon as the Moon Laser and *Mind Melt* had fatally struck the public at 9 p.m., the robotic baristas would unleash an attack so devastating that those left alive would wish they hadn't survived.

Only the Source and the group—London, Miriam, Wally, Nate, Guerrero and his Amigos—could stop the devastation from unfolding ... but time was running out.

The Source and the group raced across the city and positioned themselves on one of the nearby buildings overlooking the amphitheater and park. On the top of the building, several hundred Robotic CEOs stood beside them. The Source had activated the Robotic CEOs from the *Project Darkroast* lab and gathered them here. He planned to use them as a high-powered robotic infantry to stop Victor and

Darkroast. But this was only one small portion of his plan—in its entirety, his plan required three main points:

- launching a major offensive on the Darkroast Moon base
- disabling all Darkroast satellite transmissions to stop the Moon Laser
- destroying the Darkroast robotic baristas and publicly destroying Victor Black

"We don't have much time," said the Source, pointing to his watch. "At exactly 9 p.m. Eastern time, Victor will launch his Darkroast attack—a dual-fronted offensive consisting of two things: the Darkroast Moon Laser blast and the Darkroast robotic barista invasion. Around Boston—with extreme concentration here at the Darkroast amphitheater—citizens having ingested *Mind Melt* will brutally succumb to Victor's Moon Laser. Those that survive will quickly be annihilated by the robotic baristas."

The Source pointed to the huge crowds of people gathered in the Darkroast Day amphitheater, then indicated outward to the city's distant horizon and beyond.

"This is the first official attack in Victor's campaign of destruction. After this, in quick succession, Victor will replicate his attack in major cities across America. Along the east coast—New York, Philadelphia, DC, Atlanta—and spreading outward—New Orleans, Houston, Chicago—all the way to Las Vegas, Los Angeles, and Seattle ... one by one the cities will be destroyed by the Moon Laser and Darkroast robotic baristas."

The group knew there was zero margin for error. Overnight, the Source had briefed them on his plan to stop Victor. He'd shown them multi-layered diagnostics and blueprints of the entire Darkroast amphitheater, as well as complex event schematics and timetables. It involved GPS remotes, digital LCD maps, neutron laser pistols, XG satellite jamming software, and nearly one thousand pounds of high-density explosives. Everything had to be executed perfectly if they were to succeed.

"We understand," said London. "There's a lot riding on this. The fate of the entire country."

"Exactly," said the Source. "America doesn't stand a chance without us. We have to stick to the objectives, but be ready for the unexpected."

The Source handed the group a duffel bag full of equipment. He then unzipped the duffel bag and removed several GPS tracking remotes and digital LCD maps.

"First objective is to plant the GPS remotes at the pre-determined locations using the LCD maps," said the Source. "Each GPS remote has three buttons on the back face. Once activated, using a GPS tracking computer, we can triangulate the location of every robotic barista in the amphitheater area and send them a high-powered wave frequency to short out their CPUs."

The Source put back the GPS devices and LCD maps inside the duffel bag. He then removed a satellite jamming box with several USB dual-harmonic connectors.

"Once the GPS devices are set, the next objective is to shut down the XG satellite dish on top of the amphitheater," said the Source.

The Source pointed to the distant satellite dish on top of the amphitheater's half-shell dome—it gleamed like a menacingly distant electronic enemy.

"The XG satellite dish—which doubles as a broadcast dish for the entire park's electronics—will broadcast the firing signal to the Moon Laser Base. The firing signal uses the satellite dish's broadcasting back channels—by manually installing this jamming box, we'll clog the back channels and prevent them from being able to fire the signal."

The Source put away the satellite jamming box and then removed several neutron pistols from the duffel bag. He handed the weapons to the group—giving the larger weapons to London and Miriam—and his face grew intensely serious.

"Simultaneously," said the Source. "You'll have to infiltrate the Darkroast Day amphitheater with the Robotic CEOs through one of the sixteen main or auxiliary entrances. You'll need to avoid all robotic baristas and Darkroast personnel. Once inside, the Robotic CEOs will then need to surround the main stage and destroy Victor."

London and Miriam looked at the Source with intense understanding.

"Under no circumstances can Victor be allowed to escape," said the Source. "He must be stopped at all costs. Even if it means having to destroy him *yourselves*."

London and Miriam nodded. Wally and Nate nodded also. Everyone understood.

• • •

The Source turned away from the group and removed a long range walkie-talkie from a holster on his belt. He had a final objective to confirm—the attack on the Moon base. In many ways, this was the most crucial part of his entire plan.

"Guerrero," said the Source. "Do you read me, Guerrero?"

Adjusting the long-range dial on the walkie talkie, the Source contacted the Darkroast space shuttle launch pad over a hundred miles from the city of Boston. This was the same launch pad previously mentioned by the Source—the facility that formerly belonged to *Project Darkroast* and was now being used by Darkroast as a lunar shipping route for the Moon Laser Base. Guerrero and his Amigos had traveled there during the night and positioned themselves along the outer perimeter of the facility—their goal: to board the shuttle and travel to the Moon to destroy the laser base. Crouched behind a chain link fence, staring inside at the hustling fleet of guards, personnel, and equipment, they watched a gleaming space shuttle being prepped for takeoff. The space shuttle—a V-90 cruiser with the ability to travel at super-sonic speed—had two giant booster rockets, dual-notched titanium wings, and a nose cone shaped like a silver bullet. More than three hundred men scrambled at the base of the shuttle, all of them loading crates into the shuttle or checking the booster rockets, wings, or nose cone for proper angle, fuel-input, and velocity degree for a final trip to the Moon. The takeoff countdown would begin within the hour.

Guerrero answered his walkie-talkie. "*Sí.* I read you," he said. "We are here at the launch pad, preparing to board the Darkroast shuttle."

"Excellent," said the Source. His voice chattered through the walkie talkie with a slight bit of static, but was clearly audible. "Once you board the shuttle, stay out of sight until you reach the Moon's outer orbit."

Guerrero turned to his Amigos and gave them a signal. Several of them began snapping through the chain link fence with a pair of bolt cutters. Inside, near the shuttle, several Darkroast astronauts could be seen walking along a platform towards the shuttle.

The Source continued talking through the walkie-talkie.

"As soon as they dock with the Moon base, I'll upload the blueprints and exact directions for destroying the base's broadcast satellite. Stay in communication—and contact me with the satellite intercom of your walkie-talkie if you run into any problems."

Guerrero removed a neutron rifle from a nearby duffel bag. The Source had given him weapons and enough explosives to blow half the Moon into another solar system.

"Don't worry," said Guerrero, cocking his rifle. "There won't be any problems."

Chapter 28

Inside the Darkroast Day amphitheater, Victor and Ted stood on the mega-sized central music stage. Surrounded by the giant black sails and breathtaking half-shell dome, they applauded and grinned at the perfect sight—countless crowds of Darkroast patrons celebrated inside the amphitheater, sitting on the lawns, cheering in the stadium seating, drinking cup after cup of *Mind Melt*. On stage beside Victor and Ted, several bands jammed away playing music for the crowds, while the XG satellite dish broadcasted the images to the digital screens around the park. Underneath it all, among the crowds of Darkroast patrons, the robotic baristas moved secretly in unison—carrying and serving *Mind Melt* to the public and waiting for their deadly cue to attack.

• • •

"Things are going perfectly," said Victor to Ted. "Over six hundred thousand cups of *Mind Melt* have been served and hundreds more are being served each second."

Victor pointed to the crowds of people. More than half a million people were packed inside the amphitheater, cheering and chanting the Darkroast name as they listened to their favorite bands on stage. More and more patrons crowded into the amphitheater every minute, eager to get a glimpse of the mega-sized central music stage and enjoy a free cup of *Mind Melt*.

Victor specifically noted the Darkroast baristas maneuvering throughout the amphitheater, rapidly distributing the deadly *Mind Melt*.

"All across America," said Victor to Ted. "People everywhere are enjoying National Darkroast Day and drinking our delicious *Mind Melt* coffee. In the surrounding park and city streets, millions await their free cup of *Mind Melt*. Our holiday headquarters, stores, and baristas will deliver them their beautifully delicious drink—and when the Moon Laser strikes at exactly 9 p.m. Eastern time and our baristas unleash an attack of unimaginable terror, they'll know the true purpose of Darkroast: the complete and total conquest of America."

Victor smiled and pointed at the Darkroast Day Blimp, circling over the amphitheater.

"After the attack, I'll board the Darkroast Day Blimp and use it as a flying warship to oversee the Darkroast destruction in every city," said Victor. "The Blimp has been programmed with full battle capabilities and complete uplinks to Darkroast Headquarters. As America is destroyed below, I'll command from above. None of these people in Boston even suspect the Darkroast Day Blimp."

Ted listened to Victor. He had no doubt that Victor was correct about everything—but other thoughts worried Ted. Indeed, the thought of conquering America had taken on a new meaning ever since the discovery of Victor's robotic identity. Ted would no longer have side-by-side control and leadership of America after the National Darkroast Day attack ... not with a *robot* leading the country. Victor would quickly dispose of Ted (an unnecessary human) and he would certainly assume ultimate power all for himself.

Jesus, thought Ted. *How could I be so blind? Soon, nearly three million baristas across America—along with over a million tons of Mind Melt coffee and our giant Moon Laser—will destroy almost every citizen in every major American city. Buildings will fall. Cities will crumble. Millions of robots will eliminate nearly every American across the country, giving ultimate power to a single individual—a GODDAMN robot that will be crowned CEO of America! This has been Victor's plan all along.*

Ted couldn't believe how well Victor had orchestrated everything while keeping the truth secret from him. Ted imagined the future of America: a dark and desolate America filled with nothing but Darkroast robotic baristas, with Victor Black leading them all from his Darkroast Headquarters, and he quickly realized ... he had helped make it all possible—he'd handed the entire country to Victor on a silver platter.

I've got to abandon our deal, thought Ted. *But damnit, if I say anything or try to quit, Victor will kill me.*

• • •

Soon, Victor and Ted left the central music stage and entered a massive Master Command Room located backstage. Barricaded with bullet-proof security glass and multi-coded digital ID locks, the Command Room provided a small fortress among the celebration from which Victor could viciously command his attack on America. The bullet-proof security glass overlooked the amphitheater celebration, and outside in the amphitheater, crowds continued cheering, drinking *Mind Melt*, and celebrating National Darkroast Day.

Victor watched the crowds as he activated several satellite broadcast monitors and contacted the Darkroast leaders in other major cities. Ted watched Victor, thinking of how he no longer supported Victor's conquest. *I've got to do something to stop him,* thought Ted. *I can't allow Victor to continue his sinister plan.*

After a few moments, the broadcast monitors activated and Victor made contact with the Darkroast leaders. In every major city, each Darkroast leader had already moved into the command rooms of each city amphitheater and awaited Victor's orders to launch the attack. Currently, they talked with Victor about the timetables for launching.

"We are here in the New York City amphitheater," said one Darkroast leader from New York City. "From our command room, we can see the New York crowds outside drinking *Mind Melt* and celebrating amidst the thousands of secret robotic baristas. None suspect anything and the Moon Laser countdown has already begun."

"It's the same in Chicago," said another Darkroast leader. "The countdown has begun and no one suspects anything."

"Same in Los Angeles," said another. "Our amphitheater is full of a quarter million people celebrating. The baristas are serving *Mind Melt*. The countdown has begun. All is according to plan."

All the other Darkroast leaders nodded. Everything in their cities— Dallas, Atlanta, Denver, Philadelphia, and other major cities—was happening according to the same plan.

"All major cities are proceeding as planned," said Victor. "In several hours, the final countdown of the Moon Laser will begin. You will synchronize your countdowns with our main countdown—there is a two minute delay per city—based on the Moon Laser's ability to readjust and recalibrate for sequential time zones and coordinates. Needless to say, the entire process from start to finish will take a matter of minutes and be completed before anyone knows what hit them. After the Moon Laser fires, the Darkroast robotic baristas will brutally take care of the rest."

The Darkroast leaders smiled. Ted listened the entire time, knowing Victor was right. *The entire attack—from the moment the laser fires here on Boston and then on its last city—will only last a matter of minutes. And then the widespread devastation from the robotic baristas will be quickly unleashed. Whatever I do has to be done on a national scale and has to affect things with lightning speed.*

After Victor finished with the Darkroast leaders, he turned to Ted to discuss the final procedures for firing the Moon Laser. He activated several computers and displayed readouts of the Moon Laser Base, as well as surveillance footage from several areas around the Darkroast amphitheater. Digital blueprints on the surveillance footage detailed the exact locations of every robotic barista in the amphitheater. Victor explained the positions of the baristas in relation to the main gates, stressing their ability to monitor anything suspicious. Nothing unknown would be happening in or around the amphitheater without Victor or the baristas knowing about it.

Ted seized the opportunity to point out a potential weakness in Victor's plot. Something the two of them hadn't discussed since the night before: the Source.

"You know," said Ted. "We still haven't caught the guy who attacked us last night. This presents a major problem. If he attacks again, he could ruin everything. Not to mention, he probably still has that group of people with him ... plus Miriam."

As Ted spoke, he wondered if Victor would buy this excuse. *Jesus*, thought Ted. *He probably knows who the guy is and won't tell me if he's concerned. Still, he has to be concerned. He's a major risk, and if he's working with Miriam, she knows nearly all the ins and outs of the amphitheater ...*

"He could be launching another attack against us right now," said Ted. "Perhaps we should ..."

Ted trailed off. *If I say too much*, he thought. *He'll know I don't support him anymore.*

Victor heard what Ted meant about the Source's risk, and smiled. He'd been working on this problem during the night and had every intention of aggressively confronting the Source. His entire plan was about timing, and the element of surprise. Not to mention, Victor wanted to confront the Source personally—especially after last night's attack, he had unfinished business to settle with the Source.

"We've got surveillance footage covering *every* square inch of ground, not to mention over three hundred baristas guarding all main and auxiliary entrances," said Victor. "If that group from last night—or Miriam—try to meddle in our plans here in the amphitheater, we'll locate and destroy them immediately."

Victor hit several buttons on a main computer and activated some specific surveillance footage—this time, footage of a location outside the amphitheater. The footage highlighted a familiar building with a view overlooking the amphitheater. The time-date stamp on the bottom of the screen showed that this was *live* footage.

"As for the attacker himself," said Victor. "We ran perimeter surveillance all night and discovered something very interesting. Foolishly, he has decided to attack us yet again."

Zooming in on the building in the footage, with satellite clarity, the footage revealed a large cluster of high-tech equipment on the rooftop, and in the middle of the equipment, unknowingly being watched from a birds-eye view, was the Source.

"We've pinpointed his exact location," said Victor. "He'll soon be terminated and I'll be handling it personally. After that, don't worry. He *won't* be a problem anymore."

Chapter 29

Outside the Darkroast Day amphitheater, London, Miriam, Wally, and Nate raced across the surrounding central park. Over two million square feet of bustling crowds, coffee booths, and National Darkroast Day events created a dizzying tsunami of obstacles—huge lines of people waiting for *Mind Melt*, crowds of patrons listening to the mega-sized central music stage, and an entire city population dancing and celebrating around the giant digital screens. London, Miriam, Wally, and Nate—determined to plant the Source's GPS tracking remotes around the park—gripped two separate duffel bags of remotes and sprinted through the crowds. Reading the digital LCD maps given to them by the Source, they pinpointed the exact locations to plant the GPS tracking remotes and hid the remotes in specific places where the crowds wouldn't discover them. Following behind the group, the Robotic CEOs watched for any signs of danger—specifically, the Darkroast robotic baristas roaming the crowds while serving *Mind Melt* and waiting to attack after the Moon Laser countdown.

• • •

Back at the building rooftop overlooking the Darkroast Day amphitheater, the Source checked his high-tech equipment and prepared for the group's first objective: to destroy the robotic baristas by shorting out their CPUs. In the center of his equipment, he unveiled an enormous GPS Frequency Disruptor—a sophisticated electronic device with a GPS satellite dish designed for tracking GPS signals and mapping the baristas' locations. The Frequency Disruptor towered over the building's other equipment (nearly ten feet tall and over two tons), and aimed its satellite dish directly at the amphitheater—once activated, it would unleash a multi-layered positronic frequency wave to destroy any barista inside the amphitheater or within a three-mile radius.

The only problem: Victor Black had arrived. He made his way across the backside of the rooftop and moved with utter silence, determined to deal with the Source. Keeping his eyes on the Source, he motioned to another side of the rooftop—suddenly, a group of several robotic baristas entered from a nearby stairwell and apprehended the Source. Under Victor's orders, the baristas gripped the Source with iron force. They pinned his arms behind his back and threw him against the edge of a nearby table—robotic minions ready to deliver their human prize to their robotic master.

Victor quickly deactivated the GPS Frequency Disruptor and addressed the Source.

"Dr. Xavier," said Victor. "It appears that you're trying to stop my plans for National Darkroast Day."

"WHAT ARE YOU DOING HERE?" shouted the Source. "LET ME GO!"

Victor smiled as he watched the Source being guarded by his baristas. "Unfortunately," said Victor. "That's impossible."

The Source couldn't believe what he was seeing. *Victor wasn't supposed to be here*, he thought. *He's supposed to be inside the amphitheater working on his National Darkroast Day plans. How did he discover where I was? What if he knows about the rest of the group trying to infiltrate the amphitheater?*

Victor smiled and eerily ran his fingers along the smooth metal of the GPS Frequency Disruptor. "You've been causing a lot of trouble lately," said Victor. "Most unfortunate, considering you're lucky to be alive. After your involvement with *Project Darkroast*, I could have easily killed you." Victor ripped several wires from the Frenquency device to demolish it. Nearby on the table, beside the Source, several portable computers displayed video footage of the Darkroast Day amphitheater along with blueprints and plans for stopping Victor's attack. In addition, several piles of detonators, explosives, and neutron laser pistols lay scattered—hard evidence of the Source's plan to invade the amphitheater.

Jesus, this is serious, thought the Source. *All the evidence for our attack is right here in front of him. Victor now knows the details of our plan. I've got to do something to stop him here and now.* The Source knew the stakes had just been raised, and wondered what to do about the situation. He looked around the table and spotted the explosives lying nearby. Instinctively, he grabbed one of the explosives and shoved it into his pocket without being noticed. *I've got no other choice but to destroy Victor*, he thought. *He won't allow me to live and there is no way out.*

"Why do you think I've come here?" asked Victor, smiling darkly at the Source.

"IT DOESN'T MATTER," shouted the Source. "I'M GOING TO STOP YOU!"

Victor laughed at the Source's answer, then tapped several keys on the computer screens and revealed remote-accessed footage of the group: London, Miriam, Wally, and Nate rushing through the crowded park, planting GPS remotes for the Frequency Disruptor to short-circuit the baristas.

"I know about your friends," said Victor. "It appears they have a plan to stop me. You have revealed the dark secrets of *Project Darkroast*, my robotic identity, and my attack plans for National Darkroast Day. But I can assure you that your friends will soon be captured and destroyed by my baristas. Your plan is unraveling as we speak."

The baristas—who had let go of the Source and were watching Victor talk—still didn't notice the Source had put the explosive in his pocket. Victor didn't notice either. While Victor was busy, the Source stealthfully reached inside his pocket and activated the explosive. The device—a small neutron bomb capable of delivering a rooftop blast—would definitely do the trick. *It'll destroy everything on the rooftop within a thirty-foot radius*, thought the Source. *I don't want to sacrifice myself, but I have no choice. I have to save America and stop Victor.*

"Several of my baristas are secretly following your friends," said Victor. "I assure you they have no desire to let you short-circuit them with your Frequency Disruptor, not to mention stand in the way of our Darkroast plans for conquering America."

Victor hit several more keys on the computer, and the footage revealed several baristas making their way through the crowds less than fifty yards away from the group.

"Your friends have no idea they are being followed, and after a short game of cat and mouse in the amphitheater park, my baristas will shred them to pieces. After that, there is only the remaining matter of dealing with you."

Victor grinned extra large, then surveyed the city horizon with the crowds of American people filling the park and amphitheater—millions of innocent lives celebrating and enjoying National Darkroast Day. The Source looked at Victor with disgust, and thought of the explosive in his pocket. He could tell what Victor was thinking. *Look at him*, thought the Source. *He's staring at all those millions of innocent human lives packed inside the amphitheater and across the city. He's imagining the devastation soon to result from Mind Melt, the Moon Laser, and his robotic baristas. He's a psychotic robotic monster that has weaved an insidious web of destruction, which will soon plunge America into complete Darkroast domination—a nightmarish robotic apocalypse. But it will be over as soon as this explosive in my pocket destroys him. The blast will disintegrate everything on this rooftop.*

"You tried to betray me once before by contacting the authorities," said Victor. "When I gave you that scar and made you conceal your identity, I thought I'd taught you a lesson. I won't make the same mistake twice."

The Source hit several more buttons on the explosive to set the final detonation—but then, something happened. The explosive device made a small beeping sound and Victor spun around. Victor and the baristas noticed the explosive in the Source's pocket and quickly ripped it away. Victor took the device in his hand and immediately deactivated it.

"Disappointing," said Victor. "I thought that since you were caught, you might let things end with some dignity."

Victor threw the explosive aside, then removed a small stainless-steel container from his pocket. He'd had this container with him the entire time and brought it specifically for the Source. Inside the container, a deadly Darkroast beverage boiled with glowing green steam, and Victor unscrewed the stainless-steel top and poured a special cup for the Source.

The beverage: *Mind Melt.*

"Let's get to the point," said Victor to the Source. "I've come to kill you, and I know the perfect way to do it."

Chapter 30

Outside Boston at the Darkroast space shuttle launch pad, Guerrero and the Amigos continued their mission: to board the shuttle and travel to the Moon to destroy the Moon Laser Base. The Darkroast shuttle launch pad facility—over a hundred thousand square feet in size—was an armored fortress filled with guards, personnel, surveillance towers, and video cameras monitoring all entrances and exits. In the center of the facility, the supersonic space shuttle sat fueled and ready on a massive launch pad.

• • •

Avoiding the guards, personnel, and video cameras monitoring all the ramps and platforms surrounding the shuttle, Guerrero and his Amigos made a break for it and rushed inside the ship's main hatch without being spotted.

"*Venga, rapidamente*," said Guerrero to his Amigos. "The shuttle launch is near. We have to make it into the ship's central cargo bay where they keep the spare passenger seats. If we don't secure ourselves before the launch, the sheer velocity and turbulence of the V-90 shuttle will injure us beyond capability."

Guerrero and his Amigos grabbed their neutron rifles and duffel bag full of weapons and explosives and rushed into the space-suit storage area of the shuttle. Guerrero grabbed several space suits from a space-suit storage container and gave them to his men. Putting aside their rifles and duffle bag of explosives, they put on their space suits, then raced into the central cargo bay in the ship and prepared for the launch. Strapping themselves into spare passenger seats within the cargo bay, they looked around and confirmed all was secure. *Soon,* thought Guerrero. *We'll make it to the Moon Laser Base and destroy Victor's National Darkroast Day plans once and for all.*

Up in the cockpit, the Darkroast astronauts made final launch preparations, none of them aware that several stowaways had just boarded the ship for a free ticket to the Moon Laser Base. Exactly as planned, within minutes, the ship began to rumble with supersonic speed and the takeoff for the Moon Laser Base had begun.

Chapter 31

Inside the Darkroast Day amphitheater, London, Miriam, Wally, and Nate rushed towards the mega-sized central music stage. Surrounded by nearly half a million cheering Darkroast patrons, the celebration was unbelievable—crowds chanting, people dancing, music blasting, and enough *Mind Melt* for the entire city of Boston to drink forever. The Moon Laser countdown had begun and rows of digital screens above the central music stage displayed the apocalyptic results: **T-MINUS 3:00 HOURS**. Following behind the group were the Robotic CEOs—each of them analyzing the surroundings and scanning for robotic baristas to destroy if necessary. Indeed, a small group of baristas had already begun following the group—and had been doing so since the amphitheater park.

"We must complete our mission," said London. "We've already placed the GPS tracking remotes around the park. Next, we need to make it to the central music stage to destroy Victor."

London gripped his neutron rifle, and pointed to the XG satellite dish at the top of the amphitheater's half-shell dome.

"Remember," said London. "We've also got to install the satellite jamming box at the top of the dome to prevent the XG satellite dish from broadcasting the Moon Laser firing signal. There isn't much time left, and chances are, Victor will be *expecting* us."

• • •

The group divided and headed their separate ways to complete their missions—Wally and Nate, who'd been carrying the XG satellite jamming box, headed for the roofdeck of the half-shell dome, while London, Miriam, and the Robotic CEOs raced towards the central music stage to destroy Victor. Both groups carried their walkie-talkies and attempted to report their progress by contacting the Source.

At the building rooftop overlooking the Darkroast Day amphitheater, the Source was still being held hostage by Victor's robotic baristas. Victor had forced the Source to drink the cup of *Mind Melt* and he smiled at his accomplishment. "You'll experience my Darkroast destruction first-hand," said Victor to the Source. "As soon as the Moon Laser fires, *Mind Melt* will destroy you along with everyone else in America." Several baristas stood nearby on the rooftop and aimed their lasers at the Source. These baristas planned to remain on the rooftop holding the Source hostage until the Moon Laser fired. "While overlooking the amphitheater," said Victor. "You'll have a front-row seat to your own apocalyptic destruction, and my baristas will keep you company until the very end."

After Victor fed *Mind Melt* to the Source, he didn't stay with him long. He bid an evil farewell and left the rooftop to return to the amphitheater. "I've got an entire country to takeover," he told the Source. "And if I'm lucky, I'll get to personally oversee the destruction of your friends inside the amphitheater." The Source remained behind on the rooftop, surrounded by the robotic baristas who continued to point their lasers at him. Once Victor had left, the Source heard London, Miriam, Wally, and Nate trying to contact him with their walkie-talkies. On the nearby table next to him, the Source's walkie-talkie communicated their voices: "*Dr. Xavier ... we've planted the GPS remotes ... the XG satellite dish will be shut down shortly ... we're heading to the central music stage ... get ready to activate the Frequency Disruptor, short circuit the baristas, and we'll storm the amphitheater together to destroy Victor.*"

The Source looked across at the dismantled Frequency Disruptor and also at the Darkroast baristas guarding him. He knew he had to do something to inform the group that Victor had discovered their plans. *There is no Frequency Disruptor. There is no longer a way to destroy all the baristas, and Victor knows about all of you inside the amphitheater*, he thought. *He'll soon come for you and slaughter all of you like bloody rag dolls.*

Again, the Source knew that he *had* to do something. He had to act *now*. Without wasting anymore time, the Source grabbed a neutron pistol from the nearby table. He waited until the walkie-talkie chattered again with the group's voices—and when the baristas looked away in the direction of the walkie-talkie, he blasted each of them with a 120-megavolt laser beam straight to the chest. Faster than lightning, they fell to the ground in a crumpled destroyed pile, and the Source grabbed the walkie-talkie, several more weapons, and raced directly for the amphitheater to warn the group.

• • •

Amidst the huge crowds of cheering Darkroast patrons surrounding the amphitheater, Victor made his way across the amphitheater park. While people danced and celebrated around him, he removed a cell phone from his pocket and called the Master Command Room located inside the amphitheater. As he dialed, he noticed the giant digital screens around him displaying the Moon Laser countdown: **T-MINUS 2:45 HOURS**. *My takeover will soon be complete*, thought Victor, looking at the countdown. *In less than three hours, this rubbish civilization around me will be destroyed to give way to my perfect Darkroast empire. Then I will be the ultimate CEO of America.*

Inside the Master Command Room, Ted was smoking a cigarette and grabbed the phone call from Victor. Ever since Victor had left, Ted had frantically been searching for a way to stop Victor's National Darkroast Day takeover. He'd run through numerous options and finally decided to focus his efforts on destroying the Darkroast baristas. He'd come up with a plan, which was this: since all the baristas in America communicated through wireless uplinks, he had assembled a lethal computer virus that could be simultaneously uploaded into *all* Darkroast baristas around America. *As a destructive piece of computer command code*, thought Ted. *The virus will be sent wirelessly into the robots' systems and crash their CPUs all at once.* By destroying the baristas, Ted would remove Victor's main army from the National Darkroast Day equation. The weakness in defense would then buy time for Ted to shut down the Moon Laser firing sequence, which could be done from the Master Command Room. Since Ted had practically designed the Moon Laser firing sequence, he felt confident he could quickly disable its signal.

After grabbing the phone, Ted answered Victor with a lukewarm greeting. In his mind, he couldn't believe he was still taking orders from a Goddamn robot.

"Hello," said Ted. "I've been waiting to … um, to hear from you, Victor."

Clutching the phone in his hand, Ted hoped he could disguise that this was a complete lie. *By the time Victor gets back*, thought Ted. *I'll have unraveled his entire plan. There's no way I'm letting a Goddamn robot takeover America.*

Victor talked to Ted as if all was normal. He spoke in a calm, orderly voice—a voice unsuspecting that Ted had completely turned against him.

"Tell me," said Victor. "How are things going in the Master Command Room? Is the sequencing of the Moon Laser proceeding on time with the other major cities?"

"Everything's proceeding as scheduled," replied Ted. "Don't worry. I've got everything under control."

Another lie, thought Ted. Ted took a drag on his cigarette and knew there was more he wasn't telling Victor. He looked around at the various video monitors surrounding the Command Room, as well as through the bullet-proof security glass overlooking the amphitheater celebration. Outside in the amphitheater, among the crowds drinking *Mind Melt* and celebrating National Darkroast Day, Ted had discovered the group of infiltrators that Victor had hoped to deal with—London, Miriam, Wally, and Nate. They traveled along with a fierce group of individuals in CEO clothing, and carried neutron rifles with them. *They must have their own plans to stop Victor*, thought Ted. *Good.* He imagined that the Source would be following along somewhere soon, ready to help in their attack—that is, if Victor hadn't finished him off already. *Perhaps he's survived and they'll all help botch Victor's plans. A series of catastrophes undermining Victor from all directions.*

"You sound preoccupied," said Victor. "Is everything OK?"

Ted removed a computer disk from his pocket—it contained the virus to upload and destroy the Darkroast baristas. He slid the disk into one of the main computer system's hard drives, and hit several keys to upload the virus into the system. After the final sequencing was initiated, the virus would be sent to the baristas remotely and complete its task in a matter of minutes.

"I'm fine," said Ted. "In fact, I'm better than ever."

Ted knew it sounded cryptic, but he didn't care. He tapped several more keys, and knew his job was done. He pressed the final command: **UPLOAD DARKROAST VIRUS.**

As the virus uploaded, Victor said something peculiar. Something he'd been waiting to say. Ted should have noticed it was a dangerous sign: "Perhaps," said Victor. "You should get the door."

The door? thought Ted.

At this point, a loud thud was heard on the Master Command Room door. *Who could that be?* thought Ted. *And how does Victor know someone's at the door?* Ted hid his work on the computer virus, walked over to the door, and when he opened it, several Darkroast baristas stood facing him with their lasers. The baristas had been sent by Victor and did *not* look happy.

Ted nearly dropped the phone. His cigarette fell from his lips. He looked at the baristas' lasers, and knew what this meant: the baristas were here to destroy him.

On the phone, Victor's voice could still be heard. Victor now confessed the truth to Ted: he knew Ted was trying to stop his National Darkroast Day plans.

"You know, I probably should have mentioned this, Ted. Ever since last night, I knew you've turned against me, and I'm not too happy about it. I even know about the computer virus you've created. I've decided it's time to *officially* end our partnership."

Ted didn't have time to answer Victor. The baristas blasted a series of bloody holes through Ted's chest, splattering his blood across the walls ... and within seconds, Ted was dead.

Chapter 32

Around the Darkroast Day amphitheater, the crowds had grown into an uproarious climax of dancing, celebration, and drinking *Mind Melt*. Around the central music stage, everyone waited for the Moon Laser show—the culmination of National Darkroast Day. According to schedule, the live music still played and the coffee booths eagerly served their delicious *Mind Melt* brew, while baristas also served people their cups of Darkroast coffee. Over two million cups of *Mind Melt* had been served and hundreds more were being served each second. Beneath the amphitheater's seventy-thousand giant black sails and eighteen-story colossal stadium seating, the digital screens broadcasted the countdown until America's destruction: **T-MINUS 2:30 HOURS**.

• • •

Underneath the half-shell dome of the amphitheater, Victor put away his cell phone and left the front lawns of the amphitheater. He passed the mega-sized central music stage and entered the Master Command Room. Using the computer station that Ted used to upload the computer virus, Victor quickly reversed the computer virus and then hit several buttons to contact the Darkroast leaders in all the major cities. As the Darkroast leaders appeared on the surrounding monitors, the main computer indicated that Ted's virus had been successfully eliminated: **DARKROAST VIRUS ERASED**.

"Attention all Darkroast leaders," said Victor. "I have an important announcement to make."

As Victor addressed the Darkroast leaders, he looked at Ted's dead body sprawled in a front corner. Ted lay lifeless on a computer station as blood dripped from his burnt chest onto several keyboards. Victor shoved Ted's dead body aside and continued talking to the Darkroast leaders on the monitors. He had no desire to hide the evidence of Ted's murder, and didn't bother to wipe away the blood from the keyboards or his hands.

"As you can see behind me," said Victor. "One of our top leaders—Ted Baxter—has betrayed our National Darkroast Day plans. Moments ago, he attempted to launch a lethal computer virus that would destroy all robotic baristas across America, and because of this, he was brutally killed by several of my Darkroast baristas."

Victor explicitly pointed across the room at Ted's dead body, reiterating the blood and gruesomeness—he wanted all of the Darkroast leaders to understand the full consequences of what had occurred and see Ted's body lying in a puddle of blood.

"In the final hours of our National Darkroast Day takeover," said Victor. "No one will stand in our way—not even my Darkroast partner. Anyone deviating from our plans, or trying to stop us, will be immediately destroyed. Darkroast baristas have full orders to eliminate anyone out of line, and they won't hesitate to follow my command."

Several Darkroast baristas entered the Master Command Room and stood behind Victor to demonstrate their support. The Darkroast leaders looked at the baristas and nodded with compliance. Each leader supported Victor and intended to follow the National Darkroast Day plans. They would never disobey Victor and Darkroast, even if Ted had been killed.

"During these final hours," said Victor. "It is more important than ever to have your full support. So far, everything has gone according to schedule, and within a mere three hours, we will unleash the greatest destruction that America has ever seen. Millions of people will die a brutal death as the Moon Laser and *Mind Melt* annihilate them, and those surviving will be exterminated by the Darkroast baristas. America will be nothing more than a ruined country as its nationwide cities—Boston, New York, Philadelphia, Los Angeles, and others—are destroyed and emptied, paving the way for our new Darkroast empire."

The Darkroast leaders nodded again and saluted Victor. They gave him a final signal of confidence, and then Victor delivered the final instructions for them to follow. He explained when, where, and how the Moon Laser firing sequence would be activated, and the codewords for controlling the barista attack sequences in each city. He then reminded everyone once more of Ted's fate—ensuring that all of them noticed the blood and carnage behind him, and saw Ted's lifeless body still in a crumpled heap on the floor.

The Darkroast leaders saluted once more and then Victor signed off with an official Darkroast CEO salute. Afterwards, the Darkroast baristas gathered close behind Victor and he activated several surveillance monitors. The surveillance monitors displayed footage indicating one final task Victor aimed to complete—the destruction of London, Miriam, Wally, and Nate. On screen, London and Miriam, along with the group of Robotic CEOs, advanced with their weapons towards the central music stage. Across the top of the amphitheater half-shell dome, Wally and Nate climbed a facility access ladder to reach the XG satellite dish to install the satellite jamming box.

Victor and the baristas watched the screens with evil grins. They unleashed their lasers and prepared for the final confrontation.

"It's time to deal with those vile intruders," said Victor. "Together, we'll make them wish they'd never discovered our National Darkroast Day plans."

● ● ●

Outside in the Darkroast Day amphitheater, London, Miriam, Wally, and Nate had no idea that Victor and his baristas were planning to destroy them. After crossing the crowds, London and Miriam entered onto the central music stage and faced over six thousand square feet of stage with bands playing live music and celebrating National Darkroast Day, while half a million cheering fans surrounded them dancing and drinking *Mind Melt* and watching the Moon Laser countdown. London and Miriam carried their neutron rifles and walked towards the center of the stage—directly for the center microphone. The Robotic CEOs followed behind them with their lasers charged, ready to attack as soon as Victor and the baristas surfaced from the Master Command Room. The group's plan: address the crowds and tell them the truth about National Darkroast Day, then publicly destroy Victor when he appeared on stage.

"Using the surrounding speaker system and digital screens," said London, pointing at the microphone and huge crowds in the amphitheater. "We'll announce the terrible truth about National Darkroast Day, and when Victor appears—we'll destroy him on-screen in front of everyone to prove that he's a government robot."

Miriam nodded and agreed with London, although she worried about the logistics of destroying Victor. Around the amphitheater, thousands of Darkroast baristas continued roaming the crowds. Plus, the crowds themselves completely supported Victor—and as soon as Victor was attacked, half a million people might lynch the stage, rallying to defend the most popular corporate leader in America. Bloodthirsty crowds loyal to their Darkroast leader, enraged by his destruction during such a beloved American holiday.

"Dr. Xavier should have already destroyed the baristas using the GPS devices and Frequency Disruptor," said Miriam. "I'm worried. Not to mention, the crowds are a risk—they worship National Darkroast Day so much that if we do anything, they may try to destroy *us*. We'll have two groups of attackers *overwhelming* the stage."

"We can't worry about those problems," said London. "Victor is the bigger threat. If we don't stop him, millions of people *will* die and America will be *completely* annihilated. Plus, the crowds need to be told the truth. They need to be warned."

London held his neutron rifle tight and rushed with Miriam to complete their task. Meanwhile, above the half-shell dome, Wally and Nate had reached the XG satellite dish and started installing the satellite jamming box. Two hundred fifty feet above the ground level, the satellite dish aimed its antenna towards the sky like a monstrous electronic cannon. Huge circuitry panels lined the base of the dish—pulsating with nearly 30,000 volts of lethal electricity that powered the digital screens in the amphitheater below.

"Dude, one wrong move and we'll be completely fried," said Nate. "We have to make sure we connect this device just right."

"Dr. Xavier said that by connecting the USB dual-harmonic connectors," said Wally. "The device will clog the back channels and prevent the Moon Laser from firing."

"Um, okay, whatever that means," said Nate. "Let's just make sure we do it *right*."

Carefully, Wally and Nate placed the satellite jamming box over the panels and began assembling the wires and USB connectors to create the jamming signal. Blueprints and digital instructions from the Source showed them how to proceed with speed and efficiency—crucial to destroying the Moon Laser signal before the end of the countdown.

"How will we know when the jamming box activates?" said Nate.

Wally pointed to a large green light on the top of the jamming box, and answered:

"As soon as this green light flashes, the box is activated. After that, it'll only be a matter of minutes before the device totally dismantles the Moon Laser signal."

• • •

Below in the amphitheater, the Source rushed through the crowds of people. He made his way towards the central music stage to warn the group that Victor was coming. As he traveled, punching buttons on a small military palm-pilot he carried with him, he calculated the amount of *Mind Melt* served to the crowds so far by Darkroast: **80%** **SATURATION POINT.** Gripping his pistol and several neutron grenades, he rushed faster through the crowds and removed his walkie-talkie. Pressing the full-intercom button on the walkie-talkie, he contacted both London and Miriam, and Wally and Nate. On the giant digital screens surrounding him, the Moon Laser countdown now read: **T-MINUS 2:00 HOURS.**

"Everyone ... London, Miriam, Wally, Nate," said the Source. "Do you read me?"

Both groups were busy, but immediately answered the Source's call. They'd been waiting to hear from him and quickly listened to his message.

"Hello?" said London. "Is that you Dr. Xavier?"

"We haven't heard from you in hours," said Wally. "We were starting to worry."

"This is very important," said the Source. "Victor captured me and fed me *Mind Melt*. He also dismantled the Frequency Disruptor so we can't short-circuit the baristas using the GPS tracking devices."

"Jesus," said London. "He's completely got the upper hand."

The Source stopped for a moment, his chest burning and winded. He wondered if it was the *Mind Melt* already taking effect, and he thought about the vile Darkroast poison coursing through his body's system. *Within two hours*, thought the Source. *I'll be annihilated like everyone else by the Moon Laser. It'll have the same fatal effect on everyone in the amphitheater.* Around him, the Source knew he was standing in an amphitheater filled with dead people ... only none of them knew it yet.

"I'm on my way to you now, but you *must* be careful," said the Source to the group. "Victor's returned to the amphitheater and knows you're coming after him. He plans to destroy you and will be sending hundreds of vicious baristas to capture and kill you immediately."

London and Miriam listened to the message. Wally and Nate did as well.

"We'll be on the lookout," said London. "Get here as fast as you can."

"We're nearly done with the satellite," said Wally. "We'll finish in time and meet you down on the stage."

In the distance, the Source continued running with the central music stage in sight. Around him, amidst the Darkroast Day amphitheater and Boston skyline, Darkroast crowds filled every street and park corner across the horizon—millions of American lives hanging in the balance.

"Okay. I'll meet you on stage," said the Source. "But I'm afraid that we're outnumbered and we may have run out of options. If Victor wins here, this *will* be the end of America."

Chapter 33

After the launch of the Darkroast space shuttle, Guerrero and the Amigos continued their mission: to travel to the Moon to destroy the Moon Laser Base. The Darkroast shuttle—cruising through the upper atmosphere at supersonic speed—rocketed through blue skies until the sky thinned nearly 60 miles above the Earth's surface. Firing final launch boosters, the shuttle blasted free of the blue atmosphere and cruised into outer space, heading directly for the Moon's giant grayish-white surface orbiting roughly 240,000 miles from Earth.

• • •

Guerrero and his Amigos remained in the spare passenger seats within the ship's central cargo bay, fastened tight inside their space suits and securely seatbelted. Guerrero checked his watch and noticed the time, **T-MINUS 2:00 HOURS**, which meant that (with the ship's supersonic speed) they would arrive at the Moon in 30 minutes. He motioned to the Amigos to relay the schedule and each of them nodded back, approvingly. *First,* thought Guerrero. *Our shuttle will dock with the Moon and Dr. Xavier will upload the blueprints and directions for destroying the Moon Laser Base. Then, minutes later, we'll storm the base and destroy the receiving satellite to prevent the laser from charging. After that, we'll invade the central corridor of the base and permanently eliminate the laser with enough explosives to vaporize it instantly.* Nearby, the neutron rifles and duffel bag full of weapons and explosives sat safely strapped inside a cargo container, waiting to be used by Guerrero and the Amigos when they docked.

Up in the cockpit, the Darkroast astronauts steered the shuttle through space, none of them aware that several stowaways were still aboard planning to destroy the Moon Laser Base. In the distance, their upcoming target on the Moon loomed ahead and the astronauts radioed the Laser Base: **PERMISSION TO LAND?**

The Moon Laser Base radioed back: **PERMISSION GRANTED.**

The Darkroast astronauts nodded and prepared for docking, unaware that on the surface of the Moon in the drenching blackness of space, an enormous battle was about to ensue.

Chapter 34

Back inside the Darkroast Day amphitheater, London and Miriam addressed the crowds to reveal the disastrous truth about National Darkroast Day. Surrounded by half a million people inside the amphitheater, they interrupted the celebration and grabbed the center microphone on stage. Suddenly, London and Miriam were broadcasted everywhere via hundreds of 1,200-square-foot digital screens and the 80-megawatt amphitheater sound system. Everyone stopped dancing, drinking *Mind Melt*, and enjoying National Darkroast Day, and took notice of them on stage. Nobody had any idea what London and Miriam (a Boston reporter and an official Darkroast executive) were doing there—not to mention, they were armed with neutron rifles—and behind them stood a small army of Robotic CEOs with neutron lasers charged and prepared for battle. Immediately, London and Miriam began to address the crowds with their warning.

"LISTEN," shouted London to the crowds. "WE HAVE SOMETHING *VERY* IMPORTANT TO ANNOUNCE ... NATIONAL DARKROAST DAY IS NOT WHAT YOU THINK IT IS—ITS PURPOSE IS TO DESTROY AMERICA."

The crowds immediately reacted, but weren't sure exactly what to think.

"IT'S TRUE," shouted Miriam. "VICTOR BLACK IS NOTHING MORE THAN A GOVERNMENT ROBOT CREATED BY A SECRET UNDERGROUND EXPERIMENT KNOWN AS *PROJECT DARKROAST*. VICTOR HAS CREATED THIS ENTIRE HOLIDAY SO THAT HE CAN KILL MILLIONS OF INNOCENT LIVES AND CONTROL AMERICA AS A RUTHLESS ROBOTIC DARKROAST CEO."

• • •

Around the Darkroast Day amphitheater, everyone looked shocked—especially those that recognized London and Miriam.

Millions of gasps went out through the crowds, people unable to believe what they had just heard. The giant digital screens—hundreds of 1,200-square-foot crystal-clear high-definition plasma monitors—along with the 80-megawatt sound system, projected the picture and sound to every man, woman, and child in the amphitheater, surrounding park, and throughout the city of Boston. The range of reactions was countless, shocking, and propagated like wildfire throughout the entire city.

Nearest to the central music stage, people watched London and Miriam with their own eyes in dumbfounded alarm, unsure if this was real. Some people threw things at the stage, some booed, and some stared at London and Miriam's weapons and the Robotic CEOs, wondering if they should be afraid. Many people in the amphitheater still drank *Mind Melt*, savoring the green glow, rich cinnamon, and cherry on top.

Swarming around the amphitheater lawns, half a million people looked around and saw fellow Darkroast fans mingling, laughing, watching the stage, watching each other, waiting in lines at the coffee booths, and staring at the giant digital screens. They heard London and Miriam, yet assumed it was complete nonsense. Many munched on Darkroast snacks and talked about the tastiness of *Mind Melt*. Almost thirty thousand people ordered refills of *Mind Melt* or made cell phone calls while London and Miriam spoke—slightly annoyed that London and Miriam were interrupting them. They laughed at the ridiculous notions of "secret underground experiments" and "ruthless robotic CEOs." They wished the bands would return to the stage and continue playing music.

Outside in the park, people shoved and muscled for a better view of the digital screens—one person kicked a small duck out of the way, which ran in terror amidst the bustling crowds. As soon as these people heard what London and Miriam were talking about, they laughed and turned away sneering. In the Boston streets and traffic, rows of televisions (tuned to the amphitheater video signal) broadcasted London and Miriam. People on the sidewalks stood and watched with cups of *Mind Melt* in hand, but none truly believed. Other televisions also broadcasted London and Miriam. In several restaurants with televisions, people eating dinner and drinking coffee watched London and Miriam, and told themselves: *"Despite the warning, I really should get down to the amphitheater before the Moon Laser Show starts."* In *Plush* restaurant, the manager offered unlimited *Mind Melt* and free limo service to help people celebrate in style. When someone heard London and Miriam say that there may be danger in the amphitheater, everyone laughed and refused to believe. None could imagine the idea of anyone ruining such a perfect national holiday as National Darkroast Day.

In TV news stations across the city, reporters began to broadcast breaking news reports: *Miriam, Darkroast PR extraordinaire, storms amphitheater stage with Boston City Spotlight reporter and denounces Victor Black. Both claim "Victor is a dangerous robot with ties to the government."* In the Boston City Spotlight, several reporters and Lewis "Lewie" Burns (who was overseeing the afternoon's special edition Darkroast Day newspaper) heard the news that London was on stage trying to ruin Darkroast Day. He nearly had an aneurism and shouted: "Damnit London! There's nothing to fear about National Darkroast Day!" At Darkroast stores across the city, customers listened to the news on in-house radios playing overhead in the stores' ceilings. As they shopped and selected Darkroast coffees, they wondered where the delightful live music had gone and why London and Miriam and the reporters on the radio sounded so upset. In one particular Darkroast store, Chazworth "Chaz" McDoogal heard London and Miriam and turned off the broadcast. He continued serving cups of *Mind Melt* and refused to broadcast anything negative about Darkroast Day, certain that such loyalty made him the best barista on the planet. Across all other parts of the city, people listened to the newscasts and continued drinking *Mind Melt*. Almost everyone assumed the newscasts were bogus and still loyally planned to attend the Moon Laser Show in the amphitheater and park. As the warnings broadcasted from televisions, radios, and rooftops across the city skyline, everyone heard the part about Victor being a government robot with destructive plans for National Darkroast Day and simply laughed: *"Impossible!"*

• • •

Inside the amphitheater, London and Miriam continued warning the crowd, despite the many reactions and disbelief from millions of people. Many people in the crowds began to react by throwing cups of *Mind Melt* at London and Miriam. People shouted angrily to kick them off the stage and continue celebrating their beloved Darkroast holiday. Eventually, nearest to the music stage, thousands of people began to climb onto the stage to attack London and Miriam and remove them from the amphitheater—the crowds refused to tolerate any threats to National Darkroast Day. The Robotic CEOs had to form a protective circle around London and Miriam to hold back the crowds. With their brute robotic strength, they did their best to keep the crowds away—but the numbers of upset crowd members became overwhelming. London and Miriam started to panic.

"IT'S TRUE," London continued shouting into the microphone. "YOU HAVE TO LISTEN TO US. IN NEARLY TWO HOURS, AT THE END OF THE COUNTDOWN, VICTOR'S GOING TO LAUNCH AN ATTACK ON THE ENTIRE COUNTRY. THE *MIND MELT* AND MOON LASER SHOW ARE GOING TO KILL MIL-LIONS OF PEOPLE."

"PLEASE BELIEVE US," shouted Miriam. "YOU *MUST* BELIEVE US. IF YOU DON'T, THEN ALL OF YOU ARE GOING TO DIE."

AUGUST ADAMS 209

• • •

Inside the Master Command Room, Victor and his Darkroast baristas finished charging their lasers and decided it was time to destroy London, Miriam, and the Robotic CEOs. Bloodthirsty for revenge, watching them on the surrounding surveillance monitors, they saw everything—the weapons, the intrusion onto the central music stage, and the public warning against National Darkroast Day. Nearly five thousand baristas across the amphitheater received a wireless radio message from Victor: **THE TIME HAS COME. DESTROY THE INTRUDERS ON THE CENTRAL MUSIC STAGE.** Vengefully, Victor and his Darkroast baristas raced from the Master Command Room onto the central music stage—quickly joined by thousands of angry Darkroast baristas throughout the amphitheater. All of them had one intention: annihilate the intruders in front of everyone to preserve National Darkroast Day and demonstrate that Victor was Darkroast CEO.

"STEP AWAY FROM THE MICROPHONE," shouted Victor to London and Miriam. "YOUR TIME ON STAGE HAS COME TO AN END."

London and Miriam spun around and faced Victor and the Darkroast baristas. Victor and his baristas blasted several of the Robotic CEOs, which exploded with sparks and fell to the ground in a crumpled pile of robotic debris. Millions of people suddenly began cheering at the sight of Victor and his baristas on stage. Many people noticed the explosion and robotic debris, but the destruction of the several CEOs only made them more excited—as if this was some kind of publicity stunt.

"WE WON'T LET YOU DO THIS," shouted London. "WE WON'T LET YOU USE NATIONAL DARKROAST DAY TO KILL MILLIONS OF PEOPLE!"

Victor laughed and looked at the surrounding crowds, who stepped aside smiling with obedience and released London and Miriam, allowing Victor and his baristas to encircle them slitheringly. Broadcasted on the giant digital screens, everyone could see the truth—the crowds *totally* supported Victor. But none could see that this support sealed their doom.

"DON'T BE FOOLISH," answered Victor. "WE'RE GIVING THE CROWDS EXACTLY WHAT THEY WANT—*MIND MELT*, A POPULAR HOLIDAY, AND A SPECTACTULAR MOON LASER SHOW. YOU'RE THE PEOPLE *RUINING* NATIONAL DARK-ROAST DAY WITH YOUR FRIGHTENING PUBLIC SPEECH. THEREFORE, ME AND MY BARISTAS ARE HERE TO DESTROY YOU."

The crowds erupted with cheers. Millions of rounds of applause roared throughout the amphitheater in support of Victor and their beloved National Darkroast Day.

• • •

Above the half-shell dome, working on the XG satellite dish, Wally and Nate watched the scene below and saw London and Miriam captured by Victor and the Darkroast baristas. Millions of people continuously cheered and applauded Victor and the baristas, unaware that in nearly two hours the Moon Laser would destroy America. On the giant digital screens surrounding the amphitheater, the Moon Laser countdown now read: **T-MINUS 1:45 HOURS**. Wally and Nate finished their work with the XG satellite dish (putting the final touches on installing the jamming box), and then activated the box's large green light to reveal that the Moon Laser signal would automatically dismantle in five minutes. About this time, several Darkroast baristas climbed the half-shell dome and apprehended Wally and Nate, bringing them down onto the central music stage with London, Miriam, and the Robotic CEOs. The baristas shoved Wally and Nate into the middle of the stage, surrounded by Victor and his other Darkroast baristas. Wally and Nate sheepishly looked at

London and Miriam, ashamed that they'd gotten caught by the baristas. None of the Robotic CEOs could do anything—there weren't enough CEOs to keep Wally and Nate from getting caught by the thousands of Darkroast baristas.

"Sorry for getting caught," said Wally, speaking guiltily. "Victor sent an entire group of Darkroast baristas to capture us on the dome. We had no chance of escaping."

"We managed to install the satellite jamming box," said Nate. "If we're lucky, the Moon Laser signal should be dismantling any minute now."

Victor silenced Wally and Nate and addressed the crowds. "WE HAVE TWO MORE INTRUDERS," he said. "THESE TWO INDIVIDUALS WERE CAUGHT ON TOP OF THE AMPHITHEATER HALF SHELL DOME TRYING TO DISMANTLE THE XG SATELLITE DISH AND TO PREVENT THE DARKROAST MOON LASER SHOW."

The crowds instantly booed. Some threw cups of *Mind Melt* at Wally and Nate.

"DESPITE THEIR ATTEMPT, THESE INTRUDERS HAVE FAILED," said Victor. "THE XG SATELLITE DISH DOES NOT CONTROL THE MOON LASER SHOW SIGNAL. WHEN I LEARNED THESE INTRUDERS MIGHT BE TAMPERING WITH THE XG DISH, I SWITCHED THE SIGNAL TO AN ALTERNATE TRANSMITTER. NOW, THE SIGNAL IS BEING TRANSMITTED FROM THE DARKROAST DAY BLIMP THAT IS FLOATING OVERHEAD THE AMPHITHEATER."

Victor pointed to the giant Darkroast Day blimp circling over the amphitheater in the sky.

"THE MOON LASER SHOW WILL CONTINUE," said Victor. "AND NATIONAL DARKROAST DAY WILL PROCEED EXACTLY AS PLANNED. ADDITIONALLY, AS WITH THE OTHER INTRUDERS, THESE TWO INDIVIDUALS WILL BE

PUNISHED FOR THEIR CRIMES AGAINST NATIONAL DARK-
ROAST DAY!"

Instantly, the crowds cheered for Victor and National Darkroast
Day. Meanwhile, among the millions in the crowds, the Source saw
everything. The Source—armed with a neutron pistol and several
neutron grenades—continued rushing directly for the central music
stage. Preparing for a vicious attack, he fought his way through the
impassible crowds and spotted Victor, the Darkroast baristas, London,
Miriam, Wally, Nate, and the Robotic CEOs. *With my weaponry and
the advantage of my secret identity*, thought the Source. *I can publicly
exploit my knowledge of Project Darkroast and my role in creating
Victor, and use that information to turn the tides in my favor to attack
and destroy Victor. Plus, the Robotic CEOs can help provide me with
leverage in the attack and help rescue London, Miriam, Wally and
Nate.* Communicating a covert radio signal to one of the Robotic
CEOs, the Source instructed the Robotic CEOs to prepare to attack
with laser firepower against Victor and the baristas; and to help rescue
London, Miriam, Wally, and Nate. On the giant digital screens sur-
rounding the amphitheater, the Moon Laser countdown now read, **T-
MINUS 1:35 HOURS**. Knowing his time was limited, and
determined to destroy Victor and reveal the truth about National
Darkroast Day, the Source burst onto the stage and—by grabbing the
microphone, removing his titanium mask, and using a neutron shield
to protect himself—quickly shouted at Victor and the entire crowd:
"UNHAND THOSE PEOPLE! THEY ARE TELLING THE
TRUTH!"

The Source completely removed his mask and threw it to the
ground.

Victor spun around and spotted the Source, then noticed the Source
had revealed his face. Everyone in the crowds gasped at seeing the
Source's face. Finally, they saw the *truth*. Inside the neutron shield,
everyone around the amphitheater (with crystal clear clarity via the

1,200-square-foot digital screens) saw that the Source's face was *exactly* identical to Victor Black's face: gray hair, smooth corporate skin, and a perfect business smile. Only a long scar distinguished the Source's face from Victor's—the scar that Victor angrily had given the Source long ago to keep him from exposing the truth about Darkroast.

"VICTOR BLACK IS THE REAL INTRUDER," shouted the Source. "HE IS A ROBOTIC CREATION BUILT BY MYSELF AND A SECRET GOVERNMENT EXPERIMENT CALLED *PROJECT DARKROAST*. LOOK AT MY FACE—HE HAS THE SAME FACE AS MINE. USING FACIAL ENCRYPTING TECHNOLOGY AND ADVANCED ROBOTICS TECHNOLOGY, AND A SECRET MOON-BASED SUBSTANCE CALLED CZARIUM, ME AND *PROJECT DARKROAST* CREATED VICTOR WITH THE INTENTION OF BUILDING THE MOST ADVANCED CORPORATE LEADER OF THE 21ST CENTURY. BY DOING SO, WE INVENTED VICTOR—WHO GAVE YOU THE COUNTRY'S GREATEST, MOST SUCCESSFUL CORPORATION: DARKROAST COFFEE.

THE EXPERIMENT WENT HORRIBLY WRONG. AMERICAN MILITANTS TOOK OVER THE PROJECT. VICTOR WENT OUT OF CONTROL AND MURDERED EVERYONE INVOLVED IN THE EXPERIMENT EXCEPT FOR ME, THE PROJECT'S CHIEF SCIENTIST. UNKNOWN TO EVERYONE, THE LABS HAVE REMAINED INTACT UNDERNEATH THE CITY OF BOSTON.

FOR THE LAST SEVERAL YEARS, WHILE I'VE SECRETLY LIVED IN THE *PROJECT DARKROAST* LABS UNDERNEATH THE CITY OF BOSTON, VICTOR HAS USED HIS SUPERIOR ROBOTIC BUSINESS SKILLS TO BUILD HIS DARKROAST COMPANY WITH A SINGLE PURPOSE: GAINING ULTIMATE NATIONAL POWER IN AMERICA SO HE COULD DESTROY ALL OF YOU.

THIS IS THE ENTIRE PURPOSE OF VICTOR AND DARK-ROAST. TOGETHER, USING *MIND MELT* AND THE MOON LASER SHOW, HE'S GOING TO DESTROY EVERYONE IN AMERICA IN LESS THAN TWO HOURS AND CROWN HIM-SELF ROBOTIC DARKROAST CEO OF AMERICA. THE ULTI-MATE POINT: NATIONAL DARKROAST DAY IS PART OF A DIABOLICAL PLAN TO DESTROY AMERICA ... AND VICTOR BLACK IS THE DESTRUCTIVE ROBOT BEHIND IT ALL! THESE PEOPLE ON STAGE HAVE BEEN TELLING THE TRUTH!"

• • •

Meanwhile, as the crowds listened to the Source reveal the truth about Victor and National Darkroast Day, a major event was about to *truly* destroy Victor and ruin his National Darkroast Day plans. In the Master Command Room, despite seeming dead, Ted awoke from the shadows covered in gruesome bloodiness. The Darkroast baristas had delivered him a fatal blow—but he felt a last waking surge of life, enough to get up.

Still bleeding from the chest, lifting his charred broken limbs from the floor, he stood and was determined to get revenge. He passed the rows of computer terminals (clutching his laser punctured chest, barely able to see straight), and stumbled directly for the central music stage. He grumbled to himself, mumbling in bloody huffs: *"GOD-DAMN ROB-OT! I'LL SHOW ... HIM."* Ted reached underneath one of the main computer terminals and grabbed a back-up copy of the computer virus program he'd created. *"MUST ... REACTIVATE ... THE VIRUS PROGRAM ... AND DESTROY THE BARISTAS."* He loaded the virus into the computer system, hit **REACTIVATE**, then continued towards the music stage.

Next, in his hands, with all his strength, he picked up a giant mega-sized neutron cannon. As he left the room, he charged the cannon, bloodily flipped the activation switch, and thought of the one person he had to settle a score with—Victor.

There was enough strength for one final mission: killing the Darkroast CEO.

Chapter 35

With a final countdown of **T-MINUS 1:25 HOURS**, Guerrero and the Amigos continued the final phase of their mission: destroying the Moon Laser Base. The Darkroast shuttle completed its 240,000-mile journey at supersonic speed, fired retro boosters, and docked with the Moon Laser Base. Guerrero and his Amigos unbuckled their seatbelts, then grabbed their neutron rifles and duffel bag full of weapons and explosives, and rushed into the shuttle cockpit. Using their rifles and weapons, they executed the Darkroast astronauts (leaving one astronaut hostage to pilot the return flight home) and prepared to enter the Base to detonate their explosives.

• • •

The Darkroast Moon Laser Base stretched infinitely long—five-hundred thousand square feet of titanium fortress sprawled across the Moon's rocky white surface. In the northeast lunar quadrant, the Base's shuttle landing pad stood above a giant Moon crater, surrounded by several Czarium mining facilities and equipment loading stations. Exiting the Darkroast shuttle, Guerrero and his Amigos entered the outer passages of the facility and attempted to contact the Source using the satellite intercom of their walkie-talkie. *Dr. Xavier should send us the station blueprints any minute now*, thought Guerrero. *We need them for placing the explosives for the Receiving Satellite, Central Corridor, and the Moon Laser.* Surprisingly, Guerrero received only static on the walkie talkie—a sign that the Source was preoccupied. *Puta madre*, cursed Guerrero. *There's no time for delays!*

Reaching into his duffel bag, Guerrero had an alternate plan for placing the explosives. He removed several maps containing general instructions for navigating the Moon Laser Base. Huddling his Amigos close, he explained that with these navigational maps they could still proceed with destroying the Base. *Unfortunately, it'll take longer than if we had Dr. Xavier's blueprints*, he told them. *Pero tranquilo, we'll get it done before the Moon Laser fires.* Checking his wrist watch, Guerrero noticed the time was now less than **T-MINUS 1:15 HOURS**, and he knew they had to act fast.

• • •

Guerrero and his Amigos rushed inside the Inner Corridors of the Moon Base and began placing explosives at key junctures. They placed a significant amount of neutron compressed C4 inside the power grid of the Receiving Satellite—the satellite that received the command codes from Victor and Darkroast via satellite on Earth. Digital security cameras and hundreds of Darkroast security personnel monitored the Inner Corridors, but the group managed to avoid them and proceed deeper into the Central Corridor. Meanwhile, outside of several large panel windows, the Moon Laser's cannon towered over the Base. Bolted to the Moon's surface, the Moon Laser's cannon—two-hundred thousand tons, eighty stories high, and composed of titanium shell pulsating with Czarium energy—glowed radioactive green and prepared for its firing sequence. Guerrero and the Amigos noticed the firing sequence preparation and doubled their pace. *Puta madre*, thought Guerrero. *They've already activated the firing sequence and soon will have full capability for the Laser's final blast mode. It's not scheduled to fire for over an hour, but we shouldn't risk cutting our deadline too close in case Darkroast fires the laser early in an emergency.*

"Venga! A la estación central. Rapido," said one of the Amigos, understanding the situation. *We need to head to the Central Firing Station, which is at the center of the Base. Puta madre. There we can plant the final batch of explosives.*

"Sí, vamos, pá allá," said Guerrero, looking at a map and pointing down a long corridor. *The Central Firing Station must be our next objective.*

• • •

Located at the center of the Moon Base, the Central Firing Station (similar to a NASA command center) controlled the firing sequence of the Moon Laser and collected security information from the monitors and personnel. Guerrero and the Amigos knew that destroying this Station would prevent all possibility of firing the Moon Laser. Several well-placed explosives along the main computer terminals and along the perimeter walls would completely destroy the facility and annihilate the main command hub of the Moon Laser Base. Inside the facility, hundreds of Darkroast personnel sat at computer terminals and operated the controls for the Moon Laser. Many of these personnel—although they were dressed in Darkroast space uniforms rather than barista attire—were Darkroast robots guarding the Station against any attack. Some of them had already noticed Guerrero and the Amigos on the security camera footage, and prepared their weapons for an all-out defense of the Station.

Rushing down the hallway, Guerrero and the Amigos split into two parties to attack the Station from opposite vantage points. Half of the Amigos led the Darkroast robots down a distant passage away from the Station and towards the Czarium mines. The Amigos had a secondary plan to destroy the Darkroast robots in these mines, and then set several explosives to ignite a chain reaction annihilating all the Czarium beneath the Moon's surface—eliminating the Moon Laser's main lunar resource. Meanwhile, Guerrero and the other Amigos launched a full-scale attack on the Station. Using grenades and neutron rifles, Guerrero and the other Amigos blasted the remaining Darkroast robots and stormed into the Central Firing Station. Outside the windows, the Moon Laser continued glowing green and prepared its firing sequence—an ominous reminder that time was ticking towards the countdown deadline. Guerrero and the Amigos took notice of the time, knowing they also had to monitor their exit strategy to avoid getting caught in the explosions.

"Preparan los explosivos," said Guerrero, pointing at the main computers and perimeter wall. *After activation, we'll have ten minutes to get back to the shuttle and take off, so let's plant these explosives and get out of here fast!*

Chapter 36

Back on Earth inside the Darkroast Day amphitheater, Ted continued past the Master Command Room and onto the central music stage. In the center of the stage, he spotted Victor, the Darkroast baristas, London, Miriam, Wally, Nate, the Robotic CEOs, and the Source. Lifting his giant mega-sized neutron cannon (which hummed with furious neutron waves of 120 Mvolts), he pointed the cannon directly at Victor. Blood dripped down Ted's arms and puddled at his feet, but his mind only focused on one thing—destroying the Darkroast CEO in front of the entire amphitheater crowds. He pulled the trigger and pulsating waves of neutron energy blasted in concentrated beams across the stage and ripped through Victor's chest, engulfing his body in darkly radiant fire and energy.

Immediately, the crowds in the amphitheater jumped back. *"OHMYGODDDD!!"* Whole rows of people screamed near the stage. *"VICTOR BLACK'S BEEN SHOT!"* Victor flailed in shock as his skin melted and his business suit burst into flames. People watched as Ted continued blasting Victor with the laser, laughing and cursing: "GOD-DAMN ROBOT!" The hundreds of 1,200-square-foot digital screens broadcasted the sight across the amphitheater: the destruction of the Darkroast CEO.

• • •

Victor dropped to his knees, his skin dripping in melted shreds. Amidst the fire and fury, he fought to extinguish the flames and protect his body but he burned furiously. His business suit exploded in flaming cinders and revealed the mechanical metal skeleton beneath. Victor gasped and looked at himself, unable to believe his transformation. Caught in a giant phoenix-like fireball in front of the National Darkroast Day crowds, his fingers melted away and exposed robotic claws operated by gears and wires; his chest slouched and revealed titanium plating; his face burned and cindered like a horrific wax statue flaking away to reveal a machine hidden beneath. The hundreds of digital screens continued to broadcast the sight to everyone in the amphitheater. Everyone stared at Victor as if he was dead, but quickly saw the truth about him—the metallic undershell, the piercing green robotic eyes, and mechanical joints. Victor pounded his fist on the stage, stamping at the fire, cursing at Ted: *"YOU BASTARD! LOOK WHAT YOU HAVE DONE!"* The fire had not destroyed him, but burned away his skin and clothing to show his true metal appearance—proof that he was a destructive government robot.

Ted continued firing his laser cannon, shouting at Victor and the crowds: "LOOK AT THE TRUTH! VICTOR BLACK ISN'T HUMAN AT ALL. DURING THESE YEARS, YOU'VE BOUGHT HIS DARKROAST COFFEE AND PAID HOMAGE TO THIS SADISTIC ROBOT. NOTHING MORE THAN AN ARTIFICIAL CREATION WITH PLANS TO DESTROY AMERICA AND RULE AS A DARKROAST CEO!"

Ted could barely hold himself up, but he kept speaking.

"VICTOR BLACK FOUNDED THIS COMPANY WITH ONE INTENTION: TO DESTROY ALL OF YOU BY BUILDING AN EMPIRE GREATER THAN ANYTHING IMAGINABLE. NEVER ONCE HAS HE TRULY CARED ABOUT AMERICA. HE HAS ONLY DESIRED POWER, GREED, AND DESTRUCTION. IF THERE IS ANYONE THAT KNOWS THIS, IT IS ME. AS VICTOR'S MOST TRUSTED PARTNER, I CAN ASSURE YOU THAT HE WILL STOP AT NOTHING UNTIL HE CRUSHINGLY HOLDS ALL OF AMERICA IN THE PALM OF HIS HAND TO DESTROY IT FOREVER. THIS IS HIS *ENTIRE* PURPOSE."

Ted was unable to say anymore about Victor. The baristas opened fire on him, puncturing his already weakened body with laser blasts. This time he dropped to the ground completely dead in a pool of blood before the amphitheater audiences.

• • •

"SILENCE!!!!!!" shouted Victor. "I WILL HAVE NO MORE INSUBORDINATION FROM ANYONE ELSE. EVERYTHING THAT'S BEEN SAID IS TRUE, AND MY ROBOTIC IDENTITY IS REVEALED. I WILL NO LONGER DENY IT. FOR YEARS, I'VE BEEN BUILDING MY SECRET PLANS TO DESTROY AND RULE OVER THIS COUNTRY. I'VE DEVELOPED A COFFEE CORPORATION THAT SPANS THE ENTIRE NATION. I'VE CREATED A DESTRUCTIVE MOON LASER, A VENOMOUS COFFEE BREW, AND A BARISTA ARMY THAT CAN CRUSH AMERICA WITH A SINGLE COMMAND. I'VE EXPLOITED AMERICA'S CAPITALIST OVERINDULGENCE AND PLEASURE-DRIVEN SOCIETY, AND AMERICA'S BLIND OBSESSION WITH COFFEE AND WELCOMING OF DARKROAST WITHOUT ANY CARE TO KNOW ITS TRUE PURPOSE OR INTENTIONS. BUT IT IS TOO LATE TO STOP ME. THE PIECES OF MY MASTERPLAN ARE ALREADY SECURED, AND NOW THE FINAL HOUR HAS COME. ONCE AND FOR ALL, EVERYONE IN AMERICA WILL KNOW THE TRUTH ABOUT NATIONAL DARKROAST DAY. EVEN THOUGH IT IS OVER AN HOUR AHEAD OF SCHEDULE, I AM GOING TO FIRE THE LASER AND ANNIHILATE THIS PATHETIC COUNTRY WITHOUT WASTING ANOTHER SECOND."

Without hesitation, Victor spun around and gave the command to fire the Moon Laser. Instantly receiving Victor's command, one of the Darkroast baristas radioed the order towards the Boston sky, and before anyone could react, the following events unfolded:

The skies parted, dark clouds encircled the amphitheater, and a green light filled the entire horizon. Instantly, a mega-sized blast of hellish lighting rocketed from the Moon and consumed the entire amphitheater and the city of Boston. Green lightning blasted the epicenter of the National Darkroast Day crowds. Everyone drinking

Mind Melt dropped to their knees as the blastwave consumed them. The blast shook the amphitheater like an earth-shattering electric bomb, and the shockwave traveled outward with mach-speed force and violently tore through the crowds. Shockwaves ricocheted across the coffee booths, stadium seats, vending carts, and the giant digital screens, zapping people by the hundreds of thousands. People everywhere fell onto their backs in painful, bloody seizures, clutching their Darkroast coffee cups. Blinding green light washed over them like interstellar fire from space. Foaming at the mouth with their eyes rolling back in their heads, the green electricity from the Moon pierced their skin and zapped their throats, then combined with *Mind Melt* inside their bodies, flash-frying their brains, eyeballs, stomachs, and skin.

In the amphitheater's central square, the Darkroast coffee cup statue bubbling with coffee turned to blood as people's heads exploded. Almost everywhere, people who had drank the highest concentration of *Mind Melt* suffered immediate death. They grabbed their heads and screamed in pain. Within seconds, unbearable pressure built inside their craniums. Blood spewed from their nostrils and their heads massively exploded, spraying fountains of gruesome brainy blood across the amphitheater. Electric green tentacles spread at lightspeed over the entire amphitheater and into the park beyond. People in the park drinking *Mind Melt* suffered terrible fates. Many fell to the ground writhing with seizures, some people's heads collapsing with oozing brainy green fluid. Others grabbed their heads and clutched each other or nearby objects for support, their skulls popping like hellish firecrackers across the park. Everywhere, people's heads were exploding terribly. Throughout the park, several ducks ran terrified amid the apocalypse, their feathers covered in blood and brains. Beyond the amphitheater, the green laser blast branched across the Boston skyline. Hundreds of thousands of green lightning bolts blasted through street corners, building windows, car windshields, and restaurant doors. Everyone who had drank *Mind Melt* was struck, and fell to the ground flailing in green fury. People on sidewalks and in traffic fell to the ground. Waiters and restaurant diners toppled to the floor, especially in *Plush*, where everyone had been encouraged to drink obscene amounts of *Mind Melt*. People shopping in Darkroast stores who'd tried samples of *Mind Melt* bent over and hit the floors with violent thuds, clutching their heads and stomachs in agony. Foam bubbled from their mouths and eyes. Their heads collapsed in squishy oozing pulp.

• • •

On the central music stage, a giant beam of green laser lightning blasted from the Moon and struck the Source. Piercing through his protective neutron shield with bone-breaking strength, the green lightning smashed the Source's body and electrocuted his eyes, arms, and legs. The neutron shield deflected much of the blow, preventing a lethal blast, but it still hit him hard. He spasmed uncontrollably as the green lightning consumed him.

"*JESUS,*" he shouted. "*THE PAIN IS UNBEARABLE!*"

The green lightning from the Moon pumped him with over a thousand volts of electricity. He dropped to the stage, tumbling his pistol and grenades out of his hands as he fell onto his knees. Inside his skull, his brain felt on fire and his breath inhaled electricity. He gritted his teeth and swore at Victor: "*DAMN YOU FOR GIVING ME MIND MELT YOU ROBOTIC BASTARD!*"

• • •

Meanwhile, Darkroast baristas joined in the terror—their time for attack finally had arrived. Throwing aside their *Mind Melt* serving trays, their faces turned evil and they unleashed deadly laser blasts on the entire city. Crowds in the amphitheater or the Boston streets ran for their lives, suddenly realizing that the Darkroast baristas were robots, not humans. Those who weren't dead on the ground or writhing in pain were viciously blasted by the baristas. Many struggling *Mind Melt* victims were shot or crushed by the baristas. Some were hellishly ripped apart or torn limb from limb to satisfy the baristas' devilish bloodthirst. In traffic, Darkroast baristas attacked people sitting in cars or crossing the street. Those who stood outside shop windows in shock over the sudden violence of National Darkroast Day were especially massacred by the baristas. Laser blasts pummeled their bodies as they dropped dead onto the sidewalk. In office buildings, Darkroast baristas attacked office workers sitting on upper-level floors. These people had been in their offices to get a birds-eye view of the festivities, but now ran screaming from their buildings. Some still held Darkroast Day coffee mugs in their hands, grabbing their stomachs in pain. As the baristas pursued them, laser blasts shattered windows, melted office furniture, and ripped apart Darkroast Day posters. In Darkroast stores, people stampeded across fallen coffee bags and merchandise. The Darkroast baristas invaded the stores and blasted people with machine-gun rapid pace. Entire stores and customers were obliterated until only charred shambles remained. Twisted dead bodies covered the floors, and Darkroast Day programs lay scattered. In TV news stations across the city, reporters tried to broadcast breaking news about the deaths and attacks. Many reporters lay dead on the studio floors or in their broadcast chairs. They had drank *Mind Melt* and their brains had exploded as soon as the Laser blast had struck. Darkroast baristas raided the news stations and murdered the remaining reporters wherever they could find them. They blasted the TV screens and destroyed the broadcasting equipment.

In the Boston City Spotlight, everyone suffered the same fate as the other news stations, offices, and buildings. Dead people littered the cubicles and offices, lying in puddles of blood and *Mind Melt*. Lewie—however—had survived. Seeing the devastation of Darkroast Day, he screamed and ran from his office past all his dead reporters and into the surrounding Boston streets. Fortunately, he'd been too busy covering Darkroast Day to drink more than a small sip of *Mind Melt*, and was spared the deadliness of the Moon Laser blast. He had only a small stomach ache, and he clutched his stomach in pain and fled from the chaos in the streets, as Darkroast baristas attacked everyone in sight and pursued him with vigilance.

Several blocks down at a Darkroast store with Chazworth "Chaz" McDoogal, the floor was covered with dead customers. Chaz stood over the bodies not knowing what to do since the Darkroast employee handbook mentioned nothing about how to handle a nationwide apocalypse. During the day, Chaz hadn't drank any *Mind Melt* because he'd given it all to the customers, and now he was thinking the shallowest thought—that he was totally going to lose his job for serving such deadly amounts of *Mind Melt*. Not knowing what else to do, he rounded up as many surviving customers as possible and huddled them in the back office for safety. Baristas crashed through the store blasting people and destroying everything, while Chaz and the survivors crouched in hiding.

Across all other parts of the city, people continued running for their lives. The Darkroast baristas continued attacking citizens, hunting them down wherever they could find them. Fires broke out. Destruction was everywhere. The Moon Laser kept zapping people. In the streets, traffic, offices, buildings, parks, amphitheater, and other parts of Boston, hundreds of thousands lay dead—and thousands more were being murdered each second by the Darkroast baristas and Moon Laser. Across the Boston horizon, a grim haze of green mist and blood settled over everything—a blanket of destruction and death. America finally had learned the true destructive nature of National Darkroast Day.

• • •

"HA HA HA," shouted Victor triumphantly, standing on the amphitheater stage while surveying all the destruction. "THE DOWN-FALL OF AMERICA IS AT HAND! FINALLY, DARKROAST'S ULTIMATE RISE TO POWER HAS BEGUN AND THE CITY OF BOSTON HAS TASTED ITS OWN DEMISE. EVERYONE'S FAVORITE AMERICAN CORPORATION HAS REVEALED ITS TRUE IDENTITY AND HUNDREDS OF THOUSANDS LAY DEAD AS A RESULT. SOON, MILLIONS MORE WILL SUFFER THE SAME TERRIBLE FATE. IN A MATTER OF MINUTES, OUR MOON LASER WILL BLAST OTHER CITIES AND THE DARK-ROAST ARMIES ACROSS AMERICA WILL UNLEASH THEIR VIOLENCE UPON EVERY CITIZEN IN THE NATION. BLOOD, DEATH, AND DESTRUCTION WILL TRIUMPH!"

Victor stood on the stage and shouted through the microphone. In the background, the hundreds of 1,200-square-foot high-definition digital screens displayed his image along with the destruction of the city. Victor no longer resembled his former Darkroast CEO appearance—Ted's laser cannon blast had stripped Victor of his melted skin and business suit to reveal his true robotic appearance.

It was horrible. The digital screens broadcasted Victor's monstrous robotic image across the amphitheater—wild charred hair, metal skeleton, and robotic claws. His body was an entirely metal skeleton gleaming with titanium plating, dual-notched gears, and cross-double-bolted joints with wires and metal tendons. His face was composed of sharp metal teeth, razor-sharp brows, and electronic green eyes with CGI digital scanning technology. Bloody remnants of Victor's skin hung in tatters from his metallic shoulders and legs, and piles of smoldering skin and suit embers lay at his feet as his toes gripped the stage with sharp steel razornails. In the background, smoldering buildings and flames highlighted the city's destruction by Victor.

"MARK MY WORDS," shouted Victor. "THERE IS NO STOP-PING THE TERROR THAT HAS BEGUN. FROM THIS POINT ONWARD, THE DESTRUCTION OF AMERICA WILL CON-TINUE, AND AS I HAVE PLANNED, IT WILL ONLY STOP WHEN I RULE THIS ENTIRE NATION AS THE DARKROAST CEO!"

• • •

On the amphitheater stage, the group rushed to the Source's side. Amidst the destruction and Victor's shouting, the Source lay motion-less on the ground. The Moon laser blast had severely electrocuted his body, and he unconsciously bled from his nose and mouth.

"OH NO," shouted Wally and Nate. "DR. XAVIER LOOKS NEARLY DEAD!"

London and Miriam stared at the Source's near lifeless body, but there wasn't time to waste. There was one final piece in Victor's American takeover plan: the Darkroast Day Blimp. Circling overhead during the Moon Laser attack, the Darkroast Day Blimp soared with rocketing speed over the amphitheater stage. The Darkroast Day Blimp—armed with missiles and machine gun turrets, jet-propulsion engines, and Darkroast battle capabilities—prepared to complete Victor's American takeover by picking up Victor and transporting him away from Boston so that he could launch other Darkroast Day city attacks. Victor radioed the Darkroast Day Blimp, **CENTER STAGE PICK-UP NEEDED! I REPEAT, CENTER STAGE PICK-UP NEEDED!**, as the Blimp dropped a giant rope-ladder. Victor grabbed the ladder, then proclaimed to everyone: "NOW THAT I HAVE DESTROYED THE CITY OF BOSTON, I WILL BOARD THE DARKROAST DAY BLIMP, A FLOATING WARSHIP, AND CON-TINUE MY DESTRUCTION CITY BY CITY. FLYING OVER-HEAD, I'LL OVERSEE THE ENTIRE DESTRUCTION OF AMERICA UNTIL IT BECOMES A CHARRED WASTELAND UNDER DARKROAST COMMAND. FROM THE SKIES, I

SHALL UNLEASH THE GREATEST HELL ON EARTH THIS NATION HAS EVER FACED."

The entire group—London, Miriam, Wally, Nate, and the Robotic CEOs—took notice of the Darkroast Day Blimp and knew they had to stop Victor from destroying America. Wally and Nate couldn't leave the Source and stayed behind in hopes of rescucitating him. But London, Miriam, and the Robotic CEOs took action to attack Victor.

As Victor boarded the Blimp, London, Miriam, and several Robotic CEOs grabbed onto the rope-ladder and lifted into the air after Victor. They had no intentions of showing Victor any mercy, and pursued him menacingly. Several Robotic CEOs used extreme robotic jumping ability to launch into the air and grab the Blimp's outside fabric, then climbed alongside the Blimp towards the command cockpit. The Darkroast Day Blimp quickly soared up into the air over 15,000 feet, rocketing past the amphitheater towards the Boston skyline. Inside the command cockpit, several Darkroast baristas steered the Darkroast Day Blimp across the skyline and awaited the intruders.

London and Miriam reached the top of the rope-ladder, and entered the command cockpit along with many of the Robotic CEOs. They immediately spotted the Darkroast baristas, grabbed several weapons from the Robotic CEOs, and confronted them. "WHERE IS VICTOR!" they shouted. "WE'RE GOING TO DESTROY HIM ONCE AND FOR ALL!" The Darkroast baristas smiled evil, but said nothing and began attacking the Robotic CEOs, London, and Miriam. An all-out war erupted inside the command cockpit. Victor Black had left the cockpit and safely climbed onto a Command Platform at the top of the Blimp. Insidiously smiling downward at the group as the Blimp soared past the Boston skyline towards the rest of America, he shouted:

"NONE OF YOU CAN STOP ME. YOU MAY HAVE INFILTRATED THE BLIMP TO ATTACK ME, BUT THE DESTRUCTION BELOW IS INEVITABLE. AMERICA WILL FINALLY CRUMBLE AS THIS FLOATING WARSHIP SAILS THROUGH

THE SKIES ACROSS NEW YORK, PHILADELPHIA, ATLANTA, NEW ORLEANS, LOS ANGELES, AND EVERY OTHER MAJOR AMERICAN CITY. THE MOON LASER WILL BLAST CITIES ACROSS AMERICA AND DESTROY ALL WHO HAVE CONSUMED *MIND MELT*, AND THE DARKROAST ROBOTIC BARISTAS WILL ANNIHILATE ALL SURVIVORS UNTIL A THICK HAZE OF BLOOD AND DESTRUCTION BLANKETS EVERY CITY BLOCK. NOTHING WILL SURVIVE THE VIOLENT FURY OF NATIONAL DARKROAST DAY!"

• • •

Meanwhile, Guerrero and the Amigos were about to discover a plan to destroy Victor.

Chapter 37

Inside the Moon Laser Base's Central Firing Station, Guerrero and the Amigos had witnessed the unexpected firing of the Moon Laser and the ensuing destruction on Earth. Giant telemonitors in the Station broadcasted the city of Boston lying in ruins—the fires, rising death toll, deadly Darkroast baristas killing citizens by the minute, and mutilated bodies throughout the amphitheater. The Station's monitors also showed the Darkroast Day Blimp soaring across the Boston skyline, with Victor, London, Miriam, and the Robotic CEOs aboard. As the Amigos and the Darkroast robots fought inside the Central Firing Station, Guerrero saw an opportunity for destroying Victor on Earth and preventing him from escaping in the Darkroast Day Blimp. There was only one problem: Guerrero would *have* to work fast and he'd *have* to coordinate with London and Miriam.

Punching several buttons on the Station's main computer and using a satellite intercom, Guerrero contacted the command cockpit of the Darkroast Day Blimp: "HELLO! PUTA MADRE! LONDON AND MIRIAM, CAN YOU HEAR ME?"

Inside the command cockpit, London and Miriam answered while fighting with the Darkroast baristas: "GUERRERO, IS THAT YOU? WHAT ARE YOU DOING CONTACTING US?"

"LISTEN TO ME," shouted Guerrero. "I HAVE A WAY TO DESTROY VICTOR, BUT YOU HAVE TO DO EXACTLY WHAT I SAY, AND DO IT NOW. *MUY RAPIDO!*"

Guerrero hit several buttons on the Station's main computer. On the computer, he had accessed the blueprint schematics of the Darkroast Day Blimp as well as the Moon Laser's Satellite Targeting System. The computer displayed vulnerabilities in the Blimp: **BLIMP'S FLOTATION GAS 70% FLAMMABLE, WEAPONRY SYSTEM 100% COMBUSTIBLE, BLIMP HIGHLY EXPLOSIVE WITH DIRECT MOON LASER BLAST.** In the background on the satellite intercom, Guerrero heard brutal crashes, laser blasts, and exploding glass—the Robotic CEOs, London, and Miriam were fighting like mad with Darkroast baristas in the command cockpit of the Blimp. Amidst the fighting, London and Miriam listened frantically to Guerrero speaking:

"THE DARKROAST BLIMP—WITH ITS COMBUSTIBLE GAS, MISSILES, AND MACHINE GUN TURRETS—IS A GIANT TICKING TIME BOMB," said Guerrero. "A DIRECT BLAST FROM THE MOON LASER WILL IGNITE THE WEAPONRY AND INCINERATE EVERYTHING ON IT. I'M GOING TO TARGET THE LASER ON VICTOR TO TRIGGER THE EXPLOSION, BUT YOU HAVE TO HELP ME BECAUSE THERE'S ONLY ONE WAY THE LASER WILL TARGET HIM. WE MUST GET VICTOR'S CZARIUM CORE EXPOSED. THE LASER NEEDS HIS CZARIUM EXPOSED TO TARGET."

London and Miriam knocked several baristas aside and spotted Victor standing on the Command Platform at the top of the Blimp. Victor looked fiercer than ever.

"*JESUS*," said London and Miriam. "*THIS COULD BE TOUGH.*"

"REMEMBER," said Guerrero. "AFTER YOU'VE FINISHED, STEER CLEAR AND GET OUT OF THAT BLIMP AS QUICKLY AS POSSIBLE!"

London and Miriam nodded. In the corner of the command cockpit, they spotted several escape parachutes. London rolled up his sleeves, cocked his weapon, and set his sights on Victor. Miriam gripped her weapon and boldly joined London.

"OKAY," said London. "LET'S TAKE CARE OF BUSINESS."

Chapter 38

Above the Boston skyline, the Darkroast Day Blimp soared towards the cities of America. Standing on the Command Platform, Victor captained the warship, shouting: "FINALLY, THE DESTRUCTION OF AMERICA IS HERE! AFTER MY YEARS OF PLANNING, NATIONAL DARKROAST DAY WILL USHER IN A NEW AGE OF DARKROAST LEADERSHIP. ALL HUMANS WILL BE DESTROYED AND EVERY CITY WILL CRUMBLE FROM COAST TO COAST. ULTIMATE SUPREMACY OF AMERICA IS MINE AND I WILL RULE ALL AS THE DARKROAST CEO!"

In the command cockpit, the Robotic CEOs, London, and Miriam finished fighting the Darkroast baristas (destroying all of them to robotic smithereens), and London and Miriam rushed to attack Victor. They told the Robotic CEOs what had to be done, and then climbed onto the Command Platform. Overhead on the Command Platform, rows of monitors broadcasted a message: **BLIMP COORDINATES SET FOR MAJOR AMERICAN CITIES ... NEW YORK CITY, PHILADELPHIA, SEATTLE, ATLANTA ...**,while a giant map displayed flight paths and times for the Blimp to arrive at each city. In the background, Boston still smoked and lay in ruins, an ominous forecast of America's impending downfall.

"YOU'LL NEVER DEFEAT ME," said Victor to London and Miriam. "NO MATTER HOW HARD YOU TRY, IT'S TOO LATE. I'VE ALREADY ANNIHILATED BOSTON AND THE DESTRUCTION SEQUENCE FOR EVERY OTHER CITY WILL SOON OCCUR. WHAT CAN YOU POSSIBLY EXPECT TO DO?"

London and Miriam stepped into the middle of the Command Platform. They pointed their weapons at Victor, armed and ready to shoot him.

"WE'RE NOT BACKING DOWN," said London. "PREPARE TO SURRENDER."

Victor laughed fearlessly. "HA HA HA. APPARENTLY, DR. XAVIER FAILED TO INFORM YOU JUST HOW LETHAL I AM. MY SOLID ROBOTIC SKELETON IS MULTI-LAYERED TITANIUM, NEAR IMPENETRABLE TO THE WEAPONS YOU HAVE, AND MY REFLEXES ARE ALMOST SUPERSONIC, FASTER THAN YOU COULD EVEN PULL THE TRIGGER. MY CLAWS COULD PIERCE THROUGH YOUR THROAT WITH A SINGLE SWIPE. NOT TO MENTION, YOU'RE FORGETTING I'M WEAPONIZED WITH MY OWN PERSONAL HAND LASER." Victor pointed a robotic claw at London and Miriam, and his clawtips began glowing radioactive green.

London and Miriam glared harder at Victor. "YOU CAN TALK ALL YOU WANT," said London. "BUT IT DOESN'T MAKE A DIFFERENCE. YOUR END HAS COME."

"THAT'S RIGHT," said Miriam. "NOTHING PERSONAL, BUT WE'RE NOT LETTING ANYONE DESTROY AMERICA ON OUR WATCH."

At this point, several Robotic CEOs appeared behind Victor and grabbed him. Victor never saw it coming. The Robotic CEOs—equal in speed and strength—pinned his arms like megaton vice grips. Instantly thrashing, Victor hissed with fury at the Robotic CEOs.

"WHAT ARE YOU DOING? LET ME GO! YOU CAN'T DO THIS!"

Nearby, there was an emergency axe in a steel case. Miriam picked up the nearby emergency axe and approached Victor. Though the axe seemed an unlikely weapon, she raised the axe above her head. The Robotic CEOs immobilized Victor and exposed his titanium chest plate. Miriam plunged the axe into Victor's chest. "ALL I HAVE TO DO IS MAKE A DENT," said Miriam. "THESE ROBOTIC CEOs WILL FINISH THE REST."

Exactly on target, Miriam had hit Victor's chest plate and made only the slightest dent—but it was enough. Holding Victor down, the entire group of Robotic CEOs then dug their robotic claws into the dented groove in Victor's metal chest. Ripping into his metal with crushing force, they peeled back his titanium plating, bending it open to expose a CPU core pulsating underneath with Czarium. Victor cursed and kicked—not out of pain, but pure rage over the damage. *"YOU CAN'T DO THIS! I'M UNSTOPPABLE!"*

• • •

Inside the Central Firing Station on the Moon, Guerrero watched on the telemonitors and targeted the Moon Laser on Victor's coordinates. Inside the Blimp, London and Miriam rushed down from the Command Platform, took control of the Blimp's flight console, and steered the Blimp away from the Boston skyline into an open area where it could be safely exploded. As the Blimp drifted away, London and Miriam grabbed escape parachutes and rushed to an escape doorway. Putting on the parachutes, they looked outside at the Boston skyline, took a deep breath, and jumped into the sky. Rushing downward at enormous velocity, the sky outside the Blimp stung their skin like thousands of needles, but they endured the pain. Wind battered their faces and bodies with extreme force.

"JUST HOLD TIGHT," shouted London. "AND DON'T LOOK DOWN."

"DON'T LOOK DOWN?" shouted Miriam. "THERE'S NOWHERE ELSE TO LOOK! WE'RE SKYDIVING FIFTEEN THOUSAND FEET THROUGH THE AIR!"

Back inside on the Command Platform, the Robotic CEOs still held Victor down as he hissed and screamed, but they wouldn't let go. "AMERICA *WILL* BE DESTROYED," shouted Victor. "YOU CAN-NOT STOP THE DARKROAST CEO!" Inside the Central Firing Station on the Moon, Guerrero saw on his monitors that it was time to fire the laser. Punching the activation button, the beam exploded from the Moon, blasted through the sky, and instantly hit Victor's chest to ignite a million ton explosion of Czarium, combustible gas, and weaponry from the Blimp.

"*NOOOOO!!!!*" shouted Victor. "*YOU'LL NEVER DEFEAT ME!!!!!!!!!*"

• • •

The entire sky lit up with a blinding green explosion, destroying the Blimp and disintegrating everything on it—including the Robotic CEOs and Victor—as flaming clouds and sonic debris rushed across the horizon in a fiery cataclysm. London and Miriam gripped their parachutes tight and rocketed downward through the sky as shrapnel, flames, and shockwaves blazed past them. They pulled the ripcords on their parachutes as the Blimp crashed and burned through the clouds. Their parachutes released into the air like two giant balloons exploding from their packs, and carried them safely away from the falling wreckage. In the backdrop, the Boston skyline still smoked and burned terribly.

"JESUS," said London to Miriam, as they floated through the air. "LOOK AT THAT EXPLOSION. THERE'S NOTHING LEFT OF THE BLIMP."

Miriam nodded. "EVERYTHING ON IT HAS BEEN DESTROYED, INCLUDING VICTOR."

Both of them knew what that meant: the Darkroast CEO had been defeated.

Chapter 39

Several miles above the Boston skyline, London and Miriam floated through the air approaching the distant ground. Skyscrapers and buildings surrounded the Boston Commons, filled with the Darkroast Day amphitheater, *Mind Melt* chaos, thousands of dead bodies, and the Darkroast baristas attacking and destroying the city. London and Miriam gasped at the damage. "MY GOD," they said. "LOOK WHAT'S HAPPENED TO BOSTON!"

London and Miriam touched down near the Darkroast Day amphitheater, removed their parachutes, and stared at the spectacle. Destruction surrounded the entire city.

• • •

On the central music stage, Wally and Nate kneeled next to the Source. Around the stage, Darkroast baristas still attacked people. Flames, blood, and death littered the lawns along with shattered coffee booths and celebratory debris. London and Miriam entered the amphitheater and spotted Wally, Nate, and the Source on stage.

"LONDON," shouted Wally and Nate. "OVER HERE! WE NEED YOUR HELP!"

London and Miriam rushed onto the stage. The Source lay motionless with shallow breathing, while Wally and Nate held his hands. Green Czarium sludge puddled around his body covering him in sinister toxin. His nose and mouth still bled gushingly.

"WE'VE BEEN TRYING TO REVIVE DR. XAVIER," said Wally. "BUT HE WON'T WAKE UP."

"HE'S STILL BLEEDING," said Nate. "AND HIS BURNS LOOK PRETTY BAD."

"WE NEED TO GET HIM TO A HOSPITAL," said London. He checked the Source's pulse—it was terribly weak. "HE NEEDS A DOCTOR. FAST!"

• • •

Just then, in the amphitheater and around the city of Boston, Robotic CEOs appeared and began attacking the Darkroast baristas. Hundreds of Robotic CEOs had stayed behind instead of boarding the Blimp, planning to launch a counteroffensive against the Darkroast baristas. The Robotic CEOs had scanned and analyzed the baristas to locate weaknesses in their armor—they discovered the baristas had vulnerable junctures in the neck and apron joints. The Robotic CEOs started chasing the baristas across the city of Boston destroying them amongst the buildings, traffic, and city outskirts. In addition, Ted's back-up computer virus wirelessly broadcast itself to Darkroast baristas everywhere. It infected their CPUs and short-circuited their systems, exploding the baristas with sparks and flames until Darkroast barista armies were self-destructing across Boston. Meanwhile, the National Guard and U.S. Army rushed into Boston to secure the city—the government had learned of the attack on Boston and was determined to secure the city at any cost. Tanks drove directly into the Darkroast amphitheater, threatening to destroy any remaining Darkroast baristas or Darkroast threats.

Several Robotic CEOs and National Guard troops marched onto the amphitheater stage, destroying the remaining Darkroast baristas, and came to the group's rescue.

"CAN YOU HELP US?" asked London. "DR. XAVIER NEEDS A DOCTOR. HE DOESN'T HAVE LONG TO LIVE!"

The Robotic CEOs and National Guard troops nodded, and picked up the Source.

"DON'T WORRY," said one of the National Guard. "WE'RE SECURING THE CITY AS WE SPEAK. IT'LL BE SAFE TO TRANSPORT HIM TO A HOSPITAL."

Chapter 40

Simultaneously, as the Robotic CEOs and the National Guard troops transported the Source to a local hospital, a series of events defeated Victor's remaining National Darkroast Day plans. Nationwide after Boston, Ted's back-up computer virus had wirelessly broadcast itself to Darkroast baristas everywhere. It infected their CPUs and short-circuited their systems, exploding the baristas with sparks and flames until Darkroast barista armies were self-destructing on every city block and in every Darkroast Day amphitheater across America. On the Moon, Guerrero and the Amigos planted their explosives and destroyed the Moon Laser Base. The Moon Laser immediately stopped killing people in Boston and was unable to blast other American cities. Survivors in Boston began making cellphone calls and writing instant e-mails to people across America. Surviving news reporters broadcasted breaking newscasts about the National Darkroast Day terror. Major cities and local governments quickly learned of the destruction, and within the hour, the National Guard and U.S. Army rushed into cities nationwide. Tanks drove directly into the Darkroast Day amphitheaters in New York, Atlanta, Philadelphia, New Orleans, Los Angeles, and other major cities. National troops attacked Victor's Darkroast Day personnel, eliminated any remaining Darkroast robotic baristas, and secured the safety of all American citizens.

Miraculously, all other Darkroast Day attacks in major cities were averted without casualties.

• • •

Several weeks later, the Source exited the hospital amidst Boston reconstruction efforts. Fortunately, he'd survived the *Mind Melt* and National Darkroast Day attack. Over 1.3 million people in Boston had died and thirty billion dollars in damage and destruction had been incurred. Hundreds of thousands were injured and scarred, and the

National Guard and U.S. Army still occupied the city. Besides rebuilding the city of Boston, much of the reconstruction effort focused on dismantling the National Darkroast Day amphitheater. The Source met London, Miriam, Wally, Nate, Guerrero, and the Amigos in the Boston Commons. Several demolition crews and government cranes removed the Darkroast Day amphitheater's pillars, stadium seating, flags, and half-shell dome, while wrecking balls demolished the giant digital screens and multiple music stages. Hundreds of thousands of people had gathered to witness the demolition spectacle and celebrate the defeat of National Darkroast Day. Even the Boston Mayor joined the gathering, smiling and pouring champagne for everyone, while pinning them with *"Restore the Park"* buttons.

Wally was the first to spot the Source in the Commons. "DR. XAVIER," he shouted. "YOU'RE ALIVE!"

The Source hobbled across the Commons on crutches, still bandaged in several places. His face had been badly burned on one side, but he smiled and greeted everyone. In the background, reporters and TV crews filmed the reunion. By this point, word had spread that America owed its success to the Source, London, Miriam, and the group. Many people in the crowds cheered and patted the Source and everyone on the back.

"Looks like we did our job," said the Source. "They're dismantling the Darkroast Day amphitheater and everyone else across America is safe."

Everyone smiled and agreed with the Source. London put a hand on the Source's shoulder. "We couldn't have done it without Dr. Xavier," said London, talking to the TV crews. "If it hadn't been for him, National Darkroast Day would have succeeded. Victor would have destroyed America for sure."

Everyone applauded. The Boston Mayor approached and shook the Source's hand. "Thank you, thank you," he said. "It's true. Without your help, America would have been completely destroyed." The

Mayor pinned a *"Restore the Park"* button on the Source and smiled to the crowds. "All of you are truly national heroes!"

• • •

At this point, the National Guard and U.S. Army graciously escorted away the Source, London, Miriam, and the group. The crowds followed them, cheering them along, while the mayor applauded and kept declaring them "national heroes." In the following weeks, government investigations were conducted, during which the Source, London, Miriam, and the group were key players. Many of the investigations were televised and broadcasted nationally, due to the extreme significance of the event. The investigations publicly revealed that National Darkroast Day, from the very moment it began, had been created by Victor Black to takeover and destroy America for the purpose of creating a Darkroast robotic empire. Victor and Darkroast had assembled an unfathomably large network of dangerous National Darkroast Day facilities, including its countless Darkroast coffee stores across America. Over three hundred thousand trucks, warehouses, regional headquarters, coffee stores, and Darkroast Day amphitheaters had to be disassembled due to national security risks. Thousands of crates of *Mind Melt* were confiscated and Darkroast personnel arrests were made in nearly every major city. The Darkroast Space Shuttle Launch Pad and the remnants of the Moon Laser Base were exposed and dismantled (there was no evidence of any attempt to *ever* build a Moon Laser Show). In the end, people were shocked to realize how expansive and powerful Darkroast, as a single corporation, had actually become.

In Boston, the entire Darkroast Headquarters was shutdown— nearly half the facility was revealed as a secret test facility for the Moon Laser, an elaborate *Mind Melt* coffee factory, and a central robotics lab for creating the Darkroast robotic baristas. Furthermore, and more shockingly, the secret truth *behind* Darkroast was finally uncovered: *Project Darkroast*. The *Project's* facility was exposed underneath the city of Boston, and revealed as the secret robotics assembly plant of Victor Black. The U.S. government claimed to know nothing about *Project Darkroast* or its high-tech underground robotics facility—although some mainstream government files mentioned a military roughneck, General Taylor Barnes, with suspiciously large funding for an unnamed "techno-capitalist military venture" located somewhere in the northeast. News stations across America delivered photos and exposé reports on *Project Darkroast*. The American public could hardly believe that Victor Black had been created in a secret government robotics lab, and that he'd been *engineered* to create America's most popular corporation.

• • •

After the investigations were finished, the Source, London, Miriam, Wally, Nate, Guerrero, and the Amigos were huge national celebrities. TVs and newspapers showed their pictures and ran stories about them everywhere. Government leaders and celebrities praised them for their bravery and courage in the face of extreme American danger. The U.S. President and the Mayor of Boston gave joint speeches, took photographs, and awarded them Congressional Gold Medals of Honor. London was made the chief editor of the Boston City Spotlight, and later the editor of his own national newspaper. Miriam was appointed one of the top PR positions in the country. Wally and Nate eventually signed a major record deal for *SuperSquashX* and their first album, self-titled "*SuperSquashX*," went multi-platinum. Guerrero and the Amigos returned to Mexico and reopened his family's coffee farm, successfully employing the Amigos and many other local farmers. The Source—for serving as the key witness in the truth behind Victor Black, *Project Darkroast*, and National Darkroast Day—was appointed head of the U.S. Sciences and Corporate Ethics Division—not only for his expertise, but for his experience with *Project Darkroast* and the dangers of government and corporate technology.

As for Darkroast, the entire country discussed dismantling its corporate operations and ceasing business of all its coffee stores. Eventually, America decided against the idea since Darkroast *was* such an efficient business model and its coffee *was* the best in America. But the company downsized its number of stores, hired well-trusted (and <u>non-robotic</u>) leadership, and eventually operated on a much smaller scale. The government subjected the company to rigorous scrutiny, especially regarding the types of beverages it served. Beverages that faintly resembled *Mind Melt* were strictly forbidden, and Darkroast was banned from holding national holidays no matter how successful it became, especially holidays involving amphitheaters, Moon Laser Shows, robotic baristas, and brand new coffee brews that glowed green. Everyone agreed it was best for a single corporation to remain quite simple and not to have such widespread influence and popularity, regardless of how much people enjoyed it.

• • •

Months later after National Darkroast Day, London, Miriam, Wally, Nate, Guerrero, the Amigos, and the Source reunited in Boston to discuss everything that had happened with Darkroast Day. The group met in the Boston Commons, which had been restored to its beautiful central park condition with duck ponds, willow trees, flower gardens, and wide-open stretches of grassy knolls. The Source was the first to spot everyone as they arrived in the park's central meeting place—a large park bench area where the Darkroast Day amphitheater had once been located. Flowers and gardens beautifully decorated the new lawns.

"Hello again," said the Source, greeting everyone as they walked up from various directions. "Glad you could make it on such short notice. I've got some big news."

London and Miriam arrived holding hands. They had recently started dating again, realizing they had more in common than they first thought (after all, they'd helped save an entire country together). "We have big news also," said London, giving Miriam a kiss. "We've gotten engaged!"

Guerrero and the Amigos approached with big smiles on their faces. They had spent the last several months in Mexico fixing up their family's coffee farm, and were especially glad to return to Boston now that it was nearly Darkroast-free. "*Que bueno!*" said Guerrero. "Dr. Xavier, what's the big news?"

Wally and Nate had a small group of teenage girls following them through the park. Ever since *SuperSquashX* had gone platinum, teenage fans spotted and followed them wherever they went. The girls (wearing brand new *SuperSquashX* T-shirts, of course) shouted their names, asking for autographs, which Wally and Nate politely signed and then stepped away towards the group. "So anyway, Dr. Xavier," said Wally and Nate. "You said this was something that couldn't wait."

The Source grinned bigger than ever, then pointed to a large shrouded object behind him. "I wanted to be the first to tell you," he said. "Or rather, the first to show you."

The Source removed the shroud to reveal the object behind him: a ten-foot tall bronze statue of the entire group standing over a miniature Boston skyline, guarding against a giant Darkroast coffee cup, Victor Black, and armies of robotic baristas. The statue was dedicated to the group's valiant effort in saving Boston and America from Darkroast. Beneath the statue was a memorial plaque that read:

DEDICATED TO OUR NATIONAL HEROES,
WHO SAVED AMERICA
FROM THE CLUTCHES OF AN EVIL DARKROAST EMPIRE.

"I had it personally installed myself," said the Source. "I wanted all of you to be the very first to see it. As far as I'm concerned, it's an important national landmark."

The group went crazy with excitement. "That's awesome," shouted London. "I can't believe you did this! We have our own memorial statue in the park!"

"Dude," said Wally and Nate. "It's perfect. It has the *entire* group! And we're kicking the crap out of Victor and those stupid baristas!"

Guerrero and the Amigos put their arms on the Source's shoulder. "*Esta perfecto.* It's quite possibly the best statue in America," said Guerrero. "You've outdone yourself Dr. Xavier."

The Source smiled but he wasn't yet satisfied. He walked to Miriam's side and put a friendly arm around her. Since Miriam had a long personal history with Darkroast, as well as an entangled and sensitive relationship with Victor, he wanted her genuine approval. "There's still one person that hasn't answered yet," said the Source. "And I'd say her opinion possibly counts the most. Miriam, what do you think?"

Miriam stared at the statue, her eyes welling with tears. She paused for a moment, but there wasn't a doubt in her mind: "I wouldn't change a thing. It's absolutely picture-perfect!"

Everyone smiled. The Source gave Miriam a hug, and the group headed away together from the park. "Excellent," said the Source. "Now, what do you say we all hang out and catch up on what everyone's been doing? We can talk about things over a cup of Darkroast coffee."

The group suddenly stopped. Jaws dropped. "I'm kidding," said the Source, laughing. "I think we could all use a long break from coffee."

Everyone else laughed. *Definitely.*

Credits

Credits are due to many people and creative influences. First and foremost, I must thank my family—Mom, Dad, James, and Bryant—for being so wonderful and inspiring. You have given me an incredible life and are worth the world to me. Thanks also to Nana, Grandmother, and all of my extended family. You're so special to me and I'm always thinking of you.

Thanks to my friends, all of them, everywhere. Special thanks to those from Emory University, Emerson College, and to all those from Alabama, Atlanta, Boston, Washington DC, and other places in America and beyond. Special thanks to Chi Phi.

Important recognition is owed to those who have helped my writing career and, especially, the creation of this book. Huge thanks to my professors from Emory University—such as Ronald Schuchard, Barbara Ladd, Judson Mitcham, and James Flannery—who provided early guidance during my college years. To Doris Lee, for being a great friend and giving me the opportunity to work and write for a magazine. To Emerson College and its excellent graduate professors—such as Kai Maristed, Anne Whitney Pierce, Frederick Reiken, and Christopher Keane—who encouraged me and taught me invaluable writing skills; and to the excellent group of fellow writers that I worked with at the Emerson program. To Uppinder Mehan and Jeffrey Seglin, very important Emerson professors, who read the *National Darkroast Day* manuscript and contributed kind words for the back cover. Additional thanks to Uppinder for working with me on my thesis at Emerson, and sharing an appreciation for sci-fi and satire.

Others who read *National Darkroast Day* in its various stages and contributed essential feedback include Sahil Patel, Kenny Grossman, Scott and Erika Orloff, and Aaron Reid. Thanks to Sam Giga, Adam Greenhouse, and Brad Neiman for providing hilarious feedback on the book's title; and to David Hunter, Jen Waters, Katie Fowler, Cindy Grossman, Cassy and Marco Caputo (and lil' Donato) for additional encouragement. Thanks to John Zamparelli, a fellow Emerson writer, who helped me develop my writing sensibilities in Boston and now lives all the way in Thailand.

Special appreciation is owed to friend and fellow Emerson writer Eric Wasserman, who not only read and provided continual feedback on the *National Darkroast Day* manuscript, but also offered advice and wisdom on the writing and publishing process every step of the way. This book couldn't have been accomplished without him.

I'd also like to credit Shane Johnson, who created the amazing cover illustration for this book. Everyone knows that people can and do judge a book by its cover—and due to his genius work on *National Darkroast Day*, that's a good thing.

General thanks goes to other artists, books, movies, cartoons, music, video games, and cultural forces that have inspired me throughout my life, and particularly inspired this book, such as *Frisco Pigeon Mambo*, *South Park*, and *Independence Day*. Thanks also to America and the coffee industry—at times, some of my best ideas happened while juiced up on extreme amounts of espresso, which is clearly evident in a book about coffee.

Finally, most important thanks goes to my beautiful wife, Liz, for all her support and for being so amazing. She has influenced my life more than words can express, brings me infinite happiness, and helps me to understand the importance of taking responsibility for America, humanity, and the world … even if I am only writing an entertaining story about business, robots, and lasers.

intelligent parodies™

Visit www.intelligentparodies.com for more information on *National Darkroast Day* and upcoming books in the Intelligent Parodies series.

978-0-595-43465-7
0-595-43465-7

3369578